ANGEL OF DARKNESS

ANGEL OF DARKNESS

CYNTHIA EDEN

KENSINGTON PUBLISHING CORP.
www.kensingtonbooks.com

KENSINGTON BOOKS are published by

Kensington Publishing Corp.
119 West 40th Street
New York, NY 10018

All Kensington titles, imprints and distributed lines are available at special quantity discounts for bulk purchases for sales promotion, premiums, fund-raising, educational or institutional use. Special book excerpts or customized printings can also be created to fit specific needs. For details, write or phone the office of the Kensington Special Sales Manager: Kensington Publishing Corp., 119 West 40th Street, New York, NY, 100178. Attn. Special Sales Department. Phone: 1-800-221-2647

Kensington and the K logo Reg. U.S. Pat. & TM Off.

ISBN-13: 978-0-7582-4218-1
ISBN-10: 0-7582-4218-2
First Kensington Trade Edition: December 2011
First Kensington Mass Market Edition: April 2016

eISBN-13: 978-0-7582-7428-1
eISBN-10: 0-7582-7428-9
First Kensington Electronic Edition: December 2011

10 9 8 7 6 5 4 3 2 1

Printed in the United States of America

Once upon a time, two romance writers met for milk shakes at the RWA Conference. A bet was made. A bet was lost. And now, a promise must be kept.

Rebecca Zanetti, I bow to your mad, bad, very dangerous mentoring skills.

PROLOGUE

He'd been created for one purpose—death. He was not there to comfort or to enlighten.

Keenan's only job was to bring death to those unlucky enough to know his touch.

And on the cold, windy New Orleans night, his latest victim was in sight. He watched her from his perch high atop the St. Louis Cathedral. Mortal eyes wouldn't find him. Only those preparing to leave the earthly realm could ever glimpse his face so he didn't worry about shocking those few humans who straggled through the nearby square.

No, he worried about nothing. No one. He never had. He simply touched and he killed and he waited for his next victim.

The woman he watched tonight was small, with long, black hair, and skin a pale cream. The wind whipped her hair back, jerking it away from her face as she hurried down the stone steps of the cathedral. The doors had been locked. She hadn't made it inside. No chance to pray.

Pity.

He slipped to the side of the cathedral, still watching her as she edged down the narrow alleyway. Pirate's Alley. He'd taken others from this place before. The path seemed to scream with the memories of the past.

"No!"

That wasn't the past screaming. His body stiffened. His wings beat at the air around him. It was *her.*

Nicole St. James. Schoolteacher. Age twenty-nine. A woman who tutored children on the weekends. A woman who'd tried to live her life just right . . .

A woman who was dying tonight.

His eyes narrowed as he leapt from his perch. Time to go in closer.

Nicole's attacker had her against the wall. One of the man's hands was over her mouth, the better to make sure she didn't scream again. His other hand slammed against the front of her chest and held her pinned against the cold stone wall.

She was fighting harder than Keenan had really expected. Struggling. Kicking.

Her attacker just laughed.

And Keenan watched—as he'd always watched. So many years . . .

Tears streamed down Nicole's cheeks.

The man holding her leaned in and licked them away.

Keenan's gut clenched. Knowing that her time was at hand, he'd watched Nicole for a few weeks now. He'd slipped into her classroom and listened to the soft drawl of her voice. He'd watched as her lips curled into a smile and a dimple winked in her right cheek.

He'd seen laughter in her eyes. Seen longing. Seen . . . life.

Now her green eyes were filled with the stark, wild terror that only the helpless can truly know.

He didn't like that look in her eyes. His hands clenched.

Don't look if you don't like it. His gaze pulled away from her face. The job wasn't about what he liked. It never had been.

There'd never been a choice.

They have the choices. I only have orders to follow.

That was way it had always been. So why did it bother him, now? Because it was her? Because he'd watched too much? Slipped beside her too often?

Temptation.

"This is gonna hurt . . ."

The man's grating whisper scratched through Keenan's mind. Neither the attacker nor Nicole could see him. Not yet.

One touch—that was all it would take.

But the time hadn't come for her yet.

"The wind's so loud . . ." The man lifted his hand off Nicole's mouth. "No one's gonna hear you scream anyway."

But she still screamed—a loud, long, desperate scream—and she kept fighting.

Keenan truly hadn't realized she'd struggle so much against death. Some didn't fight at all when the time came. Others fought until he had to drag them away.

Fabric ripped. Tore. The guy had jerked her shirt, rending the material. Keenan glimpsed the soft ivory of her bra and the firm mounds of her breasts.

Help her. The urge came from deep within, but it was an urge he couldn't heed.

"Don't!" Nicole yelled. "Please—no! Just let me go!"

Her attacker lifted his head. Keenan stared at him, noting the gaunt features, the black hair, and the eyes that were too dark for a normal man. "No, baby. I'm not lettin' you go." The guy licked his lips. "I'm too damn hungry." Then he smiled and revealed sharpened teeth that no human could possess.

Vampire. Figured. Keenan had been cleaning up their messes for centuries. *A mistake.* That's what all those parasites were. An experiment gone wrong.

Nicole opened her mouth to scream again and the vamp sank his teeth into her throat. Then he started drinking from her, gulping and growling and Nicole's fingernails raked against his face as she struggled against him.

But it was too late to fight. She'd never be strong enough to break away from the vampire. She was five feet six inches tall. Maybe one hundred thirty-five pounds.

The vamp was over six feet. He was lean, but muscle mass and weight didn't really matter—not when you were talking about a vamp's strength.

Keenan stared at the narrow opening of the alley. Soon, he'd be able to touch her and her nightmare would end. *Soon.*

"You're just going to stand there?" Her voice cracked.

His head whipped back toward her. Those green eyes—fury and fear—were locked on *him.*

Impossible.

She shouldn't see him yet. It wasn't time. The vamp hadn't taken enough blood from her.

Nicole slammed her hands into the vampire's chest, but he kept his teeth in her throat and didn't so much as stumble. Her neck was tilted back, her head angled, and her stare was on—

Me.

"Help me." She mouthed the words as tears slipped down her cheeks. "Please."

Her plea seemed to slip right inside of him. "I will." The words felt rusty, and he couldn't remember the last time he'd talked to a human. No need for talk, not really. Not when you were just carting souls. "Soon . . ."

The vamp's head lifted. Her blood stained his mouth and chin. "Baby, you taste so good."

Her body slumped as her knees buckled. Keenan's wings stretched behind him even as his muscles tensed.

"Grade Fucking A," the vamp muttered and he eased back. *Why stop feeding?* The vamp planned to kill her. Keenan knew that. Nicole St. James was dying tonight.

Nicole's hand rose to her throat. Her fingers were shaking. "Y-you're not real . . ." Her eyes never left Keenan.

"Oh, I'm damn real." The vamp swiped the back of his hand over his chin. "Guess what, sweet thing? All those stories you heard? About the vamps and this city? Every damn one of 'em tales is true."

Nicole didn't look at the vamp. She kept her eyes on Keenan as she inched her way down the alley. With every slow move, her hands pressed against the wall.

"You gonna run?" The vamp taunted. "Oh, damn, I love it when they run."

Yes, he did. Most vampires did. They liked the thrill of the hunt.

"Why don't you help me?" She yelled at Keenan, and the wind took the words, making them into a whisper as they left the alley.

That was the way of Pirate's Alley. Sometimes, no one could ever hear the screams.

The vampire seemed to finally realize his prey wasn't focused on him. The vamp spun around, turning so that he nearly brushed against Keenan. "What the fuck?" The guy demanded. "Bitch, no one's—"

Nicole's footsteps pounded down the alley. *Smart.* Keenan almost smiled. Had she ever even seen him? Or had her words all been a trick to escape?

The vampire laughed, then he lunged after her. Four steps and the parasite leapt at her, tackling Nicole to the ground, and keeping her trapped in the alley. Glass shattered when she fell—a beer bottle that had been tossed aside. She crashed into it and the bottle smashed beneath her weight.

"You're gonna beg for death," the vamp promised her.

Perhaps. Keenan slowly stalked toward them. He lifted his hand, aware of the growing cold in the air. The stories about death's cold touch were true. Nicole's time was at hand.

"Please, God, no!" Nicole cried.

God had other plans. That was why an angel of death had been sent to collect her.

The vamp's hands were at her throat. His claws dug into her skin. The scent of decay and cigarettes swirled in the air around Keenan.

"Flowers," Nicole whispered. "I smell . . ."

Him. Angels often carried a floral scent. Humans caught a trace of that scent all the time, but never realized they weren't alone.

The vamp sank his teeth into Nicole's throat again. She didn't even have the voice to scream now. Tears leaked from her eyes.

Keenan knelt beside her. The first time he'd seen her, he'd thought . . .

Beautiful.

Now, covered in garbage and blood, still fighting a vampire, still struggling to live . . .

Beautiful.

It was time. His hand lifted toward her and hovered over her tangled hair. His fingers were so close to touching her. Just an inch, maybe two, separated them. But . . .

He hesitated.

Why couldn't someone else have come into the alley this night? A cop? A college kid? Someone *to help* her.

And not someone who was just supposed to watch her suffer.

A fire burned in his gut. She didn't deserve this brutal end to her human life. From what he'd seen, Nicole had been *good*. She'd tried to help others. His jaw ached and he realized he'd been clenching his teeth.

His gaze drifted to the vampire. It would be so easy to stop him and take one more monster from the world.

Forbidden. The order burned into his mind. He wasn't supposed to interfere. That wasn't the way. Wasn't allowed. He was to collect his charge and move on. Those were the rules.

He'd take Nicole St. James this night, and someone else would wait on him tomorrow. There were always more humans. More souls. More death.

Her hands fell limply to her sides as the vampire drank from her, and her head turned toward Keenan.

There was gold buried in her eyes. He'd thought her eyes were solid emerald, but now he could see the gold glinting in her eyes. Angels had strong vision—in darkness or light—but he'd never noticed that gold before.

Her eyes locked right on him. She was so close to passing. He had no doubt that she saw him then.

"Don't worry," he told her. The vampire wouldn't hear him. No one but Nicole would hear his voice. "The pain is already ending for you." His hand still reached for her. He'd wanted to touch her before. To see if her skin was as soft as it looked. But he knew just how dangerous such a touch would be—to both of them.

Keenan well understand what happened to those of his kind when they did not obey their orders.

Despite popular belief, angels were not the favored ones. They did not have choices like the humans. Angels had only duty.

"I don't . . ." Her words were barely a whisper. Had the vamp already savaged her neck too much for speech? "D-don't . . . want to . . . die . . ."

The vamp gulped down her blood, growling as he drank.

"Don't . . . let me . . ." Her lashes began to fall. The fingers of her right hand began to curl inward, and her wrist brushed against the jagged glass. "Die . . ."

There was so much desperation in her voice, but he'd heard desperation before. Heard fear. Heard lies. Promises.

But he'd never heard them from *her.*

Keenan didn't touch her. His hand eased back as he hesitated.

Hesitated.

He'd taken a thousand souls. No, far more. But her . . .

Why her? Why tonight? She's barely lived. The vamp should be the one to go, not—

Nicole let out a guttural groan. Keenan blinked and his wings rustled behind him. No, he had a job to do. He *would* do it—

Nicole grabbed a thick shard of broken glass and wrenched it up. She shoved it into the vampire's neck and caught him right in the jugular. His blood spilled over her as the vamp jerked back, howling in pain and fury.

Her throat was a mess, ripped flesh, blood—so much blood. Hers. The vamp's. Nicole grabbed another chunk of glass and swung again with a slice to the vampire's neck.

Fighting.

She was fighting desperately for every second of life

that she had left. And he was supposed to just stop her? Supposed to take her away when she struggled so hard to live?

You've done it before. Do it again.

So many humans. So little life. So much death.

"Bitch! I'll cut you open—"

The vamp would. In that instant, Keenan could see everything the vamp had planned for Nicole. Her death would be ten times more brutal now. The future had already altered for her. *Because I hesitated.*

"I'll rip your heart out—"

Yes, in the end, he'd do that, too.

She'd die with her eyes open, with fear and blood choking her.

"I'll shred that pretty face—"

Her coffin would be closed.

The fire twisting in Keenan's gut burned hotter, brighter with every slow second that passed. *Why her?* She'd . . . soothed him before. When he'd heard her voice, it had seemed to flow through him. And when she'd laughed . . .

He'd liked the sound of her laughter. Sweet, free.

"Help . . . me . . ." Her broken voice.

Keenan squared his shoulders. What did she see when she looked at him? A monster just like the vamp? Or a savior?

"No one fuckin' cares about you . . ." The vamp yanked the glass out of his neck. More blood sprayed on Nicole. "You'll die alone, and no one will even notice you're gone."

I will notice. Because she wouldn't be there for him to watch anymore. She'd be far beyond Keenan's reach. He didn't know paradise, only death.

She tried to push off the ground, but couldn't move. The blood loss had gotten to her and made her the perfect prey.

The vampire smiled at her. "I'm gonna start with that pretty face."

Nicole shook her head and swiped out with the glass. The wounds didn't stop the vampire. Nothing was going to stop him. No one. Nicole would scream and suffer and then finally—*die*.

And Keenan would watch. Every moment.

No.

His hand lifted, rising in that last, final touch. His touch could steal life and rip the soul right of a body.

He reached out—and locked his fingers around the vampire's shoulder.

The vampire jerked and shuddered as if an electric charge had blasted through him. Keenan didn't try to soften his power. He wanted the vampire to hurt. Wanted him to suffer.

And that was wrong. Angels of Death weren't supposed to want vengeance. They weren't supposed to get angry. They weren't supposed to care.

Killing the vampire was wrong. Against orders. But . . .

She will hurt no more.

The vamp would not slash her pale skin. He wouldn't carve open her chest or defile her body.

He'd just die.

The vamp fell to the ground, his body as hard as the stones beneath him.

Keenan didn't worry about the creature's soul. Those headed to the pit needed no courier. But Nicole . . .

Her breath rasped out as her chest heaved. She was still alive, but barely. His hands lifted to her savaged throat, the move an instinctual gesture.

Stop the blood.

But he didn't touch her. Couldn't. Because, this time, he didn't want to kill.

"*Help* . . ." Her desperate whisper made his chest ache.

His wings beat against the air. No humans were close enough to save her.

She was suffering, but she'd keep living. Until he touched her, she wouldn't die, no matter how bad her wounds were.

Help. Right then, killing her would be kinder than the nightmare she faced as she fought for every breath.

"L-live . . ."

But she didn't want to let go. He'd met a soldier like her once, lifetimes ago. A man who fought on, determined to hold back the cold touch of death. The soldier had been gutted, but he'd fought, desperate to stay alive, despite the pain.

Keenan hadn't expected to find that same fierce spirit in the schoolteacher. He should have remembered the lesson humans had taught him before: Appearances could be deceiving.

Her lashes began to flicker, yet her heart still beat. He could hear the too-fast rhythm.

End this. Death *would* be kinder than this pain.

But he couldn't touch her.

His hands clenched and he tossed back his head as he yelled into the night.

That was when the wind hit him with the force of an avalanche, slamming into his body, lifting him up, and tossing him in the air, higher, higher. The wind took him away from the woman who fought so valiantly below.

The night sky whipped past him as the whisper of a thousand voices filled his ears. A dim light appeared, growing brighter, brighter—beckoning him upward, then blinding him when he got too close.

Darkness.

Keenan blinked and found himself on his knees.

He'd been tossed onto a gleaming marble floor. Keenan knew who would stand before him even before he allowed his gaze to lift.

Azrael. The leader of the angels of death.

"What have you done?" Azrael—*Az*—demanded.

Keenan closed his eyes and saw a woman bleeding out in an empty alley. Shivering with cold. "She still lives." He rose to his feet, letting his wings spread behind his back.

Az shook his head. "No."

Fear gripped him. "What? I didn't touch her, I didn't—"

"You confess to disobeying your orders." Az's face tensed. "You disobey—"

She was dead? Determined to get back to Nicole, Keenan spun away from Az. No one else would take her over, not after what he'd risked.

"You knew the penalty for such an act." Az's words froze him.

Yes, he knew he had to answer for taking the vampire's soul, but—

"I'm sorry, Keenan. You . . . you were a good angel."

Wait. Keenan whirled back around to face the blond angel. "I didn't—"

"No, you did *not*. That's the problem." And there was sadness cloaking the words, when there was never any emotion in the angel's voice. Never much emotion in any of them.

No love. No fear. No hate. Only duty. That was the way it should have been.

Except when I looked at her, I . . . felt.

"Temptation can destroy us all." Az's all-seeing bright blue gaze raked him. "You had the chance to obey. You knew when the moment of her death was at hand, but you killed one not on your list."

"He was a vampire!" The rage was new—something that had developed only when he saw the pain Nicole suffered. "He was torturing, killing, he deserved—"

"We all get what we deserve." Az's chin lifted. "Beware, my friend, this will hurt."

What?

"I've heard it's the fire that makes you scream the loudest."

There was no fire—

The wind hit Keenan again, wrapping around him, but this time, its grasp felt like the edge of a hundred blades.

Az watched him with a hard stare. No more emotion. Maybe it had never been there. "Did you think we did not know the lust you held in your heart?"

What would angels know of lust? What would they know of anything but following orders, protecting the weak, living in that vast, blank world of *nothing*?

"Why do you think she was given to you?" Az asked.

And he finally understood. *A test.* One he'd failed because he hadn't been able to watch Nicole slip away.

"You broke our rules. You took a life not yours to extinguish." Az's cold voice floated to him. "And you failed in your duty."

To take Nicole's life. But, no, Az had told him that she didn't live; he'd said—*"Where is she?"* He'd had to shout to be heard over the fury of the wind.

But there was no answer. Nothing but the wind howling. And then the fire came.

The fire ripped through his body, starting at his feet, burning up, up, even as Keenan fell, plummeting from the sky.

Expelled from my home.

He flapped his wings as he tried to fight that controlling wind, but—

He cried out in agony as the fire spread to his wings.

This was no phantom fire—real flames ate at his skin and burned his flesh. Burned his wings, his *wings*— *No!*

He'd never known pain, but after this day, he would never forget it.

The wind stopped. His body hovered in the air, his shoulders hunched and his wings burning. He tried to move his wings, tried—

He dropped, falling straight for the earth below, and he burned as he fell. Burned and burned.

Az had been right. The fire made him scream the loudest as he became the one thing he'd always dreaded.

A Fallen.

Nicole St. James screamed and bolted upright. The night was quiet around her. Too quiet. Stars glittered above her and, for a moment, she didn't know where she was. Didn't know—

The alley.

Pirate's Alley. She'd taken a shortcut on her way home. She'd wanted to get inside that church. After hearing her doctor's news and crying all day, she'd *needed* to get inside.

But the doors had been locked, and she'd taken the shortcut home.

Her hand lifted to her throat. When she swallowed, it burned, and her fingers touched something wet and sticky—*blood*. But she didn't feel any wound. The skin was smooth.

She glanced around as her heart drummed way too fast now. She'd been attacked. She remembered that. One man. He'd shoved her up against the side of the alley, and then—

There was a dead man beside her.

Nicole screamed and did a fast, backward crab-walk away from him. The guy's eyes were wide open, and his throat—it had been slashed good and deep with . . . oh, damn, with the glass that was next to her.

I did that.

Vaguely she remembered her hand wrapping around the glass. She'd lifted it and—

Killed him.

She'd killed a man. Her eyes closed as nausea rose in her throat.

He tried to kill me. The reminder blasted through her head. She'd defended herself, that was all.

The guy had bitten her. He'd ripped into her throat. She'd fought back, and he'd wound up as the dead one.

But . . . but she didn't have a wound anymore.

Nicole rose on shaky feet. Her throat burned, but it wasn't so much from pain as from thirst. Her throat seemed so dry. Parched. Just how long had she been screaming?

Nicole's gaze scanned the alley once more. This time, she saw the dark liquid on the ground. Blood. Her nostrils flared a bit. The coppery scent was strong. She licked her lips and realized she was starving.

"Ma'am?" A voice called from the darkness.

Nicole's head whipped to the right. A man stood at the far end of the alley. She could see his long, tall shadow. Actually, when she narrowed her eyes, she could see his dark hair, the hard lines of his face, and the gleaming badge on his chest.

A cop. Finally.

The beam of his flashlight hit her, and she lifted a hand against the bright light.

"*Shit.* Ma'am, is that blood?"

Yes, she had blood on her hands. Her blood? His?

Probably both. "I was . . . attacked." For all the dryness of her throat, her voice came out perfectly normal. Actually, she sounded way too calm. Maybe she was in shock because she sure didn't feel calm. Her insides were churning, her heart racing, and—really, really weird—her teeth were starting to ache.

The cop crept closer. "Where are you hurt?"

Nowhere. "I-I killed him." She'd never lied to the cops before. Why start now?

Silence. Then she followed the slow sweep of his light toward the ground and the dead man.

"He was biting me . . ." But she didn't have the bite-marks anymore. And surely, she'd just imaged those too-long teeth. "He was so strong. He wouldn't let me go and I—"

Shoved a chunk of glass into his throat.

The wind whispered against her cheek and the breeze brought the scent of blood to her. Blood and . . . the faintest aroma of flowers. "Someone else was here." The certainty filled her. She tried to remember the other guy, but could only recall a dark shadow. A big, strong shadow of a man.

And . . . his eyes had been blue. Bright blue.

"A second assailant?" The cop came even closer. "Ma'am, I want you to lift both hands for me."

She lifted them, aware of the clench in her gut. Why was she so hungry?

"That's good, that's real good . . ."

A pounding filled her ears. A fast, wild pounding. And suddenly, she could smell everything—blood, flowers, sweat, cigarettes, alcohol, and even incense from the cathedral. Too much.

"I'm gonna radio for backup and we're gonna get you taken care of, okay?" The cop was right in front of her now, and Nicole realized the pounding seemed to come from him. Her eyes drifted over his face and on down the strong column of his throat. *There*. His pulse hammered against his flesh in a double-time beat.

His pulse. His blood. So close.

Her hand lifted toward him.

"Is all that blood his, ma'am?"

She shook her head and the move made her feel dizzy. "I-I think some of it's mine." Nicole couldn't take her eyes off his neck. Then the ache in her mouth turned into pain, and she cried out as she slapped a hand over her lips and tasted the blood on her fingers. As she hunched over, Nicole's hair formed a curtain over her face, blocking her from the cop's view.

The blood slipped into her mouth.

More.

The cop reached for her. She snarled as she jumped forward. Something wild and desperate broke loose inside of her. She grabbed the cop's throat and pushed him back, back. Nicole slammed him into the alley wall.

"Lady, lady *what the hell?*"

That pounding was even faster now.

"S-sorry . . ." The word sounded funny. When had she gotten a lisp? And what was she doing? He was a cop, she couldn't—

"What's wrong with your teeth?" He demanded, and he was fighting her, pushing and shoving, but she barely felt his struggles.

The beat of his heart drowned out his voice. She leaned in closer, so thirsty—*no, hungry*—and she just needed to *bite*.

Her teeth sank into his throat. His blood spilled onto her tongue, and it was good. Better than good. The best thing she'd ever had in her life. Warm and hot; life, and it was—

Nicole staggered back, gagging, horrified as she fought through the blinding hunger. *No, no. This wasn't right.*

The cop watched her with terror filling his brown eyes.

"I-I'm sorry!" She'd attacked him and shoved him against the dirty wall, just like—

Just like that bastard did to me. She'd even bitten the guy. Her tongue ran over her lips and felt the too-long and too-sharp points of her teeth. *No.*

She'd bit him and drank his blood. *Drank his freaking blood!*

Nicole backed up, quickly, trying to get away from the sight and smell of the cop's blood. His blood tempted her and right then what she wanted more than anything was—*another bite.*

She tripped over the body and crashed hard onto the ground. Her attacker's body was so stiff and hard, as if he'd been dead for hours. But, no, wait, it had been just moments. She hadn't been out that long, so . . .

"Don't move."

The cop had lost his flashlight, but she could see him perfectly in the dim lamplight. He had his gun out and aimed at her.

"I don't know what the fuck you are, lady, but I'll put a bullet in your heart if you come at me again."

I don't know what the fuck you are.

Fear had her heart racing because she didn't know, either.

The *hunger* was ripping her apart. *One more drink, one more . . .*

She had to get away from the cop. If she didn't, Nicole was very afraid that even the threat of a bullet wouldn't keep her from his throat.

She'd never hurt anyone in her life, until tonight.

Now one man was dead and another man's throat was torn open and his blood tempted her.

She pushed to her feet.

"Don't move." His gun trembled a bit. "Unless you want a bullet in your chest, just . . . don't . . . move." He expelled a rough rasp of air. "Hell, you did this same routine on that poor bastard, didn't you? You lured him in here, then went right for his throat."

No. He'd gone for hers. He'd attacked with dark eyes and fangs like some bad horror movie vampire or something.

Vampire.

Her body iced.

Fangs. Blood. Thirst.

No. No!

I don't know what the fuck you are.

That damn pounding filled her ears. Calling. Urging her to take another bite.

Escape. She wasn't going to kill a cop. She wasn't drinking blood! Nicole spun away and ran toward the square.

"*No! Dammit, stop!*"

Nicole couldn't stop. Her teeth were *fangs*, her nails were sharpening into claws, and something was very, very wrong. Tears trekked down her cheeks as she raced for safety.

"*I said stop!*"

The bullet hit her in the back, but Nicole kept going. She didn't cry out—too scared, too fueled by panic and the choking terror.

She ran faster as she thundered through the nearby square. Then she snaked through the streets. The sights blurred around her as she pushed herself faster, faster . . .

And all the while, his words echoed in her mind.

I don't know what the fuck you are.

She glanced at the claws—claws that had formed from her short fingernails.

Claws.

Fangs.

Consuming thirst for blood.

Oh, God. The cop might not know what she was, but Nicole was very, very afraid that she did. And she was also afraid that she'd soon be just like the bastard who'd attacked her.

A killer. A monster.

A vampire.

CHAPTER ONE

Six months later . . .

When the woman with the midnight-black hair and dark red lips strolled into the cantina, he knew his hunt was finally at an end.

Keenan lifted the tequila to his lips, barely feeling the fire of the liquid as he tossed it down his throat. It had been a long hunt, but after all this time, he'd found her.

Nicole St. James.

The only charge who'd ever escaped him. The woman that, sure as the devil, had changed his life. The rage began to heat his blood because it shouldn't have been like this. Not for him. Not for her.

He slammed the glass down on the countertop. She hadn't even glanced his way. She'd just sauntered to the old, scarred tables in the back. What was she doing?

Nicole St. James was a schoolteacher. She was a woman who wore long skirts and loose, gauzy tops. She wasn't a woman who wore torn and faded blue jeans, jeans so tight they hugged her thighs and hips, and she didn't wear tops like that—tops that barely covered her breasts and left her midriff bare.

Too much flesh.

He yanked his gaze back up. Did she even realize how much danger surrounded her? And why was the woman in Mexico? She should have been home in New Orleans, enjoying the *life* he'd given her.

The one he'd sacrificed so much to make certain she had.

But no, she was leaning over some man and skimming her fingers down the guy's tanned neck as she whispered to him.

Seduction.

The man rose, laughing, and turned away from his friends. Someone called out, *"Mamacita!"* as Nicole and the man disappeared through the small back door.

Keenan's shoulders straightened as he rose from this chair. Okay, so he'd expected . . . more. The woman hadn't even glanced his way. Not once. She'd found her stud, taken his hand, and led the guy right outside.

Eyes narrowing, Keenan stalked after them. The man could find another lover. *He* had plans for Nicole St. James.

He didn't bother going out softly. Keenan wanted them to know he was coming. He shoved his palm against the door and the wood splintered beneath his touch.

Then he was outside. The night air, thick with humidity and musky with the scent of wild animals, hit him. One more step forward and Keenan caught the soft whispers in the air.

A woman's husky voice.

A man's hungry mutters.

The heat inside of Keenan flared hotter.

He turned the corner, and he could see them half-hidden in the shadows. Kissing. Nicole's hands were all over the man. She was up on her toes, and her head lowered as she began to kiss her way down the man's neck.

Keenan crossed his arms over his chest. He cleared his throat. "Uh . . . sorry to interrupt." No, not sorry at all.

Nicole glanced back at him. *Same deep green eyes.* But there was no surprise in her stare. So she'd known he was there? Well, it was pretty hard to disguise the smash and splinter of wood.

But Romeo must have been too far gone to hear because he whirled in surprise with his beady eyes narrowed. The guy's shoulders blocked Keenan's view of Nicole. The guy snarled, *"Vete a la chingada!"*

Right. Been there. He didn't exactly plan to be taking another trip to hell. "You need to leave."

The guy blinked.

"I want her." Keenan's voice rumbled too much when he spoke, but fury churned inside of him, demanding release.

So he was having trouble controlling his emotions. Getting slapped with all these feelings hadn't really been part of his game plan.

"Too bad," the guy snapped, his English tipped with his Mexican accent. "She's busy tonight."

Her fingers curved over the would-be-lover's shoulders. "Let's get out of here."

Keenan shook his head. "No, Nicole, you're not going anywhere."

Silence.

Then, slowly, her fingers unfurled from the man. She shifted her stance, took a step forward, and Keenan stared right into those green eyes—eyes that had haunted him for so many nights.

"How do you know my name?" She whispered.

He smiled. "You'd be surprised at the things I know about you."

"I'll take care of this *cabron!*" Romeo promised.

Cabron. Bastard. Keenan lifted a brow at the guy. "You should leave now." Nicole didn't glance at Romeo. Her stare stayed focused on Keenan. "Really fast. *Leave.*"

"What? No, we're—"

Her head turned toward the man. "Leave."

His eyelids flickered. "*Puta.*"

"Yeah, great, call me whatever you want, but just go." Her hand came up and pressed against the guy's chest. He stumbled back about five feet. "*Go.*"

"How did you—" Romeo's eyes widened and then he turned and ran back into the bar.

Nicole shoved her hair back over her shoulder. Then she braced her legs apart and kept her arms loose at her sides.

Interesting. When had the little schoolteacher learned to prepare for an attack?

"Who are you?" She asked him, her face showing no hint of fear.

"I'm someone who's been looking for you." True enough. "For a very long time."

She gave a little shrug. "And here it is, your lucky night. Looks like you found me."

No, he hadn't found the woman he'd expected.

"So what are you going to do now?" She murmured as she walked closer to him. The moonlight spilled onto her face. His eyes narrowed. Her face was a little thinner. Her cheekbones were more defined. Her eyes were still as wide and dark, but her lips appeared redder and plumper than before. The woman was still beautiful, no doubt, but . . . a darkness seemed to cling to her.

Her body was as slender as he remembered. Her breasts still round and firm and her hips—*no*. He shouldn't be noticing that. Her body didn't matter.

"Like what you see?" She whispered, and her slow drawling voice sounded like . . .

Temptation.

He backed up a step.

One black brow lifted. "Now, surely, you aren't afraid of me."

"I fear nothing." After what he'd seen, what he'd done, there was simply nothing left to stir fear in his heart.

"Good for you," she muttered and the words didn't seem sexy. More . . . annoyed then. But then she blinked and the heavy-lidded mask came back. "Tell me how you know my name."

She was almost close enough to touch right now, but he wouldn't touch her. No, he never touched. Touching was far too dangerous.

You didn't touch unless you were ready to kill. He wasn't ready . . . yet.

"I've known your name for a long time." No sense lying. Besides, lies weren't possible for his kind. "Ever since you were put on my list."

He heard the hard inhale of her breath.

"L-list?" Now there was fear flickering in her eyes. Her voice hardened as she said, "You're one of *them.*"

"Them?" Curiosity stirred within him.

"A hunter." Her bow lips tightened in distaste when she spoke the term.

But she was right. Now he was a hunter and she was his prey.

"I haven't done anything wrong! I haven't killed anyone—not since—" She broke off and tears filled her gaze. "I thought if I didn't hurt anyone else, you were just supposed to leave me alone."

He could only stare back at her. "Leaving you on your own isn't an option for me."

Her chin snapped up. "I won't make this easy for you."

"No, I didn't expect you would." Nothing had been easy with her.

"I'm not going to be the weak target you think." Her hands were fisted at her sides. "You want to take me in, then come and try."

He blinked at that. "I—"

"You're not takin' her! Get the *gringo!*" The shout had Keenan tensing. He glanced back and saw that Romeo was back, and he'd brought friends. The drunks from inside—only they didn't look so drunk now. No, they looked furious and very, very determined.

They were also armed with knives and guns. What? *Why?* Because one of them had lost a potential lover for the night?

"*We're* taking her. Not you," Romeo threw out as he and his men strode forward. "We didn't wait this long to find her just to have some *gringo* get in our way."

Nicole hurriedly backed up.

The men brushed past Keenan, barely seeming to notice him.

"I know what you are," Romeo called to Nicole. "A monster like you . . ." He spat on the ground. "Killed my mother."

Nicole wasn't a monster. She was just a woman.

"Your kind thinks you're so safe . . . so much better than the rest of us . . ." This came from an older man with graying black hair and cold brown eyes. "Think again, *señorita.*" His long fingernails looked almost clawlike.

"I-I don't . . . I don't want to hurt you." Nicole retreated a few more feet. A fence stood behind her. An old wooden fence that had to be at least six feet tall. *Trapped.*

Keenan watched—and waited. The men weren't even glancing at him now as they closed in on Nicole. Six men against one woman. Were those fair odds?

I had to just stand back before. For so many years. Just stand and watch.

He was done with watching.

"You don't want to hurt me?" Romeo repeated. "Then what the hell were you planning to do to me tonight, *puta*? I know damn well what you were—"

She shook her head. "I had to— I didn't mean—"

And it must have been a trick of the light, because her green eyes seemed to darken with her fear.

Then she spun around and leapt over the fence.

Leapt over that six-foot-high fence in one bound.

"Get her!" The old man screamed.

"Don't even *think* of touching her," Keenan said, his voice quiet, but cutting through the guy's scream like a knife. He could hear the thud of Nicole's foot-steps as she fled—she was rushing away far faster than a human could run.

But Nicole was human.

No, she *had* been human.

The men paused, for just a moment, then they sprang for the fence.

"I said," Keenan growled, the fury breaking through his control because he still hadn't fully mastered the whole control concept, "don't even think of—"

The old guy lifted his gun and pointed it at Keenan's chest. "This fight ain't yours."

Romeo made it over the fence. Two others were right on his heels.

Keenan stepped toward the gun. "Yes. It is."

"She would've killed you tonight." The gun barrel trembled in the old man's hands. "You're lucky, we saved you—"

Keenan grabbed the gun in a move too fast for the human's eyes to track. He slammed the butt of the weapon into the man's head and heard the thud of impact even as the guy fell to the ground. And as the man fell, Keenan turned fast and fired the gun—once, twice—and took down the men still in the back alley.

He didn't kill them. He just gave them something painful to remember him by. "Go after her again," he promised, "and the bullets will be in your hearts."

They didn't answer because they were too busy groaning in pain and writhing on the ground. Keenan stared at them a moment longer as he memorized their faces. He always kept his promises.

He turned, holding the gun close, and jumped right over the fence. He followed the sound of the screams and the scent of the blood as he tracked his prey once more.

Nicole wasn't getting away from him, and those bastards after her would learn that when an angel spoke— they damn well better listen.

Even if that angel had fallen.

Outrunning humans wasn't normally hard. But when the humans in question had baited a trap and you'd walked right into it because you were so freaking thirsty—well, then things became considerably more difficult.

Nicole's knees barely buckled as she cleared the fence, and, seconds later, she started streaking across the empty lot as she rushed for the darkness on the other side.

Then the growl reached her. A deep rumble of sound—a truck's engine. The truck's headlights flashed on, coming right out of that waiting darkness, and she realized just how good the trap truly was for her.

They'd known she'd come to the bar. They'd known she'd be hungry. They'd known she'd take a man outside for her drink.

Then all they'd had to do was make certain her escape path was cut off.

The truck roared toward her, tossing up dust and dirt in its wake as it aimed right for her.

Nicole lunged to the left. A gunshot fired behind her and she felt the close rush of the bullet as it whipped by her arm. Dammit, why couldn't they let her go?

The truck swerved and followed right behind her. She was fast, but not faster than a truck.

The bumper hit her and she went down. Nicole slammed into the dirt, but she rolled quickly so those wheels didn't plow right over her.

Dirt filled her lungs. Blood poured from the gashes in her arms. And the thirst grew. *I went too long between feedings. Shouldn't have waited.*

But she hated to drink blood. It reminded her too much of what she was. *Monster.*

And when she drank, the dark temptation to take and *take* welled within her.

A truck door squeaked open. "We hit her!" Not a Mexican accent this time. She recognized Texas when she heard it.

The other door groaned open. "Keep yer gun on her. It'll take more than a smack from my Chevy to put one like her down."

Yes, it would, but Nicole kept her eyes closed and kept her breathing light. The men eased closer. She could smell their sweat and their fear.

And excitement.

Other footsteps pounded in the distance—her would-be victim and his buddies must be coming in.

Then she heard the thunder of a gunshot. One. Two. But she didn't flinch at the blasts. If they wanted to shoot at each other, fine with her. Infighting meant fewer guys for her to fight off later.

The ground vibrated with the footsteps of her hunters. She waited, *held steady,* waited and—

The first man nudged her with his boot. No, not a nudge. The jerk kicked her with his boot. She turned, moving fast in an instant, and caught his legs. Twisting hard, she broke his right leg, then his left. He was screaming before he hit the ground.

And she was up. Nicole slammed her fist into the other attacker's face. Bones crunched. Blood spurted, and oh, she would have taken a drink. Fitting punishment for them running her down like a wild dog, but . . .

But she needed to get the hell out of there.

More bullets were flying, but they weren't even coming near her. Someone must have real crappy aim. She darted around the truck and ran for the shrouding darkness once more. *There'd better not be another truck waiting there.*

Nicole risked one quick glance over her shoulder, and when she did, shock had her tripping.

Only one man followed her now. *What had happened to the others?* She'd counted at least six before she'd run like the devil was chasing her.

Been there, done that.

The man striding so calmly across that barren field had a gun in his hand. But as she looked at him, he tossed the gun onto the ground. Wait, wait, that wasn't the guy she'd intended to steal a few sips from in that dark lot. That was . . . *him.* The stranger with the voice like thunder's rumble. Deep and dark and, oh, damn, she was in trouble.

Nicole made it into the darkness in the tattered remains of the woods. She pushed inside the trees, still hurrying. She'd scouted this area earlier. There was a turn up ahead that would lead her back to the old sedan she'd parked and—

The thirst.

Nicole swallowed and kept moving. Her mantra these days was *just keep moving*. That was the way she'd been living her life. One wild step at a time.

As she broke from the woods, she saw her sedan waiting. Lucky for her, that beaten-up gray shell still managed to drive. Her breath expelled in a hard whoosh as she sprinted forward. She'd head to the next town. There was just enough time to get there before dawn. She'd drive over and find more prey.

Going without blood wasn't a possibility that night. She couldn't afford to be pushed to the edge. Not with the hunters after her.

"Nicole."

A shiver worked over her at his voice. *Don't look back*. She wrenched open the car door and jumped inside. Her hands were shaking when she shoved the key into the ignition. *Hurry.*

She slammed the car into reverse, spun it around and—

Her headlights burned right on the man standing in the middle of the road.

Tall. Muscled. Dressed all in black, he should have looked like a devil. He didn't. He looked like the best sin she'd ever seen.

And that fact terrified her. Because, until six months ago, Nicole had never sinned. Now she couldn't seem to stop, no matter how hard she tried.

He tilted his head and his blond hair, too long,

too thick, brushed against his sharp cheekbones. The man's face was perfect. Better than any photo she'd ever seen in a magazine. Not handsome, *perfect*. He had strong, high cheekbones, a positively lickable square jaw, and wide, bright blue eyes. Oh, just a come-here glance from those eyes would probably be enough to seduce most women.

Good thing she wasn't most women.

"Get out of the way!" She warned. Her foot lifted off the brake.

His lips curved slowly in a crooked half-smile that sent a chill over her.

"Move!" She yelled at him.

He stepped closer.

Her hand shoved out the driver's-side window. She'd broken the window weeks before. "Don't push me!" He'd already admitted to being a hunter, and she wasn't going to sit back and let him haul her away.

This life might not be the one she would have chosen, but she wasn't letting death take her.

Tall and sexy kept walking toward her.

Not human. She was ninety percent sure of that fact. She revved the engine and shoved down on the gas pedal.

He was headed right for her with that smile still on his face—

Okay, she was eighty percent sure. And she wasn't going that fast. If she hit him—

Seventy percent?

Her hands tightened on the wheel.

Then he leapt into the air. Her foot pushed that gas pedal all the way to the ground and she blazed straight ahead, going as fast as she could.

One hundred percent certain.

She risked a glance in the rearview mirror. The

hunter stood behind her car, staring after her with his head tilted to the side.

Thanks to her new vampire senses, she could easily see him—and the grim smile that still curved his lips as he watched her drive away.

The light streaks of dawn shot across the sky. Nicole glanced up at them, eyes narrowing. Time had nearly run out for her.

"Baby, I'm gonna rock your world."

But luckily, she'd found a drunk frat boy just in time. Thank God for spring break and boys who wanted to walk on the wild side.

Music from the club blared into the air. So dawn was coming. Apparently, the party had barely started for the folks in that place.

And for the folks *outside* . . . Nicole ran her fingers up the frat boy's throat. His pulse raced beneath her touch and she could almost smell his blood.

Next time, she wouldn't go so long between feedings. The fear wouldn't hold her back again.

The guy pressed a kiss to her cheek. A wet, rough kiss that had her hissing out a breath and shoving him back against the side of the building. Her enhanced strength could sure be handy.

"We don't have time to waste," she told him. She didn't trust that hunter not to show up. He hadn't looked like the type who would give up easily.

I should have hit him with the car.

But she'd been trying for the whole don't-kill lifestyle. And if she'd taken out a hunter, well, hunters were like weeds. A dozen more probably would have sprung up after her.

"Baby, I'm all for fast," her frat boy promised as his

hands made a grab for her. She caught them, pushed his hands back, and pinned his wrists to the wall.

He groaned. "Oh, God, yes, I like it rough."

He would. Nicole's eyes squeezed shut and she pushed onto her tiptoes even as she opened her mouth over his throat. She'd try hard not to hurt him, and she *would* keep her control. The sharp edges of her teeth pricked his skin.

The faintest whisper of sound reached her ears. A footstep. The soft rustle of clothing.

No.

Nicole spun around and saw her nightmare walking out of the darkness.

"*Get away from her,*" the hunter ordered, that voice still a dark rumble that she could almost feel.

She realized her right hand still held the frat boy. Nicole let her hand fall away from him. No way would she put a human—well, a semi-innocent one anyway—in the middle of this fight. "Go back inside."

Her college snack blinked at her. "But we were—" A few drops of blood trailed down his throat. "I thought you were gonna . . ."

"You thought wrong." She stepped away from him, and her gaze turned back to the hunter. "And unless you want to die, I'd recommend that you get your butt back in that bar."

"D-die?" The word sounded like a frog's croak.

The hunter was closing in. She took a deep breath. Yes, vampires still breathed. Their hearts still beat. Blood still flowed in their bodies. They died when they were transformed, but that death lasted only for an instant. All those tales about stone-cold vamps were false.

"Look," frat boy blustered, "I'm not going—"

She glanced over her shoulder. This time, she let the guy see the monster in her eyes and the sharp teeth that had been ready to rip open his throat.

"Holy shit!" Frat boy ran, nearly falling twice as he hurried back to the bar.

She shook her head. Flexed her wrists. And waited.

The hunter kept coming toward her with his slow, stalking steps. She wasn't going to run this time. Not when the odds were better. One against one now. And she might even be able to take him. Well, she might, depending on exactly *what* he was.

Because, as Nicole had unfortunately discovered over the last six months, monsters were real. Demons walked the earth, vamps hunted at night, and werewolves really did howl under the light of the full moon.

Her rose-colored glasses had smashed the night a vamp attacked her in New Orleans. She'd woken to a new world, new terrors, and the understanding that everything she'd known was really a lie.

Humans weren't at the top of the food chain in the real world. They were just prey for the *Other*, for all of the supernaturals who lived in the shadows and who hunted whenever they damn well wanted to hunt.

Hunt.

Her hunter stopped less than a foot away. His gaze raked her.

"This is the second time tonight that you've taken my food away." She licked her lips. Really, was a good meal so much to ask for? "Guess what that means."

He stared back at her. A faint line appeared between his brows. "Your eyes . . . they should be green."

A vamp's eyes changed color—to fuck or to fight, that's what she'd been told. The irises faded to pitch-black. "My eyes change, the better to see you," she whispered and smiled. Actually, they changed the better to hone in on prey, so she was telling the asshole the truth.

His gaze dipped to her mouth. He stiffened. "Your teeth . . ."

Her smile widened, and she knew he'd have a better view of her fangs. "They change . . . the better to bite you." She wasn't Little Red Riding Hood. She was the wolf. A hunter should know that. But while he stared at her, she took that moment and attacked.

Nicole leapt forward and wrapped her hands around his arms. Her mouth rose to his throat. "You took away my food, so that means you're dinner."

And Nicole did the only thing she could. She bit.

After all, vampires had to survive, too.

CHAPTER TWO

When Nicole flew toward him, Keenan lifted his hands and tried to step back. But she reached him anyway. *Too fast for a human.* She reached him, she *touched* him—and she didn't die.

That fact floored him.

For so many centuries, no one had been able to touch him and live.

Even though he'd fallen, Keenan had thought he still possessed the Death Touch. According to the tales he'd heard, he *should* have still—

Her teeth sank into his throat. A razor-sharp slash of pain burned his skin and then—and then, sweet fire . . .

Pleasure.

Her mouth was on him, her lips whispering over his flesh, and he could feel the delicate lick of her tongue on his neck.

Touching.

His cock began to swell, the need, the lust, rising within him. Her breasts brushed against his chest. Her nipples were tight as they pebbled against him.

Her mouth was on him, her breasts against him, and she was still *alive*.

Well, sort of, anyway.

When her tongue licked over his skin again, fire shot from his neck right to his aroused cock. *Aroused*.

Angels didn't—

The hunger grew deeper. He wanted to touch. He wanted to run his hands down her arms and feel her soft skin. He wanted to tangle his fingers in her hair. He wanted—

She wrenched back. Those eyes of hers—not green anymore, a deep, turbulent black—stared up at him. "Who are you?"

"Keenan." The name would mean nothing to her.

"Okay, Keenan." She sucked in a sharp breath. "Better question. *What* are you?" She asked and licked her lips, probably catching more of his blood on her pink tongue.

Nicole might not understand the truth about him, but he knew *exactly* what she was.

When he didn't answer immediately, her brows furrowed and she tried to pull back. *No.* He caught her wrists and held tight.

Touching.

His thumbs tracked over the delicate inner flesh of her wrists. "When did you change?" The question slipped from him, but the kick in his gut told him the answer. No wonder he'd been expelled. His crime hadn't just been refusing to take orders.

He'd made another monster for the world.

No, she wasn't a monster.

I am.

Her slightly-pointed chin lifted a bit. "I asked my question first." She swiped her tongue over her lips once more. "You don't taste like a human."

Of course not.

"You're not bitter enough to be a demon."

So she'd been sampling the supernatural delicacies?

"Are you a shifter?" She tried to pull her hands free. She probably expected to break away easily. The strength she had must trump most supernaturals.

He wasn't most.

"I'm not a shifter." He'd give her honesty there.

"Then what in the hell are you?"

"Not in hell," he murmured and pulled her closer. "Not anymore." Then, because he could, because if he wanted he could do anything now and not have to worry about the consequences, he kissed her.

Her lips were open just the way they should be for a kiss. He pressed his mouth to hers. Probably too hard, but he couldn't seem to hold back. His mouth crashed onto hers, his tongue thrust past her plump lips, and he tasted her.

Yes.

His cock ached now, so thick and hard he hurt. Humans took their pleasure whenever they wanted. He could be like them. He'd already paid the price, so *he* should be able to take what he wanted.

And in all his time, Keenan had never wanted anyone the way he wanted her.

So this is a kiss. The thought floated through his mind. Hot. Wet. Wild. He liked it. A lot.

She wrenched her head away from him. Nicole was breathing hard, her breath rasping. "What the hell was that?"

He blinked, then let his eyes narrow. His cheeks seemed to burn as he stared down at her. "I bled for you. I thought a kiss was the least I deserved as payment."

She pulled free from his hold but only because he let her go. "You thought wrong."

"Didn't you kiss your other prey?" And that had the

rage stirring again. So many emotions churned inside him now. Sometimes it seemed as if they'd rip him apart. "Weren't you rubbing against them, promising sex, when you—"

"I wasn't going to sleep with them!" Her hands flew up into the air, and he saw the small, deadly claws on the ends of her fingers. "I didn't want to scare them, so I was . . ." She broke off, shaking her head. "Never mind. I don't have to explain myself to *you*."

"You were seducing them." The words fell between them. He lifted a brow. "You think seducing the blood away is any better than holding down your prey and just taking what you want?"

She flinched. "Maybe I don't have a choice." Nicole spun around and gave him one truly glorious view of her butt as she stormed away.

But she wasn't really going anywhere. They weren't done.

"Why didn't you try seducing me?" Probably not what he should have asked then, but . . . did she not find him appealing at all? Did she truly prefer the boy she'd had against the wall?

Perhaps the kiss had been wrong. He, too, could try seduction instead of force. If it worked for her . . .

"There's no point in seducing hunters." She threw this over her shoulder. "You'd screw me, then still kill me."

Maybe. But . . . "If you walk away from me now, you *will* die."

Those words stopped her. She glanced back. "That's a threat, huh? What are you gonna do? Jump me? I'm not so easy to take down."

She would be.

"I'm not the threat right now." He went closer because her scent drew him in. Lush woman. But . . . something else. Soft. Light. A wisp of . . . vanilla?

"You look like a threat to me," she said, turning slowly to face him.

"In about five minutes, more of Romeo's friends will be here. I told them to stay away." Keenan tilted his head and his nostrils flared. "But I don't guess they listened."

She licked her lips, a fast flash of pink tongue. "Romeo? Who's that?"

His jaw tightened. "The first idiot you had ready to donate blood tonight." And Keenan guessed he counted as idiot number three. "I took down him and his men, but I didn't kill them." He hadn't touched any of them with his hands because he'd been afraid that one touch would shove them all straight to hell.

But that particular power was gone. A very, very good thing.

"You walk away from me," he continued, "and they'll have you long before you can make it to that broken-down Chevy."

"It's not broken—"

"It is now." What? Had it not been gentlemanly to tear up her motor? He'd needed to cut off her escape.

Her chin tipped up again. "I can always get another ride." She whirled and started marching away.

"They want to slice you into pieces."

She was still walking. He wouldn't chase her. This time, she'd come to him.

"They know you're a vampire, Nicole."

"You don't have to say it like that!" She snapped but didn't stop. "It's not like I can help what I am!"

That gave him pause. Had he said the word with distaste? Hatred? Sure, he'd never been a fan of the undead, but she wasn't like the others.

When had she changed? Must have been that night. Az had said . . .

Headlights cut into the lot and Keenan saw her tense. "That's not them," he said. "Not yet."

Her gaze darted toward him as she fired a fast glare over her shoulder. "You just want to take me down, too. You want to kill me just like they do."

"No." There were many things he wanted from her, but her death wasn't his priority right then. "If I'd wanted you dead, trust me, sweet, you would have been in the ground by now."

And he wouldn't have needed to crawl out of it.

"Then what do you want?"

Ah, she wasn't moving away now. He closed in on her and she faced him.

The faintest rays of red light trickled over the sky above her. Dawn. The vampire's weakest hours were at hand. "If you don't come with me, they'll kill you today."

"What do you want?"

He stared back at her. *You.* "Does it really matter? I'm offering you protection for the day. I'm offering you life. You just have to step forward . . ." He raised his hand toward her. "And take it."

She inched closer. "Nothing is free in this world."

"Nothing's free in *any* world." Every action led to consequences. Punishment.

"I'm supposed to just take you at your word?" She laughed, a bitter, mocking sound. So unlike the laughter he remembered from her. "Right. The minute my guard lowers, I'll find a stake in my heart."

"Then don't lower your guard." Seemed simple enough. "But come with me. We don't have any more time to waste." His gaze rose to the sky once more. "They know your weakness." Just as he did.

"I don't trust you," she whispered.

"Good." His hand was still up. "You have five more seconds, and then you can fight them all on your own." She hadn't taken more than a few sips of blood from him. She wouldn't be strong enough to battle her enemies during the daytime. Surely she'd realize that.

But she was backing away. "I know better than to trust a man with such a beautiful face."

That had him blinking in surprise.

"Especially when I know what lies faces like that hold. The last man who looked like you—handsome and perfect—he taught me about hell."

His heart slammed into his ribs. "What man?"

But she kept talking and he wasn't sure she even heard his question. "He got into my head. Took away my choice. Made me . . ." She swallowed. "I don't trust anyone now. And surely not someone who looks like *you*."

Then she ran from him. Again. Right into the night.

He stood there with his hand still up. He waited a few moments. Just a few, and then—

Keenan heard her scream. He heard the telltale thuds of fists in battle. He heard a man cry out in agony.

If only she had trusted him . . .

Then the squeal of tires echoed in the dying night and burnt rubber filled his nose. The men had gotten their prize. They'd captured their vamp.

Pity. They should have listened to him. He never lied. Never made idle threats.

Now it was time for them to die.

The jerks had tossed her into the trunk. Like that was going to hold her inside. Maybe if they'd waited until the sun was higher in the sky she'd have been trapped, but not now.

She lifted her knees up and slammed them into the

metal above her. The lock popped with a shriek and the trunk flew open.

The car immediately swerved, jerking to the right, then to the left. Nicole sat up and grabbed the back of the car. She knew she'd have to jump for it, and hitting that pavement would *hurt*. But it wasn't like it would be the first time she'd had some flesh ripped away.

A bullet zinged by her head. She ducked, seeing too late the pickup truck that was zooming behind her. The pickup—and the man hanging out the passenger's side with the gun pointed at her.

Where the hell were cops when she needed them?

And, of course, no one else was on the road. Those awake at this hour were still straggling out of the bars, and they sure as hell weren't on this lonely stretch of road.

On my own. Maybe she should have listened to the hunter.

And maybe he would have just staked her the moment she let down her guard.

Oh, well. She heaved up and jumped out of the car.

The guy fired again. *Missed*.

She hit the pavement, and, yes, that flesh tore right off her arm. She rolled, then hit again. *Rolled*.

The truck came charging right for her.

She kept tumbling, aiming her body for the edge of the highway and that incline she could see waiting.

The car's driver slammed on the brakes and the squeal hurt her ears.

They'd have to hunt her on foot once she made it off the highway. *If* she could make it off the highway.

The sun was creeping up in the sky, and she could feel the weakness starting to leaden her limbs.

Carlos—the guy she'd thought was such an prime mark back at the cantina—ran toward her. Dammit, she should have realized that setup had been too easy. When would she learn?

She rolled down the ravine, and after a few bumps, she sank into the shelter of the trees. Those jerks wouldn't have a target now. Not a clear one, anyway. The rasp of her breath seemed too loud.

Vampires weren't supposed to hide. *They* were supposed to be the big, tough badasses.

But she was still new to this whole vampire business and being a badass had never come easy to her. She couldn't even get her claws out right then. That damn sun . . .

Silence.

Nicole blinked. There'd been shouting a moment before. Yells in Spanish to get the "Devil's whore!" The coming sun hadn't drained her strength when they'd first attacked. She'd still had enough power that when she'd swung out with her right fist, she'd broken the older guy's jaw. But then they'd all swarmed her and tossed her into that trunk.

But now . . .

Silence.

Her nose twitched. She knew that smell. It was a scent every vampire craved. Blood.

A car engine roared to life. She lifted up a bit and saw the vehicle fishtail as it tore down the road.

And there were two dead bodies in the middle of the highway.

Nicole glanced to the left . . .

"You should have listened to me."

Keenan. The hunter she couldn't shake.

He tossed a stake onto the ground. It rolled toward her. "Guess what Romeo wanted to shove into your heart?"

Not Romeo—*Carlos.* That was the name he'd given her. "You . . . killed him?"

"No. He got away with some of his men."

Some. Yes, a look at the bodies had told her that some hadn't been lucky enough to escape. "You killed them."

His lips twisted. "I didn't have to. Your humans were piss-poor shots. When they were aiming at you, they took out their own men."

She didn't believe him. Not really. But . . . Her gaze trekked back to the dead men. The blood pooled beneath their bodies.

There had been so many shots while she ran.

"I didn't touch them," he said, and her stare snapped back to him. "There was no need. They killed each other. Humans are good at that."

His lifted his hand toward her, palm up. "Every second you stay out here, you grow weaker."

Weaker—almost human. If those men came back . . .

"You have my word, I'm not here to kill you."

"What's your word worth?" That hand was tempting. How long had it been since she'd actually been able to trust someone else?

She pushed to her feet. Swayed.

And realized something was very, very wrong.

Nicole blinked and glanced down at her arm. Bleeding. Wha—

"They shot you." Fury thickened his words.

She hadn't even felt the sting of the bullet. But her arm was coated in blood.

One surefire way to kill a vampire . . . blood loss.

"Not the . . . first time . . ." She could heal from a bullet wound, provided she didn't bleed to death first. Her left hand rose, pressing against the shoulder. The bullet had gone right in and right out.

I didn't take enough blood from him.

But something had been off about Keenan's blood.

The flavor was so different from anything she'd had before. Not sweet, but more like an old wine flavored with a hint of spice.

Human blood didn't taste like that—and most *Other*, well, they were too smart to let vampires bite them. Unless they were baiting some kind of trap.

"What is . . ." His hand was still up, and she wasn't sure how much longer she'd be able to stand on her own feet. "What is your word worth?" She asked again.

He moved toward her and caught her close. His scent—man, power—wrapped around her. "You don't have a choice."

The rays of the sun trickled down on her. If he'd wanted, he could have killed her. Bleeding, weakened by the sun—she was such easy prey.

Not that she'd admit that. "If you try to hurt me, I'll take your head." Such a big, bold bluff. Almost badass. If her voice hadn't broken in the middle of the threat, it probably would have sounded more intimidating.

"You can try," he said and lifted her into his arms. Her breath hissed out as the wound in her shoulder began to throb.

"How'd you get here . . . so fast?" The only vehicle she spotted was the old truck that had been following behind the sedan. "Where's your car?"

"Didn't need a car." But he was heading toward the abandoned truck now. He eased her inside, then hurried around the front, and jumped into the driver's side.

The keys were still in the ignition. His strong, tanned fingers reached for the keys.

She touched his hand. "Thank you." The words sounded hoarse.

He glanced at her with one brow rising. "You don't need to thank me."

But he'd saved her life. Perhaps twice in one night.

And once upon a time, her sweet Southern mother *had* taught her manners. Some instincts couldn't die.

She closed her eyes and leaned back against the torn seat. "I'm not going to wake up handcuffed to your bed or anything . . . am I?"

Silence. The thick, uncomfortable kind that normally would make her squirm.

But right then, she could barely even hang on to consciousness.

"Fair warning . . ." She licked her lips. "When the sun goes down, I'm a different girl." One who'd had to learn to fight back the nausea and drink blood from a live source. One who knew how to seduce and hide the shaking in her knees.

If only she weren't so tired now . . .

But she'd been running for months. Been so desperate.

If he wanted to kill me, I'd be dead by now.

Grim comfort, but the only comfort she had. Because in that instant, Nicole knew there was *no* choice. There hadn't been from the moment she'd crawled back up to the road. She needed him.

But what would he do with her?

The hotel's walls were paper-thin. The bedding was old and faded.

And there were no handcuffs in sight.

Keenan carried Nicole to the bed and placed her carefully onto the sagging mattress. She didn't stir. She'd gone to sleep—passed out—about three hours ago. He'd kept driving, wanting to get her to relative safety.

He hadn't stopped all the men who'd taken her. Romeo and a sidekick had fled. Since Keenan didn't want those two charging after her again, he'd made sure he crossed the border.

Not that Texas would be that much safer for his little vampire.

Vampire.

He stared down at her, frowning. Blood soaked her shirt, and vampires couldn't afford that much blood loss. When she woke, she'd be desperate to drink again.

Food for a vamp. Looked like the mighty had fallen. Not that he minded having her mouth on him. No, that had been . . .

Pleasurable.

Handcuffed to the bed.

His jaw clenched. He didn't need handcuffs to keep her by his side. Soon enough, she'd realize that he was the only thing standing between her and the monsters on her trail. *Now* he understood the whispers he'd heard—the stories about the *Other* who were tracking his runaway teacher.

He reached for her shirt. One pull and the fabric ripped. Her skin was stained red with blood, but the wound had started to close. Good. He'd clean her up, let her sleep and . . .

And figure out just what he was supposed to do with her.

Her lips were parted as her breath gently eased out. She was so pale. Far paler than she'd been back in New Orleans. Back then, she'd had sun-kissed skin and laughing eyes.

Now, her skin was like every vampire's he'd ever met. Too pale. And her eyes, when she fed—pitch-black.

His fingers skimmed down her arm. The flesh was as soft as he'd imagined. Smooth. Chilled.

She was—

Her lashes flew up. Her eyes were green, that deep green he remembered so well. "I don't want to die . . ." She whispered, her voice fretful.

"You won't." Not that day. He'd make sure of it.

Her left hand rose to her throat. "Hurt me . . ."

Did she even know what she was saying? Doubtful. Her eyes were already starting to sag closed again, and her voice had slurred on the words.

But he leaned close to her anyway and let his mouth hover near her ear. "I won't."

At least, not any more than he already had.

It seemed that nearly everything had been taken from him. Even the life—*her life*—that he'd meant to save.

Vampire.

CHAPTER THREE

It was the thirst that woke her. The pain of her parched throat and the grumble of her stomach trickled through her consciousness. Thirst/hunger . . . for vamps it was one and the same.

Then the other sounds registered. The soft expulsions of breath in the air. The squeak of beds, close, probably within one hundred feet. The rumble of cars on a highway.

She licked her lips. The move didn't help the thirst any. Nicole opened her eyes. *He* was beside her. Keenan's long lashes cast dark shadows against his cheeks.

His chest was bare, the muscles strong and toned and his flesh tanned a golden brown. The thin sheet lay just over his hips, barely covering his waist and legs.

Nicole glanced down. Her clothes were gone. Right. She'd figured that when she felt the cold air on her breasts. She grabbed the sheet and yanked it up.

And that thirst had her teeth stretching, burning . . .

He was still asleep. So close. If she was careful, he wouldn't even realize what she was doing.

Maybe.

Nicole leaned over him and her hair fell forward to brush against his arm. She could hear his heartbeat drumming. Such a strong, powerful beat. He'd tasted so good before. If she could just get a few more sips of blood, she'd have enough strength to head back into the night and disappear.

Her mouth lowered toward his throat. Just a few drops . . .

"So I had to promise not to hurt you, but as soon as you wake, *you* go right for my throat."

She froze. Her gaze lifted, and she saw his lashes slowly rise. He turned his head a fraction and met her gaze. "Hardly seems fair, sweet."

She swallowed—tried to, anyway. "You don't . . . understand the thirst." For a human, it would feel as if the person had gone a week without food. So consuming. Overwhelming.

"I understand more than you can imagine."

No, he didn't. She wrenched away, keeping that sheet clutched to her as she rolled for the edge of the bed.

He grabbed her wrist in a lightning-fast move. Now it was her turn to freeze.

"Where are you going?" He demanded, but his hand wasn't rough on her flesh. His thumb was . . . stroking her. Like he was enjoying the feel of her skin. Weird.

Sexy.

A shiver skated over her. "If I can't take from you, then I have to find someone else."

Now his hold tightened. "Going to seduce another human?"

Her head whipped back toward him. "Would you rather I ripped out their throats?"

"I'd rather you didn't do anything with them. Humans are dangerous."

She laughed at that. "Of all the monsters out there, I fear them the least."

"Then you're being a fool." He still didn't let her go.

And, great, he'd called her a fool. Way to sweet-talk.

"Humans hunted you last night," he said. "When humans realize what you are, they want you dead."

"*Everyone* wants me dead." Why did he think she'd been running for so long? "I've been running from shifters, demons, and hunters like you ever since I became one of the undead." And she was tired.

If they'd just leave her alone . . .

But since she'd risen as a vampire, she seemed to have some kind of beacon on her back. They kept coming after her. Before she'd left New Orleans, a group of demons had broken into her house. Screaming, fighting, they'd tried to force her to leave with them.

They hadn't expected her vampire strength. She hadn't expected it either. But when she'd nearly ripped a demon's arm from his body, the others had finally backed off.

"How long have you been a vampire?"

Not a growl now. A deep, rumbling question. His thumb still stroked her wrist.

Her breasts tightened. "About six months." She licked her lips. *Thirsty.* The sheet had dipped near his waist. She wouldn't look down there, well, not again, anyway. "One day, I was your average almost thirty-year-old, walking in the sun, eating chocolate cake, drinking margaritas after work. Then . . ."

She shrugged. A careless move when she cared too much.

"Then one night, I became something else." She wouldn't talk about that night. The hunter wasn't going to pity her and offer to let her walk away. Hunters had no pity.

"A vampire bit you."

She rolled her eyes. "Yes, well, that's usually the way it works. He bit, I fought back and—"

"You had to ingest his blood in order to change."

She drove the broken glass into his throat. Blood poured from the wound. On her hands. Her face. Her shirt. Nicole cleared her throat. "I guess I did." She paused, and her hands clenched around the sheet. "His, but not the other bastard's."

"The other—"

"There were two of them there that night. One who attacked and one who just *watched*." No matter how much she'd pleaded, he hadn't helped her. "When I fought back, the other one got out of there fast enough. He ran, but one day I'll find him."

"Will you?"

Her head jerked in a nod. "Damn right. And he'll pay for what he did." No, what he *hadn't* done.

Help me.

Keenan turned his hand over and offered his wrist. "Take the blood."

Nicole blinked. "Why—"

"You can't hunt. Those humans might have tracked us and if you go out to hunt, they'll find you." He paused, then said, "And if you don't drink, you'll just slow me down."

"Uh, I don't have to slow anything with you, we're not—"

"*Drink.*"

Right, like she was going to refuse a buffet. She yanked his wrist toward her mouth. Her teeth scraped over his flesh. Her tongue tasted him and then she bit.

"*Nicole.*"

Her gaze flew to his face. His blue eyes glittered at her and, as she watched, a dark flush covered his cheeks.

So good. No taste had ever hit her like this, and with

every delicious drop of his blood, strength seemed to pour back into her.

"Is it . . . supposed to feel like this?" His voice was gravel-rough.

Was she hurting him? Her fingers were curled tight around his wrist, but she'd tried to be careful when she bit.

His teeth ground together. "Your mouth . . ." His breath hissed out.

Her head lifted at once. "Pain? I'm sorry, I—"

Keenan gave a hard negative shake of his head. "*Pleasure*."

Oh. She hadn't felt pleasure when she'd been bitten. Only terror and agony. But the men she'd tasted over the last few months had seemed to enjoy the bite, and—

He pushed his wrist toward her mouth. "More."

She wanted more, but . . . There was always a price. "Do you know what happens when I drink?"

His eyes narrowed.

The sheet had started to rise at his waist. *Aroused*. Oh, damn, she'd meant to keep her eyes up. She yanked her stare to his face. "When they drink, vampires link with their victims." Another lesson she'd learned. "The more I drink, the more control I'll have over you." Maybe she should have just shut her mouth. Having control over a hunter could only be a good thing.

But . . . she remembered what it was like when someone else had the control. When someone else had been in her mind, forcing her actions, and yanking her around like a puppet on a string. *I won't do that to him.* She dropped Keenan's hand.

There were two kinds of vampires in the world. Those that had been born to the blood, and those that had been taken, like her. The Taken had been transformed, but if you traced the bloodline—the literal, actual line of blood that had been spilled and drunk—a Taken would always track back to a Born.

And the Borns . . . they were the ones with the absolute control. They could link with every person in their sick blood family tree. Link and control.

The Born's thoughts would whisper through his family's minds, slipping inside, weakening, compelling, controlling . . .

No, no, I don't want to kill!

But she'd been made to kill.

No control.

She wouldn't do the same to Keenan. No matter what else he was, he'd saved her the night before.

"You won't have control over me."

He sounded so certain that she almost laughed. But when she glanced at his eyes, she found his gaze burning on her.

"It doesn't work that way for my kind," he said. "Only one thing can control us and that one thing isn't a vampire. Vamps have no power over me." He stared down at his wrist a moment, at the faint marks on his skin, then he glanced back at her. "So drink up because you can't hurt me, you can't kill me, and you can't control me."

Her fingers reached for him and curled around his strong wrist. "Sounds like you're my perfect food supply." The words were meant to be mocking.

She lifted his wrist to her mouth and sucked the skin. Her eyes were still on him, and she saw the flare of his pupils. Her teeth rasped over the flesh. "Too bad you're a bounty hunter and all you want is to turn me over to your boss for a quick payment." Because she was a wanted woman.

Some blood could never be washed away.

Nicole bit him. His breathing deepened and his drumming heartbeat filled her ears as she drank.

Strength filled her. Strength and . . . need.

Lust.

She'd never physically wanted her other prey. She'd just taken a few sips from them and hadn't indulged long enough to truly enjoy the taste of their blood.

Keenan was . . . different.

She licked his flesh and stole away the last few drops of blood. Their eyes held. There was no mistaking the raw desire on his face or in his eyes.

"I'm not a bounty hunter."

She lowered his hand. "You . . . you're with Night Watch." Night Watch was *the* bounty-hunting agency when it came to paranormals. The Night Watch agents were often *Other*, too. Who better to catch the supernaturals than the shifters with their enhanced senses? The witches with their magic?

And she'd already been warned once by a Night Watch agent. Dee Daniels had sent all the vamps a warning when she slayed Grim, the Born Master who'd been controlling them.

Cross the line and die.

"I know about Night Watch, but I don't work for them." His head cocked. "I don't work for anyone."

Now *her* heart raced too fast. "But you said . . ."

"No, *you* said. And I was hunting at the time, so I guess that did make me a hunter." His lips twisted. "Of sorts."

"What were you hunting?" Her fast heartbeat seemed to shake her chest.

"You."

She jumped off the bed. The sheet ripped, but she kept a hold on just enough fabric to cover her body.

"I've been chasing after you for a while now."

"Chasing me . . . but not because you were hired to find me."

He shook his head.

Where were her clothes? "Then why?"

"Because you're the key."

No, um, she was a vampire. Not some kind of shiny—

"I lost something very, very important, and you can help me get it back."

—magical—what?

He rose from the bed. The sheet dropped. Oh, damn, she looked. *Very* impressive.

Too bad he was crazy. "I'm not a key to anything."

He walked around the bed and gave her a real nice view of his sculpted ass. Then he snagged a pair of jeans from the back of a chair. Well, that was probably for the best. He yanked up the jeans and kept stalking toward her. "Actually, I think you're the key to everything."

Her gaze searched his. "You're wrong. I'm a schoolteacher. I-I—"

"You *were* a teacher. Now you're a vampire." He shook his head and studied her a little too clinically. "I don't know if that will make things easier or harder."

Nicole started creeping away from him. "Look, I really wish you luck on finding your lost key, but I think it's time for me to leave." Her back bumped into the door. "Thanks for the, ah, blood, and the bed, but now—"

His gaze flew to the door behind her.

Then the door shook. Hard. Someone was banging a very powerful fist against that wood.

"I'm not the only one who thinks you're the key," he growled. "You ever wonder why all those demons were after you?"

"I just thought I had really crappy luck." Even before her change, she'd been dealt one raw hand by fate. *If the vampire hadn't taken me out . . .*

"Actually, you may be the luckiest woman I've ever met."

Bull.

The door shook again.

"There's a demon on the other side of that door," he told her. "He knows you're here, but he thinks I'm just some human, so that means we'll both be easy prey."

She sidled away from the door. "I don't care much for demons." Not since that gang had jumped her.

His eyelids flickered just a bit.

"But I'm not scared of them," she continued quickly. "I—"

The door smashed as wood splintered beneath the force of the intruder's blow. Nicole jumped back as the demon shoved his way inside.

The guy was muscled and tall and had angry, pitch-black eyes. A demon's real eyes were always black. The iris, the sclera—everything was black. But usually the demons used glamour magic to hide that telling indicator.

Guess this guy didn't care that she knew what he was.

"Vamp," his voice thundered, "I'm tired of chasing—"

His head snapped up. His eyes zeroed in on Keenan. And the demon paled. "You . . . you're not . . ."

Keenan stepped forward and a grim smile curved his lips. "I'm her guardian."

The demon's black eyes seemed to double in size. "Bullshit! She's a vamp, she don't have—"

"No one touches her, no one hurts her, without going through me first."

Oh, wait, that was . . . Nicole's breath rushed out.

Nice. But she was a vamp with superhuman strength, and she could certainly manage to handle a demon or two.

Even if the guy in her doorway looked to be close to six foot four and made of bricks. Size didn't equal strength. Not in this new world she lived in.

So she stepped forward, still holding her thin sheet. Her arm brushed Keenan's because their bodies were so close.

The demon couldn't seem to tear his gaze off Keenan, and yes, that was fear in the guy's eyes.

She slanted a quick glance at her hero. He didn't look particularly scary to her. Sexy and strong? Double check. Scary? No.

But he was sure making the demon tremble.

"You don't want me as an enemy," the demon finally said, but he made no move to approach them. Actually, she was wondering if the guy *could* move.

"Yes," Keenan said flatly, "I do. You . . . and your boss."

Why did everyone but her seem to know what was happening here?

"So go run back to Sam and tell him that she's off-limits. There'll be no more vamp hunting, not unless he wants to lose his demons."

The demon's head jerked in a fast nod, but as he stepped back, his gaze darted to Nicole.

Her breath sucked in on a hard gasp. *Hate.* There was no mistaking the hatred and fury in that demon's stare.

Even as the guy turned and ran, she knew she'd be seeing him again. She also knew that if she faced him alone, he wouldn't hesitate to go for her throat.

"We have to get out of here." Keenan's eyes were still drilling through that broken doorway. "Even in a dump like this, that crash would've attracted attention, and the cops are the last thing we need now."

Right. She realized her claws were out and that burning black eyes were imprinted in her memory. "He was scared of you."

"He should be."

"*I'm* the vampire, but he was scared of you." She turned and caught his arm with her right hand. Her left still gripped the sheet and held it just above her breasts. "Before I go anywhere with you, I want to know just what the hell you are."

That same grim smile tilted the corners of his perfect lips. "I just told you, sweet, I'm your guardian."

"Bull."

He turned away, those strong shoulders shrugging, and her gaze dipped down the taut lines of his back. Golden flesh, muscle, and—scars.

Bright, angry red scars. Two of them—each about seven inches long—sliced right along his shoulder blades.

"What happened to you?" The scars were still fresh and damn vicious.

He grabbed a T-shirt and yanked it over his head. "I made a mistake." He pulled another shirt out of a small gray duffel bag and tossed it to her.

She caught it and her fingers squeezed the soft cotton. "What kind of mistake?"

This time he tossed her underwear—her bra and panties. His gaze lasered on her. "The kind I won't make again."

Right. Nice and mysterious and broody. Keenan was sure striking her as a broody kind of guy. She let the sheet fall and saw his eyes widen when he stared at her naked flesh. *Uh, huh. Look.* "You realize that tells me nothing."

He didn't speak. His eyes locked on her breasts as he took a step forward.

"Don't even think about it," she whispered. "Guardians are supposed to guard, not touch."

That light flush stained his cheeks again. "Maybe we do both."

Her nipples pebbled. *Down, girl.* She still didn't know him. Sure, she'd tasted him, but she hadn't gotten so much as a whiff of his past or his current life with that drink.

He could be anyone. Anything.

No matter how sexy, she *couldn't*.

Yet.

"Why'd you strip me?" She put the shirt he'd given her on the table, then pulled up her panties. She took her time hooking her bra.

He licked his lips. "I had to bathe you . . . to get the blood off."

Nicole didn't remember that. Actually, the last thing she remembered was that truck ride from hell. "Guess I should thank you for that." She just kept on owing the guy. At this rate, her tab was going to be huge. Suspicion whispered through her. "Just what all did you touch while you were bathing me?"

The bra was in place, pushing up her breasts. Yes, his gaze was still on them. Men, supernaturals or humans, were always the same.

"Not enough," he muttered.

Her eyes narrowed.

"When I touch you with sex in mind, you'll know it, sweet."

He seemed so confident. But why did she see a slight tremble in his fingers?

He spun, giving her his back and showing her those red scars again. "If we stay any longer, the cops will be here."

"I can handle Mexican cops."

He laughed, a rusty, rough sound. "Maybe, if we were in Mexico."

Oh, no. She shoved her hands into the sleeves of the shirt and popped her head through the top. The shirt swallowed her and smelled like him. Her fingers rubbed the bottom of the T-shirt. "Tell me, *please* tell me that you didn't drag me into the U.S."

"Yeah, you're welcome. When you passed out, I saved your butt and got you out of Mexico—and away from the locals there who were out for *your* blood."

She yanked up her jeans. In seconds, she'd found her boots. Nicole managed to shove her feet inside them just before he grabbed her arm and they stumbled through the broken door.

And, yes, sure enough, the wail of a siren was already cutting through the night. She stayed quiet while they stuck to the shadows and hurriedly jumped into the truck. They eased out of the lot, driving nice and slow, and cruised right by the black-and-white patrol car that raced into the hotel's parking zone.

Nicole waited a minute, then five more, and as the truck ate up the miles, she finally spoke the words she *had* to say. "I've heard demons recognize each other on sight. That they can look right past the glamour and see the monster inside." Her nails tapped against the rough armrest.

The truck sped up.

It was the way of the paranormal world. Like recognized like. She always knew when she was near another vamp. She'd heard that witches felt the power pull of their brethren.

"That demon," she continued, "he took one look at you, and he got *scared.*"

"Because he was smart."

Right. "But just what did he see?" She asked, letting

her eyes sweep over him. "When he looked at you, what did he see that made him back off?" Not just back off—*run away*.

Keenan's head turned toward her. Even in the dim lighting, she could see him clearly with her vampire vision. He had such beautiful blue eyes—wait, those eyes were getting darker. Darker . . .

Demon eyes.

"I guess he saw through the glamour," Keenan told her, his voice quiet.

Oh, damn.

She was in trouble.

Sam stared up at the night sky. So many fucking stars. Millions of them glittered down on him.

Humans looked at the stars and they wished and they dreamed.

He looked at the stars and knew they didn't matter. The stars were just chunks of glass in the black sky. No, the stars were meaningless.

Others were up there, though, nestled in the heavens. Powerful beings were pulling all the strings and making the puppets dance.

Footsteps thudded behind him. Sam inhaled, catching the scents of the one who approached. Alcohol. Cigarettes. Demon. *Elijah*.

No vampire. Fuck. The bastard would bleed for failing again. How hard was it to bag one newbie vamp? The lady was so fresh she'd probably barely cut her fangs.

Sam turned around, ready to slam a burst of power right at the demon, but the fear in Elijah's black gaze stopped him.

And made him smile. *Finally*.

"Y-you never said she'd have backup."

Because Sam hadn't thought the vamp would. He'd worked so hard to cut her off from the rest of the world. Her silly little comfort system she'd had in New Orleans—ripped away. Her job—gone. Her home—destroyed. No family, no friends—they were all terrified of her now. No one wanted to be close to a killer.

When you isolated your prey, it was always so much easier to take 'em down.

"He could have fuckin' killed me!" Elijah snarled, spittle flying from his mouth.

Sam raised a brow. "He?" His voice came out mild, as always.

"Him—yeah that fuckin' *angel* that was at her side. And she smelled like him. Shit, ain't there some rule about angels fuckin' around?"

"Probably." Undoubtedly. Another way to get cast out. Angels didn't enjoy nearly the preferential treatment that the humans did. Screw up once ... get ready to burn.

"And fuckin' with vampires?" Disgust etched deep lines on the demon's face. "What the hell?" Elijah didn't much care for vampires. Who did? And as for angels ...

Demons were right to fear them.

Sam took a deep breath and asked, "You're sure the man with her was an angel?"

Elijah's head bobbed in a quick nod. "There's no damn way to kill one of 'em, you know that!"

"Everything dies," he snapped, sick of the lies that the *Other* chose to spread, particularly lies about themselves. Only one being was immortal. All the others ... *we can all die.* Some of them just had the unfortunate pleasure of perishing over and over again.

Yeah, life could be one fucking blast.

Elijah yanked a hand through his thick blond hair. "Well, I don't want to be that *everything.*"

Too bad. Elijah was already marked for death. Sam had seen the bastard's end coming for days. Mostly because he'd planned it. Elijah had his uses. The guy was strong, evil, and usually ready to rip and tear. But even a killer had to die some time.

"Describe him to me." There were hundreds of angels. Thousands. Could be any—

"Blond, black eyes, with black wings that hung over his shoulders . . ."

Black wings. An angel of death.

"I didn't even see the wings at first. They moved behind him, like weird-ass shadows." A pause. "Just like yours."

Sam rolled his shoulders and slowly stretched his back as he felt the ghostly flutter of wings that weren't there anymore, not really.

Elijah hissed out a breath. *"Weird-ass . . ."*

The shadow wings were just an illusion. A magic memory. Only seen by demons or angels . . . any who had the blood of the celestial beings in them.

Lucifer hadn't been the only angel to fall. So many others had lost their grace. Or traded it for the chance to be like the humans.

No, the demons who walked the earth now weren't puppets of the devil. They were descendants of the Fallen. Not as favored as humans, but not as cursed as most of the monsters, no matter what some of the zealots liked to think.

"Did he have any unusual marks?" Sam pressed. Who was he up against? You couldn't fight a battle without knowing your enemy.

He'd been right. The vamp had been the link. The key. The Fallen had gone after her, just as Sam had suspected he would.

"No," Elijah said with a shake of his shaggy head.

"He was blond, and he had black eyes. He was one of them damn pretty-boy angels but . . ." The demon's eyes narrowed. "When I first saw him, I swear I felt a cold wind blow right over me."

Sam's breath expelled. *Perfect.* There were so many angels out there, so many different kinds—some harmless and some very, very dangerous. He didn't want to waste his time with the harmless variety.

"How did he act with the woman?" A freshly-fallen angel would be confused. Unprepared for the onslaught of emotion—and need. Lust.

Easy pickings.

Elijah glanced over his shoulder. But, the demon didn't need to check for a threat behind him. The real menace was right in front of him. Was the guy truly becoming a trusting sort now? Fatal mistake.

"His eyes kept going to her . . ."

Interesting.

"And he said he was her *guardian.*"

Sam's lips quirked at that. He suspected the guy was far from a benevolent guardian angel. But if that was the spin the Fallen wanted to play, then who was he to bust the vamp's bubble? At least, not yet.

"I'm all about killing a vamp." Elijah crossed his arms over his bulky chest. "But I ain't taking on that bastard."

"You're that sure he'll take you out?" The demon's fear was new. Elijah had never been afraid of a hunt before.

But Elijah was backing down. "I know Death when I see him."

Yes, Sam was rather betting that he did.

"We're done," Elijah said, turning away and giving Sam his back. Oh, bad move. "I'm sick of dancing on your damn string . . ."

Right. Same song, different fucking dance. "And where will you get your special brew, Elijah? When you walk away from me, who will help you?"

Now that stopped him.

Elijah looked back, and the struggle was clearly etched on his face. Like so many of his kind, Elijah had a bit of an addiction. *Demons and addictions.* When Elijah used his drugs, he could focus his thirst for blood and violence. With the drugs, he didn't kill just anyone—he killed specific targets.

Without the drugs . . . women, children—*everyone* became his prey.

Sam liked to think he'd been doing his part to keep the dog on the leash these last few months. But if Elijah was ready to bite the hand that had been feeding him . . .

"You're not the only game in town," Elijah muttered and kept walking.

Oh, but I am.

"When you change your mind," Sam called after him. "Maybe I'll help you."

Elijah was nearing the top of the small hill, his body a dark shadow.

"And maybe I'll just kill you," Sam whispered, smiling, because he knew that the demon couldn't hear him.

His dog would be back. Probably within forty-eight hours. And if he wasn't . . . there were always other demons. Others who needed what he could give them. Others who were weaker, and so easy to control.

Demons came in every size, color, and power. Some barely tipped the scales, those with powers between one and three. Those poor bastards might as well be humans. A power scale of ten was supposed to be the strongest. A level ten, or L-10, was the alpha of the demon land. So the stories said.

The stories were bullshit.

He glanced back up at the sky and all those glittering stars and he began to whistle.

It took a while for a Fallen's powers to come back. The crash and burn wiped out an angel. This new opponent wouldn't be at full strength yet.

It was the perfect time to play.

And time to see just how attached the "guardian" truly was to his charge.

Would he kill for her? Bleed for her? Die for her?

One way to find out . . .

A star fell, blazing a trail across the sky.

CHAPTER FOUR

Nicole lunged across the truck and grabbed the wheel. She jerked it hard to the right and the truck careened across the road.

Keenan fought to push her back, but he'd been totally unprepared for her attack. "Nicole, what are you—"

The truck plowed into a wooden fence and fought to hurtle forward.

Keenan shoved his foot down on the brake and the vehicle bounced twice, then steam exploded from the engine as the truck finally stopped.

Of course, Nicole had already flown from the truck by then. Her door hung open, swaying in the breeze, and he caught sight of her curving, come-get-me hips as she ran away from him.

Again.

He jumped out of the truck. Yeah, that piece of crap wasn't going anywhere, but if he didn't hurry, Nicole could easily vanish.

"Nicole!" He shouted. Great. He couldn't see her now. With a vamp's speed, she could be anywhere.

"I'm trying to help you!" Keenan called out into the night.

The hit came from behind. A hard, fast tackle that sent him slamming into the ground. He rolled, moving in a blink, but it still wasn't fast enough. Nicole pinned his hands to the ground and loomed over him.

"Why do I need help from a demon?" She demanded and her teeth lengthened as he watched.

She straddled his body. Her hips and sex pushed down onto him. Keenan had never been in this particular position with a woman. He rather . . . liked it.

A lot.

His cock began to swell. "I don't . . . I'm not here to hurt you." He didn't bother letting his eyes change back to blue. She'd see him as he was. Probably would be better that way. Keenan could break from her hold in an instant, vampire strength or not, but he lay on the ground beneath her and let his gaze slowly rise to her face. "If I'd wanted you dead, I could have killed you back at the hotel. You couldn't fight back in your sleep."

"Maybe killing me isn't the plan." Her eyes narrowed to slits. "Death is the easy part."

He'd always thought so. Until her.

"If this is all some trick that you and your demon buddies are working, think again."

Now she was starting to offend him. "I have no demon friends." Come to think of it, he wasn't sure that he actually had *any* friends.

She leaned closer to him, and her thighs slid against his hips.

Like it.

"What's so special about me, huh?" The darkness shone in her eyes. *To fight or fuck.* He'd heard the whisper before. A vamp's eyes changed to black when she was either getting ready to battle or to screw.

"Tell me, Keenan . . . Why do I get a guardian? You don't know me. You know *nothing* about me."

Her scent surrounded him. Her hair brushed his cheek. If he wanted, he could lunge up and reverse their positions in about two seconds. Maybe one.

If he wanted.

I want.

He put a stranglehold on the beast that was growing inside of him. A beast he hadn't even known about until her.

Lust.

"You're not special," he managed to grit from between his teeth.

She blinked at him. "Uh, I—"

"You're just like every other human out there." If he said it enough, it would be true.

"Wrong answer, hotshot. I'm not exactly human." And she let her claws scratch his flesh. A light, painful sting.

It shouldn't have made his cock twitch.

It did.

He sucked in a breath and tasted her. His eyes squeezed shut. But now . . . now he could feel her. Supple thighs. Slender, soft body. *Control.* "You . . . you were just like the others." His words came out as a growl. "Going to work. Teaching at that school. Work. Home. Over and over."

He caught the hitch of her breath. "What school?"

His eyes opened. "St. Mary's. Down in the Quarter. You'd stay late with the kids, then hurry home, change and meet—who was it? Donna—for drinks at the bar on—"

"*How do you know this?*"

"You never went home with any of the men." Not while he'd been watching. "You flirted. You drank.

Wore skirts a bit shorter than the ones you used to wear at St. Mary's—"

A shiver skated down her body—the shiver trembled over him like a silken touch.

"You weren't any different from a hundred other women in the city. Work, job, friends . . ." *No different.* No different from the thousands of other charges he'd taken, but when he'd looked into her eyes . . .

He'd lost everything.

The rage hit him then, a hard fire that burned with the lust. Keenan lunged up, spun them, and pushed her onto the ground.

"I'm not a human you can jerk around," he told her, bringing his face in close to hers. "Your strength isn't going to work on me. Your bite isn't going to make me weak." Right then, he was the one wanting to take a bite. And why couldn't he? Why couldn't he take what he wanted from her?

He'd *burned* for her.

"That's bullshit!" She tried to shove away from him. When would she realize he wasn't letting her go anywhere? "A vamp can drain a demon, a vamp can kill—"

He stared into her eyes. No, she wasn't the same woman she'd been. In her stare, he now saw the secrets, the pain, the fury. A fury that matched his own because he wasn't the same, either. "Sweet, I don't remember saying I was a demon. Just that the bastard had seen through my glamour."

Her lips parted.

And he took.

His mouth crashed onto hers, a deep, hard kiss. This need, this consuming hunger—it was what had led the humans into temptation.

Sin.

Oh, yes, he wanted to sin with her.

She didn't wrench her head away from him. Didn't bite him with those too-sharp teeth.

But she didn't kiss him back.

He *wanted* her to kiss him back.

"*Nicole* . . ." His hold gentled on her wrists. Her breasts were tight. Her hips pressing up against him. Keenan knew the signs of a woman's arousal but he didn't know how to get her to give in to her need.

His hands freed hers. He kept his lips on hers and managed to soften the kiss. His tongue swept inside her mouth. *Yes.* That rich taste that was pure Nicole tormented him. He wanted more. Wanted everything.

And her hands were on him now. In his hair. Not pushing away. Pulling closer.

Her tongue met his. She gave a little moan in her throat, a hungry, hot sound that had all the blood in his body rushing right to his erection.

Lust.

Men had killed for this. Died.

He could understand. Finally.

His hands pushed between their bodies and found the snap of her jeans. *Touch.*

He had to know what she felt like. Had to see if she was wet. Hot. Would she taste as sweet there?

Her zipper hissed down. His fingers pushed inside and found the soft cotton of her underwear. Her hips arched against him, and her tongue licked across his lips.

And a car's engine growled in the distance. Coming closer. Closer.

No.

His head snapped up. His breath heaved out, and he couldn't look away from her. On the ground. Lips red from his mouth. Her arms around him, her claws digging into his skin.

His gaze trekked down her body. His stare lingered

on the pebbled nipples that thrust against her borrowed shirt. Slowly, slowly, his gaze dropped down to the jeans that were unsnapped, revealing the pale skin of her abdomen, the dark black of her panties.

More.

The car's engine idled closer. A siren blared on, a slow, droning wail.

"A cop . . ." Her husky voice was like a stroke right over his flesh. "If he sees the truck, he'll think we're hurt. He's not going to leave . . ."

No. "This isn't over." His thumb brushed over her lips. Her eyes widened and then her tongue snaked out, licking him.

His heart shoved into his ribs. "Nicole, *don't run from me again.*"

The cop was getting closer. Keenan could hear the tread and roll of the tires.

Her head moved in the slightest of nods. "After we get rid of him, you tell me everything, okay? Because if you're not a demon, then what are you?"

He would tell her this much. "Once upon a time," he rose, stretching to his feet and pulling her up with him. "I was an angel."

Her lips parted in surprise, but then she immediately shook her head. "What? Come on, no way. Angels aren't—"

"Vampires can be real. Demons can live. Werewolves can howl." He raised a brow. "Why can't angels exist?"

A car door slammed. Footsteps thudded toward them. *"Oh, shit,"* a rumbling male voice said. *"Hello! Hello! It's all right, I can help you!"*

Keenan glanced back toward the wrecked truck. In the dark, a human wouldn't be able to see them. The beam of headlights from the patrol car illuminated the truck's wreckage. He turned toward the cop.

Nicole grabbed his hand. "Guardian . . . angel?"

Not quite.

"There's something you should know," he said, but didn't look at her. Her hand felt cool against his overheated flesh.

"Wh-what?"

"Sometimes, angels really do fall." She deserved the warning.

Nicole sucked in a sharp breath.

"And when we do, we bring hell on earth in our wake."

She backed up a step. "So are you the good guy—"

He laughed at that. "Not even close." But he leaned in toward her and pulled up her zipper, then snapped her jeans. His fingers lingered too long. He couldn't help that. "But I'm not here to hurt you. Those bastards who come after you, yeah, I'll hurt them, but *not you.*"

"Because I'm your key?"

He'd told her that in a weak moment. The truth should have stayed hidden. Too late now. He gave a grim nod.

The cop was swearing and yelling. They'd have to talk more later.

Keenan headed for the truck.

"If it's all true . . ."

Her voice followed him. She didn't.

"If it's true," she said again, and, so, what, a vampire doubted an angel's word? The world really was screwed. "Then, Keenan, what made you fall?"

He froze.

"Angels don't just . . . fall. It had to be something big, right? Something very, very bad."

The cop's flashlight hit him them. *"Sonofabitch!"* The guy exclaimed and ran toward Keenan. "Take it easy, sir, I'll get you help, I can—"

Keenan lifted his hand. "I'm not hurt."

"Neither am I," Nicole murmured as she came slowly to his side.

The flashlight jerked toward her and illuminated her pale face.

"Ma'am, you sure about that?" The cop's voice held an edge of worry. "That truck was smashed to hell and back."

Apt.

"Not a scratch on me," she said, her lips rising in a smile.

The cop—no, that wasn't a cop. The older man approaching them so cautiously wore a brown sheriff's uniform, complete with a shining silver star. The sheriff raised his brows. "Mind telling me what happened out here?" The worry had faded from his voice, and suspicion coated the words. His right hand began to inch toward his hip and the gun holstered there.

Nicole stepped forward.

After we get rid of him, you tell me everything, okay?

Keenan grabbed her wrist. Nicole wasn't the same woman she'd been in New Orleans. He didn't know what she'd been doing for the last six months. Drinking from prey, killing them?

Don't know, but I still want her just as much.

That was the problem.

"Don't hurt him," he ordered, his voice a whisper.

Her expression never altered.

"*Let go of that woman,*" the sheriff barked. "And you both put your hands up high in the air."

Keenan let her go and raised his hands. After a moment, Nicole followed suit.

The sheriff came closer, sniffing as he neared them. "Don't smell no alcohol." He peered at Nicole. "Ma'am, you been drinking?"

Keenan nearly smiled.

"No, I—"

"*Holy shit.*"

Now that gun of the sheriff's was up and out—and aimed directly at Nicole.

"*I know who you are.*"

Keenan saw the fear flash on Nicole's face.

The sheriff jumped back and pointed the gun right at her heart. "I got a fax in my office earlier today— one with your picture. You're wanted for murder in Louisiana."

Keenan heard the hitch in Nicole's breathing. A faint sound, but one he caught.

"And you nearly killed a cop . . ." The deep lines around the sheriff's eyes tightened and his lips thinned. "He came to help you, and you nearly killed him."

"No, I didn't!"

Keenan didn't know this story. "Perhaps you have the wrong woman."

The cop's eyes darted to him. "You don't want to be with her, mister."

He held that stare. "Yes, I do."

The sheriff yanked out a set of handcuffs and crept carefully toward Nicole. "No, no, if you'd seen what she—"

Nicole's hands flew up and she punched the cop, her fist catching him under his jaw. The blow sent him stumbling back.

When the sheriff hit the ground, his eyes were closed and he was out.

"I can't go to jail," Nicole whispered with her eyes on the cop. "I didn't want to hurt him, but I can't—"

"A vampire would never survive in jail." Or rather, the powers that be wouldn't let her. He knew how the game was played. Some supernaturals—generally the low-level demons and the charmers—could handle prison. Vamps couldn't. They'd start feeding on the other inmates and eventually, they'd have to be put down. Besides, it wasn't like the jails could really hold them. Or the shifters, for that matter.

He bent next to the sheriff. Still breathing. His jaw wasn't broken, though it must have been made of glass. Keenan glanced back up at Nicole. "You up for a run?" The faintest scent of flowers teased his nose and he tensed, his gaze sharpening.

But no one else was there.

Just Nicole, with her wide, worried gaze. And the sheriff, but he was all but dead to the world.

That scent . . .

Time to get out of there.

They couldn't take the sheriff's car. Too obvious. But with their power and speed, they could put a whole lot of distance between them and the man on the ground.

She gave a grim nod. "What about him? When he wakes up, he'll put out an APB on me. More deputies will start searching."

"Then I guess we need to make sure they don't find you." He rose and scanned the dark area around them. "We run until we find the nearest house. We take any car we find."

"Steal it?" She bit her lip as her stare landed on the sheriff. The guy did look rather defenseless, knocked out like that. His arms were spread. His hat had fallen onto the ground near his head, and his thinning gray hair stuck to his forehead. "Isn't that breaking one of the commandments and not very, um, angel like?"

Going to dwell on that, was she?

"Told you, sweet, I fell." Now they had to move. Sleeping Beauty wasn't going to stay out for long. "You ready to run or do you want him to toss your butt in jail?"

She swallowed. "Run."

Good. He laced his fingers through hers, and they raced into the night.

The angel watched them run. Keenan was so fast he could have easily left the vampire, had that been what the Fallen wanted.

But he knew Keenan didn't want to leave her.

That was the whole crux of this nightmare. Keenan didn't want to leave the one who'd lied, fucked, and killed.

Sad. He'd had so much potential. So much promise. And for Keenan to now fall so low . . .

The vampire would suffer for this. Tempting. Making the strong weak.

She'd suffer.

Wings flapped as the angel prepared to soar above his charges. Death was coming. Sweeping closer in the air. This time, Death wouldn't be denied. No last-minute reprieve would be given because of temptation.

Not for the vampire, anyway. There was still a chance for Keenan. Grace could be regained.

It just took one selfless act. One courageous, determined act.

And all would be forgiven.

Sins . . . wiped clean.

As the angel soared into the night sky, his black wings merged with the darkness.

Sheriff Tom Duggley pushed up, flexing his jaw. That little lady had one damn devil of a punch. But then, he should have expected that.

He rose and shuffled toward his car. The scent of flowers hung in the air, a light scent, totally out of place in the all but barren land.

Tom was surprised they'd left his keys—and the car. Bad move. They'd be on foot, and so much easier to track now.

He grabbed the radio. "Need an APB . . ." He spit out a mouthful of blood. That punch had been *real* hard.

But she hadn't killed him.

Odd, that.

"We got us a wanted fugitive in the area. A Nicole St. James . . ." He rattled off her description.

Killing him would have been so easy for her. Child's play, especially with him knocked out.

But she'd let him live.

And that big hoss of a protective shadow she'd had with her hadn't gone for his head, either.

"Approach with extreme caution," he said as his fingers tightened around the radio. The deputies wouldn't understand just how extreme the situation would be.

They didn't know about vampires. He did.

Good thing he'd taken the liberty of ordering special bullets for his department. A sweet little batch made just for situations like this.

A silver bullet/holy water combination—a mix that had trickled through law enforcement personnel a few years back.

A mix that worked wonders on the border. You never knew exactly what you'd see on a Texas night, not when you'd been patrolling for as long as he had.

But she'd let him live.

Damn odd for a vamp.

Damn odd. Especially since, if the stories were true, Nicole St. James had killed two men since her vampire transformation.

* * *

The motorcycle roared down the road. The engine vibrated between Nicole's legs as she held tight to her angel.

Angel.

Impossible.

But she'd spent her life as a semi-good Catholic girl. She'd been taught about angels since the time she learned her first few words. She'd always believed, until . . .

Until she'd thought God turned away from her.

Not when she'd gotten the news from the doctor. No, she'd still believed. Still hoped. Still wanted to pray.

But . . .

That alley. That blood-soaked hell of an alley had convinced her. And then, the things she'd done . . .

Her eyes squeezed shut as she pressed her forehead against Keenan's strong back. No helmets, of course. They'd been lucky to steal the bike. The bike's owner hadn't been forgetful enough to leave helmets behind. Now they were just driving hard and driving fast. Her arms were around Keenan, holding tight.

Trusting him didn't seem wise, but what choice did she have? She'd been thrown into this new world, with no damn clue how to survive. She'd barely scraped by the last few months. There'd been so many times she'd come close to death.

And she'd changed. The woman she'd been—yes, she really had died in that alley. The woman holding onto the back of a fallen angel had fallen herself.

He'd said that if she drank his blood, it wouldn't weaken him, so the man seemed to be her perfect prey.

Perfect, but . . .

I can't trust him.

When a vamp took from prey, a link was formed. A link that allowed the vamp to slip into the prey's mind.

Sometimes to control, other times to steal thoughts or memories.

When you had control over someone, trust wasn't exactly an issue. So most vamps didn't worry about trusting their prey.

But she didn't want control. Never had. She knew too well what it was like to be a puppet on someone else's string.

Soon the lights of a city glittered in the distance. *San Antonio*. Good. The bigger the city, the easier it was for a paranormal to hide. And to feed.

Keenan snaked through the streets, guiding the bike easily, and she held him tighter. Whether she wanted it or not, her fate was being tied to his.

Keenan braked on a busy corner lined with bars, drunk humans, and cars.

Nicole eased off the motorcycle. "Thanks for—"

He turned toward her with his eyes glittering. "We get weapons here."

Weapons? They were in front of a bar, not—

"Weapons," his gaze swept her, "and clothes for you." He left the motorcycle, not glancing back, and caught her hand as they pushed through the crowd. No standing in line for her angel. Just a determined stride forward.

The bouncer at the door was too smart to try and stop him, or maybe the guy saw the hint of fang she flashed.

But then they were inside. Music blared. Smoke drifted in the air and the scent of—

Blood.

Nicole froze. The scent of blood was everywhere. She hadn't smelled so much as a drop outside, but *in* the bar—*everywhere*.

"What? Haven't you ever been to a feeding room

before?" He murmured. "Would have thought it was your kind of place."

Nausea and need tightened her belly. "F-feeding room." Right. She knew what these places were. She'd heard about them. They were—

"Your one-stop dining shop for vamps," he said, his gaze sweeping the crowd. She followed his stare and saw that a woman had a man pinned against the far wall, and her fangs were in his throat. Two men fed off another woman in the corner. A few feet away, a female vamp bit the wrist of the blond with her.

Blood.

"I don't . . . like feeding rooms," she managed. Her teeth were burning, an instinctive response to all the blood. Like a dog salivating. *Want. Need.*

But the prey in feeding rooms—they were expendable. Used, tossed away. Killed.

"I'm not . . ." *Like this*. Right. Who was she kidding?

His steady gaze—once again that bright blue—seemed to say the same thing.

"Why are we here?" She demanded. *Weapons.* That's what he'd said, but the only deadly weapons she saw in that place were fangs.

"You've got demons after you. And I don't quite have the skills I used to possess." His head cocked and his attention drifted to the bar. "If we're going to fight the ones coming after you, we'll need to be armed."

Right. Because she wasn't exactly kick-ass. He'd probably noticed that. "How did you even know this place was here?"

But he was already walking toward the bar as he tossed his answer back to her. "Oh, you'd be surprised at the things I've seen."

No, she wouldn't be.

Keenan reached the bar. He flattened his hands on the surface. "Max."

The bartender glanced up with one brow raised. Keenan knew the guy's name?

"I want to see the goods in the back room," Keenan said.

Nicole put her elbow on the bar and let her stare dart around the room. The humans there had come in willingly, but with one bite, the vamps had taken control of them. There'd be no running back home and telling friends about the cool new club now. From here on out, the humans—those who made it out alive—would say nothing without the vampire's permission.

Control.

She hated it.

"Listen, buddy," the bartender snapped, "I don't know you and I don't know what the hell you're talking about—"

His voice choked off.

Nicole glanced back at him. Keenan had gone over the bar. His hand was around the guy's throat, and he was squeezing, hard.

"Don't bullshit me," Keenan ordered. "I know about the stash, and I need weapons."

The angel wasn't so good with finesse. Nicole cleared her throat. The bartender was a vamp. Maybe she could deal with him. She flashed a smile. A vampy one. "What my boyfriend means—sorry, he's still new to the scene—is that I want to make a purchase from you."

The vamp's black eyes measured her, and he gave a jerky nod, as much of a nod as he could manage right then, anyway. "I'll deal . . ." He rasped. "With . . . you."

"You'll deal with us both, Max," Keenan promised as he shoved the guy back.

"How do you know me?" Max asked, his eyes narrowing.

"Word about you gets around."

Okay, that sounded ominous.

Max straightened up quickly, cast a quick eye around the bar, and then shoved his thumb toward the door on the left. "This way."

They couldn't go that way fast enough. That blood smell was getting to her. Her control had never been that good and right then, that scent was sweeter than any candy she'd ever had.

She hurried behind Max and Keenan, her stare quickly sweeping back once more and—

Oh, shit.

Nicole's eyes met a pitch-black stare that belonged to a vampire she'd hoped to never see again. Handsome face, arctic black eyes, and a smile so cold and cruel . . .

A lover. A killer.

Connor.

Her breath seemed to choke in her lungs. Then Connor lifted his hand and crooked his finger at her, urging her closer. Bastard.

She spun on her heel and hurried after Keenan.

But she knew the vampire would follow her. Damn him. *She knew.*

Some monsters never stopped hunting.

Not until you shoved a stake into their hearts.

CHAPTER FIVE

Max pulled out the gun and offered it, handle first, to Nicole. She took it, her hold hesitant, but the gun felt solid in her grip. Almost . . . reassuring.

"Silver bullets," he said, giving a nod. "It works best on wolf shifters, but all them damn animals will have some reaction to it. Fire and they'll go down." His lips kicked up a bit. "At least for a little while. Long enough for you to take their heads."

Her lashes lifted and she met his stare. "Long enough," she repeated quietly. The words came out weak because it seemed like her throat might be closing up.

Connor could come in at any moment. They didn't have time to waste. "How much?" Why was she even asking? She had about one hundred bucks shoved in her back pocket. Well, she'd had it shoved there last night. She hadn't even checked today.

Max ran his tongue over his fangs. "Well, now . . ."

"We're not worried about shifters." Keenan took the gun from her and slammed it back down on the wooden table. "What have you got that will take out a demon?"

Max's black eyes narrowed. "That would depend on just how strong your demon is." He shrugged. "If you're talking low level, maybe one or two . . ." He lifted his claws. "These will work well enough."

Her hands fisted.

"I'm not talking about a level two." Keenan glanced over his shoulder and his gaze tracked to the door. That thin wooden door wouldn't keep out anyone for long. Surely not someone like Connor McQueen.

"Then what are you talkin'?" Max demanded, crossing his arms over his chest.

"Powerful." Keenan looked back at him. "High-end. Strong enough to burn the city to the ground around you."

"Wh-what?" Nicole gasped. The demon who'd come hunting for her had been that strong? No, no way, he'd turned tail and ran. The strong didn't run. Just the weak.

Me.

The faint smile slipped from Max's face. His eyes measured Keenan. "What are you?"

Nicole stepped closer to him. "I already told you, he's with me."

"He's no pet."

Pet—the slang for human prey that a vamp drank and fucked. She swallowed. "Yes, he is." Nicole felt Keenan's gaze dip to her face.

But Max didn't seem to be buying her story. A muscle flexed in his jaw. "I want you both out of here. I don't care how much money you have, you get the fuck out!" He ran a shaking hand through his hair. "I don't want no level-ten demon comin' after my ass."

"But if he did," Keenan murmured, "how would you fight him?"

Max's lips parted on a surprised breath.

A soft knock sounded at the door. Soft—such a lie. Nicole moved fast as she spun and put her back against Keenan's. The better to fight and defend.

So two seconds later, when the lock shattered and the door burst open, she was ready to meet Connor's black stare.

"Hello, there, love," he told her, his voice flowing with the faintest of English accents. "Fancy meeting you in a hellhole like this."

Hard fingers squeezed her shoulder. Keenan. *No.* He'd whirled around at Connor's entrance, giving his back to Max. A fatal mistake with a vampire.

Nicole grabbed Keenan's arm and yanked him out of the way—just as Max came at him, with claws and teeth ready. Max hit her instead, taking her down to the floor. His claws scraped down her arm, but she punched at him and slammed her fist into his jaw. Max's head snapped back, and she twisted as she managed to roll away from him.

When she leapt back to her feet, she saw that Connor stood in the doorway, fangs glinting. Two other vamps waited behind him. Figured. Connor had always liked an audience.

"You're bleeding." Keenan's too-calm voice came from her right.

She didn't want to think about her arm. Those claws had stung like a bitch. "I'm fine." Actually, they were screwed. Connor was blocking the only way out.

Coming there had been a serious mistake.

"You shouldn't have brought your *pet,*" Max sneered as he circled her and Keenan. He wiped away the blood that trickled from his lips, then he licked his bloodstained fingers. "Only vamps dine here. Everyone else is on the menu."

"Yeah, coming here was a great idea," she muttered,

trying to put her body in front of Keenan's. She offered a big, fake smile to the others. "My mistake. Won't happen again."

"*Nicole*." Connor purred her name. "Of all the vamps, you're the last one I expected to see tonight."

"Who is he?" Keenan growled.

Connor's smile was too knowing. "I'm the one who taught her about the sweet mix of pleasure and pain."

She would *not* go there.

"We killed together . . ." He said, voice dipping with the memories. "Then I drank from her, and—"

And Keenan was on him. Holy shit, she hadn't even seen the guy move! Keenan had his hand wrapped around Connor's throat and Connor's minions were staring with wide eyes because—damn—he'd moved *fast*.

"Nicole doesn't kill." Keenan's dark, rumbling voice filled the room.

Connor's claws slashed down Keenan's arms. "Yes, mate . . . she does. Not that she . . . had much . . . choice . . ."

Max tried to run at Keenan's back. Again. This time, Nicole just grabbed the gun he'd been fool enough to leave out, and she shot him.

Max howled and fell to the ground. Silver might not kill their kind, but any bullet, especially one fired at close range and right into a man's spine, would hurt like hell.

The gunshot had every eye turning to her. She readjusted her aim as she pointed at the minions. "Step toward him, and you'll be digging out silver."

They didn't move.

"You're . . . defending me?" Keenan's brows rose. "I didn't expect that."

"Yeah, well," *neither did I,* "you saved my ass, so I figure now it's my turn."

He nodded. "But I didn't need your help."

Ungrateful much?

Keenan stared into Connor's eyes. "Do you want to die?"

Connor jerked free. He'd always been strong. "Bastard, I *am* dead. And so are you. Nikki doesn't have the balls to shoot me, not after what we went through. So I'll cut you up, I'll drain you and then—"

Nicole shot Connor right in the chest. He stumbled back, then fell, screaming her name.

"It's because of what we went through," she whispered, aware that her fingers were shaking, "that I *can* shoot you." Because she knew just how vicious Connor could be. *Shoot or die.* She didn't want to die.

"Bitch!" Connor shoved a hand against his chest, and his fingers were immediately stained with blood.

Shouts echoed from the bar. Of course, the other vampires had heard the gunshots. With their enhanced hearing, there had been no way for them to miss the shots. Even humans wouldn't miss the sounds of gunfire. Getting out of that place would be a nightmare.

Keenan stepped back.

"There's got to be another way out of here," Nicole said, her gaze sweeping the room and her hands still trembling. *Didn't kill him.* She'd just slowed Connor down. He'd recover the moment he got his fangs into one of his bimbos' throats.

Not a human. Not dead. She tried to take a deep breath.

The minions had slipped away. They'd probably be back with reinforcements. "Maybe another door—"

"*No, shit, no, leave me alone!*"

Her head snapped to the left. Keenan was crouched next to Max, and the angel had a knife in his hand. Where had Keenan gotten that? And he'd just sliced the vamp.

"It's blood loss, right?" Keenan asked in that same quiet, calm voice he'd used when he told her that she was bleeding. A really creepy voice. "That'll kill a vamp every time." He lifted the knife to Max's throat. "You could bleed to death slowly . . . or else I could just take your head." The blade cut Max's skin.

"*No!*"

Nicole didn't move. "Keenan . . ."

"You never answered my question, Max."

The shouts from outside grew louder. More vamps were creeping toward the door. She glanced down at the weapon she still held. How many more bullets were in the gun? How many vamps could she hold back?

"Tell me what you've got that will take out a level-ten demon."

That was what Keenan still wanted to know? Her gaze whipped back up. "Tell him," she snapped, her heart racing. Oh, they needed to get out of there. *Fast*.

Another vamp tried to come through the doorway. Nicole fired. Missed him.

Laughter teased her ears.

"You're just . . ." Connor rasped. "Makin' 'em . . . hungrier . . ." His red hand pressed to his chest once more. He offered his twisted grin. "Missed my . . . heart."

Because she'd planned to. Once, he'd helped her to push away the misery and hate that had nearly consumed her. "I owed you." Was there a price for pleasure? "I don't anymore. You come at me or at Keenan and I'll—" What? Could she really kill him?

Connor's gaze held hers. "You never had the killer instinct, did you?"

"*What will take out the demons?*" Keenan demanded.

"N . . . nothin' . . ."

The blade dug deeper. More blood flowed. Nicole's hand was sweating around the gun. "Weapons like this . . ." She lifted her gun. "They aren't supposed to work against the stronger demons."

"Nothin' made by man . . ." This came from Connor. His eyes had slipped closed. He'd lost a lot of blood, but she knew he'd gulp more down at the first opportunity. The man loved his blood.

He was right, though. The stories said that no weapons made by man could kill those all-powerful level tens.

If one came after you, then you were pretty much screwed.

But why would a level ten want her?

You're the key.

To a very broken lock.

"If you can't help me," Keenan gritted, "then you're no good to me." Blood poured down the bright edge of the knife.

What was he doing? He shouldn't kill. He was an—

"Angel!" Max's choked gasp froze them all.

Keenan leaned in close. "What about angels?"

"Angel's . . . Dust . . ."

The knife lifted a bit. The blood still flowed.

"Heard . . ." Max licked his lips. "Heard talk there was a voodoo priestess in LA—she mixed angel's blood with some herbs—m-made the Dust." He was talking fast now. "It's poison to demons. Even the badasses . . ."

"You don't have any of that Dust here?" Keenan wanted to know.

"No." A rough laugh. "Takes *a lot* of their blood . . . to make it . . . And I ain't seen no fuckin' angels to kill."

The knife trembled over Max's throat. She knew

just how badly Keenan wanted to do some killing of his own then.

She hurried to him and brushed her left hand over his arm. "We need to get out of here."

Keenan nodded and rose, his body stone hard.

Nicole looked at the door. Vamps stood there. Smiling, waiting. They'd have to fight their way out. Pity she wasn't a very good fighter.

"You shouldn't turn on your kind," the blond woman in front of the pack said, her teeth stained red. "Not very loyal."

Nicole forced a shrug. "Guess I'm just not the loyal type—"

Fire exploded. A red-hot ball of flames flew right at the blonde and the other waiting vamps. They screamed and ran, fighting each other in their fury to escape from the fire.

A fire that had come from nowhere.

No, not *nowhere*. Keenan's hand was up and his fingers pointed right at the fire. Wisps of smoke surrounded his hand. The smoke curled over him and seemed to hold him tight.

Because the fire had come from him.

Damn.

Demons could control fire. Apparently, angels could, too.

Nicole managed to shut her mouth. Then she shook her head. "You should have mentioned that little talent sooner." She could have saved some bullets. Actually, she *would* save some. Silver would definitely come in handy for her at some point.

The vamps were running, really hauling butt now. Nicole tucked the weapon into the back waistband of her jeans.

Keenan glanced at his smoking fingers. "Didn't realize I had the talent."

She pushed him toward the door. "Keep that hand up. You might have to burn us a way out of here."

But, no, the vamps had scattered. The humans were still there, and they stared with dazed eyes and bloody bodies.

Nicole's jaw locked. *Why do they choose to be prey?*

"Come on," Keenan said, and his fingers wrapped around her wrist. She jerked at the contact because his touch was so hot. Not hot enough to burn, but . . .

She swallowed and her gaze met his. "Keenan . . ."

He'd already looked away. "I should burn this place to the ground."

"They won't leave," she said, waving her hand toward the humans. "They're too far gone. You burn it, and they'll die."

He stalked toward the door. She glanced back, that blood tempting her . . .

Until she met those vacant stares. Lost. Helpless. Desperate.

Me.

The motorcycle was still parked outside. A miracle in this neighborhood. She secured the gun in the saddlebags, and they climbed onto the bike. He revved the engine, then they streaked forward. She held on tight, as tight as she could, and drunk in the heat that flowed off his body the way she'd normally drink in blood.

A shudder shook him, a long, hard shudder. Her hold tightened on him. "Keenan?"

The motorcycle sped faster as it ate up the pavement. She glanced back. No sign of vamps.

He snaked to the left. To the right. Then he turned down an alley and the motorcycle snarled to a stop. He jumped off the bike at once and stormed away from her.

"Keenan?" She sat on the bike, uncertain as she watched him. "What's wrong?"

He jerked at his shirt and ripped the material from collar to waist, a long, jagged tear that revealed his chest. "*So . . . hot.*"

She cleared her throat. When you conjured fire, it stood to reason you might get a bit . . . warm.

But, wait, he was *sweating*. His cheeks were flushed and his eyes kept flickering from blue to black.

Not good.

Her gaze swept the alley. "We're not safe here." Understatement of the century. She didn't see anyone, but thanks to her vamp-enhanced hearing, could hear the slight shuffle of footsteps. Someone hunted here.

Of course, these days, someone hunted everywhere.

"*So . . . damn . . . hot.*"

She jumped off the motorcycle and went to him. One touch and, oh yes, he was hot. Burning as if he had a fever. "You really haven't ever conjured fire before?" She didn't know how this whole creating fire thing worked.

He jerked his head in a *no*.

"Great. Okay." She pulled him a little closer and let her gaze sweep down the alley once more. "I saw a little motel a few turns back." One of those no-tell motels that charged by the hour. "We'll hide out there, dunk you under a cold shower, and you'll be fine in no time." Maybe. He'd be fine or . . .

He'd start burning everything around him.

Uh, oh. Right then, she was the closest thing to him.

That blue/black gaze bored into her. "You need to get away from me."

Because he'd obviously had the same thought. If he couldn't pull this power back, she'd be feeling the burn up close and personal. Like witches, vamps burned too fast.

Despite the rumors out there, vamps actually weren't that hard to kill. An old-fashioned stake and a beheading worked. Bleeding out—yeah, that would give you a dead vamp, too. Or . . . you could always let the flames take a vamp straight to hell. *Trade one fire for another.*

She swallowed. "You need me." Because the guy seemed to be having trouble standing. He hadn't left her when she was at her breaking point, and she wouldn't leave him.

Unless the fire got too close.

Nicole pulled him back toward the motorcycle. She climbed on first. "Just . . . put your arms around me. Hold on, for a little while."

He eased down behind her. The bike dipped beneath his weight. Then his hands came up and curled around her stomach. His heat lanced right through her T-shirt. But it wasn't painful. Not even close.

Pleasure.

It took her two tries to start the bike. They almost fell once, and then she got the motorcycle to a weaving acceleration. They didn't go fast. It wasn't a smooth ride, but she managed to get them back to the motel.

A fifty on the counter got them room number seven. Lucky seven. She pushed him inside, flipped the lock, and then started to strip him.

The angel studied the chaos at the feeding room. Humans—so pale and listless. Ready for death.

Good. Death was ready for them.

One touch, and a soul was his. Ready for the afterlife and any judgment that would come.

So many souls . . . so easy to take.

But, no, Death didn't get to pick and choose. Death took only the ones on the list.

So he walked past the vamp with the bloody chest, the one that seemed to actually see him. He took the humans who were marked and let the others escape.

The taint of the Fallen hung in the air, mixing with the scent of ash that clung to the floor, to the walls.

The Fallen was discovering his power. A dangerous thing . . . for those around Keenan. He'd be out of control with the initial rush of power.

The first taste was always the most tempting—and therefore the most dangerous.

Keenan would want more, *need* more.

Demons weren't the only ones who became addicted too quickly.

His gaze searched the room. *Take another.*

They all had their addictions.

He was strong enough to fight his. The Fallen wasn't.

More death would come.

Her hands were on him, soft, cool hands that stroked—and ripped away his clothes.

"Nicole . . ." Keenan's tongue felt thick and swollen in his mouth, but, right then, his whole body felt that way. Courtesy of the fire and her stripping hands.

She tossed his shirt onto the floor. "Kick out of your shoes," she ordered.

He nearly fell, but he managed to get the shoes off.

Then her hands went for the waist of his jeans. The heat inside flared hotter. The air around them crackled with sparks.

She froze. He saw the pulse racing at the base of her throat. "You in control?" She whispered.

Barely. He nodded.

Her hands brushed against his abdomen. Keenan sucked in a sharp breath. The fire seemed to burn his entire body from the inside out, but the need—that was centered in his throbbing cock. Her fingers were so close, and he wanted her hand on his flesh.

No, he wanted his flesh *in* her.

She pushed down his jeans. Her tongue swiped over her lips as her gaze dipped. "We, ah . . ." She stepped back, turned, and hurried toward the bathroom. "We need to get you cooled down."

He stood there, hands clenching, naked. Hungry, hot, *wanting her.*

The roar of water filled the room.

"Keenan?"

He kicked out of the jeans that had locked around his ankles. He put one foot in front of the other and forced his body to walk into that bathroom. She stood next to the shower, and water pumped down in a hard stream.

"I—it's ice cold. It should help you." Her voice was husky, sexy, and her gaze fell to his cock.

Need.

He wasn't supposed to need her. He'd never wanted another. Never craved. Never wanted to take.

But he wanted to take her more than he wanted another breath.

He stepped into the shower. Like icy needles, the water pelted his body.

But the heat didn't fade. The lust didn't ease away. And he couldn't take his eyes off her.

Water poured over his shoulders, slid down his chest, and he found his hand lifting toward her.

Her own eyes had begun to slowly darken and fade to black. In that stare, he saw the same raw need and lust he felt.

"Nicole . . ." *Forbidden.* This wasn't the way for angels.

But he wasn't an angel anymore. If he'd already paid the price for his lust, then shouldn't he take the pleasure that waited for him?

She stepped closer to the shower. Water sprayed on

her and dampened her T-shirt. Then her hands lifted. Not to reach for him, but to yank off that T-shirt.

The heat consumed him. Burning hot, so hot from within, and he *ached*.

His gaze raked her. *Sweet flesh. Pale. Smooth. The plain black bra hugged her curving breasts . . .*

In mere moments, the bra hit the floor. So did her boots, her socks, her jeans . . . the soft cotton panties.

Steam began to rise in the ice-cold shower—the steam rose from his flesh.

"You have to cool down," she whispered.

The sight of her naked body wasn't going to cool him off. Right then, he didn't think anything could.

Flat stomach, flaring hips. Legs that were long, sensual . . .

She stepped into the shower. Her nipples—dark pink—pebbled at the lash of cold water.

Take. Taste.

He wanted her so badly, but when he looked down, he realized that he'd clenched his hands. The better not to touch.

She shivered at the cold even as she came closer. Her breasts brushed against his chest.

His eyes closed. The touch was agony. A sensual hell.

More.

He wanted her nipples in his mouth. He'd seen humans fuck. Once, he'd thought it looked messy. Hot.

Now he wanted that—the shove of bodies, the pant of breath, and the hot clasp of her sex.

He wanted it all.

"You're not cooling down," she said, voice husky, and her hands rose to clasp his shoulders.

Keenan laughed, a rough bark of sound. "When you touch me, there's no way I can't burn."

She rose onto her toes. "Maybe—maybe that's what you need to do . . . just let the fire out."

Her lips were so close he could taste the sweetness of the kiss that would be. "And if it scorches you?"

Nicole shook her head. Her dark locks were already soaked. "It won't." The icy water had her trembling, but she still leaned in ever closer to him. "*It won't.*" Her words sounded certain, but there was so much she didn't know.

Her lips—cold from the kiss of water—touched his. Her mouth was open, her lips soft, and her tongue pushed into his mouth.

He was lost. But then, with her, he always had been.

His hands were rough with need as he held her tight. He wanted every inch of her body against his. His tongue met hers and tasted. His mouth opened wider because he needed more of her. Wanted *everything*.

Her hand slid between their bodies. Slick, sure. Her fingers skated over his nipples and a growl vibrated in his throat. She pushed between them, sliding her hand down, down . . .

When she touched his cock, his body jerked.

"Easy," she whispered as she pulled back and lifted her gaze to meet his. The water wasn't as cold now. He'd made it hot. Couldn't control it.

No control.

Her fingers wrapped around his cock, curving over the base of his erection, and she began to pump. Long, slow pumps as her lips skimmed down his neck.

Bite. He wanted her mouth on him as her hands squeezed his flesh. Because her touch . . . *burning hell* . . . nothing had ever been so good. The pressure was just right, her fingers tight and sure, and now, moving faster, *faster*.

"It's okay," she said, her voice stronger, and she

pushed him back so that his shoulders hit the tile. "You won't hurt me." Her lips curved in a wan smile. "I'm stronger than I look."

So am I. He was strong, but still, with her, close to breaking.

His breath came harder and his heart thudded against his chest. Her tongue licked his throat. A hot lick that had his need spiking.

Then she began to slip down his body. Steam rose off her, and her lips feathered down his chest. Down his abdomen.

His muscles locked and when her lips closed over his cock . . .

The pleasure erupted inside of him. One lick of her tongue, just one, and Keenan lost control. Lost everything.

His vision dimmed to red. A distant roar filled his ears. The pleasure mixed with the fire in his body, burning, sweeping away his past, sweeping him into the maelstrom of need and hunger and . . .

Yes.

Pleasure.

So much pleasure.

She licked him again. Trailed her fingers over his cock and looked up at him.

He knew then he wouldn't get enough. That lash of wild pleasure—it had only been the beginning and he needed, *had* to get more.

Everything.

No wonder humans lied and killed for sex. *No wonder*.

He caught her under her arms, lifted her up high, and barely felt her weight.

"Keenan, we should—"

He kissed her, thrusting his tongue deep and loving the soft moan that trembled in her throat.

His arms moved to cradle her, and, keeping his mouth crushed to hers, he carried her from the bathroom.

The heat that had seemed to burn his body from the inside out had channeled, focused now—and the focus was on her.

Easing her down carefully, he put her on the bed. His gaze swept her body, noting every curve, every small freckle, every inch of perfect skin.

Her legs shifted on the bed, parting, and he swallowed. "I want . . ."

Her right hand eased down her stomach, but paused over the light covering of hair that shielded her sex from his view.

The roar was back, filling his ears. No, not a roar this time. His heartbeat. Pounding so fast.

"I want you," Nicole said, and with that, *nothing* would have kept him from her.

He leaned over her and his right knee pushed down on the sagging mattress. He didn't touch her, was almost afraid to. After having her haunt his dreams—*just like this*—he didn't want to risk reaching out and having her vanish.

But this wasn't a dream. Or a nightmare. This was real. He could just glimpse the edge of her fangs and her eyes were still pitch-black.

Not quite like his fantasies.

But she was still Nicole.

His fingers trailed down her arm. He'd always loved her skin. He bent and his breath blew lightly over her nipple.

She arched toward him. "*Keenan!*"

That was how a woman should say his name. With need and lust and hunger.

Not fear.

His tongue snaked out and licked her nipple. Sampled it and he found that he loved the taste. His mouth opened wider and he closed his lips over her flesh. Sucking. Tasting.

More.

His teeth scored her flesh. Perhaps there was a reason why vamps liked to bite so much. The biting was . . . pleasurable.

Her legs shifted as her breath came faster. He liked that.

His fingers found her other breast and lightly caressed the nipple. But then he had to taste it, too. Her breasts were sweet, the tips like ripe strawberries—a new temptation he'd discovered.

The world was meant to tempt.

The scent of her arousal filled his nostrils. *She wants me.* This wasn't a game. No trick. Nicole wanted him just as much as he wanted her. His head lifted. He stared into her eyes.

"Don't worry," she told him, her voice pure sin, "I won't bite you . . . I'm in control."

He wasn't. And as for biting, "I will." Then he began to lick his way down her stomach as he explored every inch of her flesh. He couldn't touch her enough. Couldn't taste her enough. And, yes, he had to bite. Had to nip the flesh because he liked the way she gasped his name when she felt the edge of his teeth. Not enough pressure to hurt, not for her, just enough to make the need mount.

He pushed her legs apart more and settled between them. His heart was heavy in his chest, his muscles tense and his flesh was so aroused and swollen he felt like he'd explode at any minute.

His fingers shook when he touched her. She gasped, and he looked up, his gaze shooting to her face. But no pain was there, only pleasure.

He touched her again, letting his finger stroke her

flesh, learning the hidden curves, and finding the spots that made her moan and arch.

He leaned in even closer because there was more he needed to know.

How does she taste?

"Keenan." Her nails dug into shoulders. "I need . . ."

"I need to taste you." He'd never thought to have her like this. Fantasies were one thing, reality another. But now that he had her, spread beneath him, open, ready, he wasn't going to back away.

One taste.

Would one be enough?

His lips skimmed over her sex. His tongue licked.

Not even close to enough.

A hungry growl burst from his lips as his hands clamped down tighter on her hips. He opened her more, tasting, licking, savoring every inch of her hot core.

Her moans were in his ears, her claws digging into his shoulders, and her hips pushing closer to him.

He heard her call his name. He heard the broken rasp of her breaths, but he wasn't done.

Her body tensed, and he looked up just in time to see the blind pleasure flow across her face—and he pressed his mouth harder to her and savored the taste of her release as she came.

Then he slowly climbed back up her body. Her breath heaved, and her hands reached for him. He kissed her. Keenan drove his tongue into her mouth and let that wild hunger build and build.

He wanted to plunge into her body. To take and take and let the release rip through him.

Forbidden.

Like he gave a damn about the rules anymore. Those rules were for angels, and he didn't have a chance of ever flying again, not with his wings burned off.

Take.

He couldn't fly, but he could have her. He *would* have her.

Then the scent reached him. The light, almost sweet scent of flowers in the air.

The scent that always came when an angel was near.

He tore his mouth from hers and spun around. His hand automatically went to the thin sheet, and he yanked it over her body. "Get out of here!" He thundered.

"What?" Nicole demanded. "After what we just— you want me to *leave?*"

He grabbed her wrist and chained her to him. "Not you." His gaze swept the room. His nose followed that scent. His eyes narrowed as he focused his stare on the far corner. "You into watching now?" A dark taunt directed at the one waiting.

"Uh, Keenan?" Worry had entered Nicole's voice. "No one else is here."

"He's here." Keenan rose from the bed and didn't bother to cover his body. Angels weren't supposed to care about nudity. And he didn't care about his—just hers. "Unless he's here to kill me, then he needs to drag his winged ass out of here."

He felt the wind whisper against his face. Angel power. "Can't you smell him?" He asked her because a vamp's enhanced senses should at least be able to pick up that light scent. Most humans—those who stopped to pay attention—caught the telltale fragrance.

The sheets rustled. "I . . . *yes.*"

Keenan glanced back at her.

Her gaze was wide, her lips open. "I know that smell. In the alley, when that vampire attacked me . . ." She jumped from the bed and clutched the sheet tightly to her. "I smelled it then." Now it was her turn to sweep the room with her gaze. "There was so much blood, I couldn't figure out why I just . . . smelled flowers."

Because an angel had been near.

"Is he the one who was there?" The worry was gone from her voice. Only fury remained. "This jerk in here—is he the one who stood there and watched while that vamp attacked me?"

Another whisper of wind blew on his face. Then the floral scent began to fade as the angel vanished. What had been the purpose of that visit?

A threat?

He didn't take so well to those angelic threats anymore.

"He's leaving," Nicole whispered. She grabbed Keenan's arm. "I can tell. The scent is almost gone." She turned and her gaze tracked all around the room. "Why can't I see him?"

"Because you're not dead." He exhaled slowly. Time for more truth. "You can only see an angel when you're dying—in those last few seconds before death."

Her lips curved down. "Haven't you heard? I *am* dead."

"No, you're *un*dead. There's a difference." She'd died only for a few seconds. Not long enough for her soul to leave. Just long enough for her body to change when the virus got inside her.

That's what vampirism really was. A virus. One that—if it wasn't monitored—could be passed along until the whole human race died out. Died out—or transformed.

He rolled his shoulders and forced himself to meet her eyes. "He's gone."

"He?" Her brows rose. "Could you see him?" She pressed.

No lies. "I saw enough."

"Was he the one that was there that night?" Her delicate jaw locked. "Was he the bastard that just stood there while the vamp tried to kill me?"

"No." One of the things about angels—fallen or those still in grace—they could never lie. He exhaled. "That bastard . . . well, that would have been me."

CHAPTER SIX

"What?" Her voice had gone flat and cold, just like her eyes.

And her teeth were getting longer and sharper. When the fangs came out, trouble was calling.

But it was time to reveal this to her. After what he'd done tonight, she deserved to know. "I was the angel there that night. I was the one you sensed."

"*You?*" Her knuckles whitened around the sheet. "You saw what he did—"

His muscles locked at the memory. "I saw everything."

"And you just stood there?" Disbelief. Disgust.

His spine straightened. He'd expected this.

"You stood there," she repeated, "and let him hurt me? He clawed me, he bit me, hell, I even thought he was going to rape me—"

Keenan spun away from her. "He didn't." *I didn't let him. I broke the rules. Took him when I should have taken you.*

"Wait. I get it now."

Keenan glanced over his shoulder. "I doubt it."

Wrong thing to say.

She lunged forward. The sheet dropped. "You were my *guardian*. My guardian angel, right? So your job was to watch me."

No. He'd never been a guardian angel, and he shouldn't have watched her so much. Since he couldn't lie, he just didn't speak.

"I thought guardian angels were supposed to keep their charges safe."

They were. Except when he was around. Then the guardians were given other charges. No one could stop death.

He ran a hand over his face. *I did*.

Hadn't he? Or had that angel been there tonight for a different reason? To finish the job?

No.

Keenan grabbed his jeans. Jerked them on. Shoved into his shoes.

"What are you doing?" she demanded.

"I have to find someone."

"No, you're not leaving right now." She stood in front of him. Naked. Furious. So sexy. The bed was just steps away. He'd been so close to the paradise of her body, but now he'd lost that chance.

Thanks, Az, you asshole. The human curses and insults were coming much easier to him now.

"You were there." It was too easy to read the disgust on her face as she grabbed his arm. "Why didn't you stop him? Why didn't you *help me*?" Her claws bit into his skin, drawing blood.

He stared back at her and barely felt the pain. "You were supposed to die that night."

Her eyelids flickered.

"I *wasn't* supposed to help you. No one was." Cold, hard truth.

Her body shuddered.

He had to get out of there. Get away from her. Because he wanted to pull her close. Keenan wanted to hold her and protect her.

But the truth, the real truth . . . he'd been the biggest threat to her all along. He was the darkness that had come to take her away.

Her worst moment—he'd been there. *Watching*.

All that rage and despair she had was directed right at him.

A fist seemed to shove into his chest. "I didn't . . . want to hurt you." Another painful truth.

"You said I was a damn key." Her lower lip trembled. "A key to what?"

His lashes lowered.

"Eyes up, angel."

His gaze snapped up.

"What kind of key am I? Why were you guarding me? Why's another angel spying on me now?"

"I don't know why he's here." But he'd find out. "And you're the key because . . ." *Tell her.* "The night you changed, I fell."

She blinked.

He pulled away from her and in a flash, he was at the door. Angels—even the Fallen—could always move fast.

"Keenan!"

"Stay here." He didn't look back. "You're weak now." Because the sun was rising.

"Oh, don't throw that up at me! I can't control the freaking sunlight!"

"Rest," he said quietly. "I'll be back." That was a promise.

"No, you're not leaving me! If you're going after that angel, I'm coming, too."

The wood was chipping off the old door. His gaze bored into that wood. "If he touches you, you're dead." Simple truth—an angel of death killed with a touch. "A vamp can't even begin to compete with his power." He opened the door and left her.

Elijah knew that dawn was coming. Sweat trickled down his back as he stared at the women easing out of the bar, their bodies held tightly by the men with them.

His heart raced too fast, his hands shook almost constantly, and a fist twisted his guts.

Withdrawal. He knew all the fucking signs. If he didn't get the drugs again soon, he'd rip apart. No, he'd rip apart any fool who got in his path.

He'd been so sure Sam would hook him up. So fucking sure.

He tasted ash in his mouth. No matter what he drank or ate, ash was all he got.

And the whispers were calling to him. Taunting.

He'd first heard those whispers when he was fourteen. Those mocking whispers told him that the humans could see right through his glamour, that they *knew* what he was.

He needed to stop the humans from seeing.

Had to stop them.

Like he'd stopped the others. So many others before . . .

No.

Elijah spun away from the crowd. He just needed his drugs. Once he had those, he'd be in control. He'd pick the prey he wanted—screw the voices. They couldn't tell him who needed to die.

He needed drugs. The drugs shut up the fucking voices.

Drugs.

He just had to find the right dealer. Someone willing to trade with a demon.

* * *

Nicole didn't stay in the hotel room—she wasn't some well-trained dog to do what she was told.

She grabbed the gun she'd taken from that feeding room and ran outside. It only took her a few seconds to get the weapon, but by the time she made it outside, Nicole discovered Keenan hadn't left so much as a whisper of scent behind.

Damn him.

He'd seen. Everything. Her worst nightmare. Her pain and humiliation. Her terror.

He'd seen . . . and he hadn't helped her.

Damn the bastard.

He'd gone—fine. He'd better stay gone. She didn't *want* to see him again. Because if she did, she'd kill him herself.

He'd been there . . . and, moments before, he'd almost fucked her.

The rage built as the hours passed. She found a small shop. Bought some new clothes and ditched his shirt because she was tired of his scent clinging to her. Her new jeans were tight, her T-shirt hugged her body, and the boots made her feel like maybe, just maybe, she could kick some ass. Angel ass.

She walked onto the street and felt the heat of the sun on her skin. Her body was tired, her moves sluggish. She'd get cover—any place but that cheap motel room—and crash.

Her fury had given her the strength to stay out in the daylight, but her emotions were churning now, and they were draining her energy.

Betrayal. Yes, that's what stabbed her right in the heart. She'd been so weak that long-ago night. If he'd just reached out and helped her . . .

"I'd still be alive," she whispered.

"No, Nicole, you wouldn't be . . . that would have been against the rules."

She spun at the hard, male voice.

A man stood there, his dark hair loose around his shoulders. He wore dark sunglasses, glasses that cast her reflection right back at her. Broad shoulders stretched the black T-shirt he wore. His back was pressed against the brick wall on the side of the building and a faint smile curved his lips.

"Stopping you from going into that alley, saving you . . . those weren't options for our boy," he said as his grin stretched.

Our boy.

Suddenly, the day wasn't quite as warm. She stepped forward, just a small step, aware of the few humans strolling down the street. *No help there.* "Who are you?"

One black brow rose. His thumbs were hooked in the loops of his jeans. "I'm a friend of Keenan's."

"An angel?" She'd been raised her whole life to believe in angels. She just hadn't expected angels to look like Keenan . . . or like this guy.

But I believe.

It was vamps and the other monsters she hadn't believed in. That disbelief had come back to bite her in the ass.

He laughed softly at her question, and the sound sent a shiver over her. "I'm no more an angel than Keenan is."

But Keenan was . . .

"Once an angel falls, he becomes something very, very different." He pulled off his sunglasses. His eyes were the same bright blue as Keenan's. His blue gaze trekked to the left, then to the right as it swept past the pedestrians. "Why don't you come closer," he invited, "so we can . . . talk . . . without worrying that the humans will overhear."

She didn't move. The gun was tucked in the waistband of her jeans, hidden beneath her shirt. But what would the silver bullets do against someone like him? *Probably not much.* "I'm fine right here."

His eyes slit. "Are you?"

Nicole swallowed. "What do you want?"

He took a step toward her. She tensed.

"Where is Keenan?" he asked.

She braced her legs apart. "You're not really his friend, are you?" Her right hand began to edge toward the gun. So what if the humans saw? She wasn't dying on this street.

He didn't blink. "No, I'm not."

Great.

"He left you all alone." His lips—sensual but cruel, just like the rest of him—pulled down. "Didn't expect that. I thought you mattered more."

"Why would I matter to him?" *I begged for help.* Help Keenan hadn't given her. "We barely know each other." Fury thickened her voice.

He took another slow, gliding step toward her. She was reminded of a snake slithering up on his prey. "Oh, you might not know him well," he said, "but Keenan knows you."

Then he was in front of her. Mere inches away. He'd moved in a blink—as fast as Keenan had at the motel.

Her hand flew for the gun.

He caught her wrist. Held tight. "I can't let you do that." His head came close, and his lips feathered against her ear as he spoke. To everyone else on the street, it would look like they were lovers whispering secrets and promises. "Digging those bullets out," he told her as his breath stroked over her, "can be a real bitch."

She'd lost feeling in the tips of her fingers. He wasn't hurting her—there was just no feeling. *"Who are you?"*

His left hand rose and brushed back the hair from her cheek. "You can call me Sam."

That told her nothing.

He eased back and gazed down at her. "He should have been with you." There actually seemed to be some sadness in his voice. "I thought he was going to protect you."

"Why would he?" She fired, refusing to cower. For all she knew, this guy was a low-level demon, just bull-shitting his way around and trying to screw with her head. "He has no link to me." Even though she could still feel his hands on her body. Still taste him. *Bastard.* "We're not—"

His laughter cut through her words. "Don't bother lying to me."

"I'm not."

Faint lines appeared around his eyes, then his brows shot up. "You don't know."

She snapped her lips closed.

Once more, his fingers brushed down her cheek. "I bet he likes to touch you, doesn't he?"

Two giggling teenage girls passed them.

"Everything's so new when you fall. Touch . . . it can bring so much pleasure." To be so bright, those eyes of his were so cold. "Or so much pain."

"Let go of my hand," she gritted. A cop was walking down the sidewalk now. The last thing she needed was to get caught between this jerk and a cop.

He didn't let go. "The emotions hit next. Anger. Hate. Fury." His gaze dropped to her mouth. "Lust. I bet he knows all about that, thanks to you."

She jumped back, and was surprised to see that she actually broke his hold. "I don't mean anything to

Keenan. So if you're trying to get back at him by taking hits at me . . ."

"*Stop lying.*"

The real fury in his voice had her heart slamming into her chest.

"He *fell* for you. Of course, he's damn well linked to you."

He fell—

"And because of that link . . ." He sighed. "I'm afraid you're gonna have to suffer."

She really didn't like the sound of that.

"Don't say I didn't warn you," he told her.

That was when the punch hit her—not a punch, an electric shock. Her head whipped to the right, and she saw the cop who'd been approaching—and the bastard had a *Taser* out. The volts were hitting her, hard, jolting her body, and the cop was screaming something.

If she'd been at full strength, the shock wouldn't have even slowed her down. She would have laughed at him. Jerked out the electrodes and *laughed*.

But the sun was out. She was weak. And she went down.

The motel room door was ajar. Keenan frowned as unease slipped over him. This wasn't right. He didn't knock. He just pushed the door open with his knuckles.

Empty.

Of course, she'd left him again. Figured. Especially after his big reveal. Not like she'd want to stick around with the man who'd been responsible for her undead transformation.

You just stood there and watched.

Story of his existence.

He turned away from the room. The place smelled

of her. His gaze swept the street. The sun was up. She shouldn't have gone out during the day.

Easy prey.

Maybe he should just walk away. The obsession he had with her . . . no way could that be a good thing.

He stalked back toward the motorcycle with his hands shoved deep into the pockets of his jeans. He'd bought new clothes. Even gotten some for her. Nicole's were tucked into the saddlebags of the bike.

He kicked up the stand on the motorcycle. Where would she have gone?

I should have stayed with her.

"Lose something?" A voice drawled.

His hands tightened around the handlebars. Slowly, he glanced up and to the left.

A man stood there. He was tall and dressed all in black. His eyes were covered by a pair of sunglasses.

"Maybe it's not something you've lost . . ." The guy said, sauntering forward as if he didn't have a care in the world. "Maybe it's someone."

"*Sam.*"

Sammael flashed a crooked grin. "Good to see you haven't forgotten your old friends."

Keenan jumped off the bike. "We were never friends." No one would be dumb enough to be Sam's friend. Sam's friends had a way of ending up in hell.

Sam shrugged. "My mistake. I forgot . . . you always thought you were better than me. Just like all the others."

"No." He readied for an attack because he knew one would be coming. "I just think a random slaughter of the humans wasn't the best way to go." That slaughter was why Sammael had fallen so many centuries before. Once, he'd been the strongest, his power ready to rival even Az.

But then Sammael had made the decision to kill those not on the death list. He'd strayed . . .

The Fallen laughed. "Just put the pieces together, huh? They threw my ass out because I killed those not on their list—just like you, Keenan. *Just like you.*"

"I'm nothing like you." Sam hadn't just killed one person, he'd killed dozens. "I was trying to save her, I didn't—"

The grin faded from Sam's face. "You broke the rules, same as me." A muscle jerked in his jaw. "Did they give you a chance to explain or did they just toss you out, too?" Sam stalked closer. "Do you still think you can feel your wings? Do you try to fly, only to remember they fucking *burned them off you?*"

Yes. Sometimes, he could feel them stretching in the air behind him. A lie. An illusion. "Why are you here?" He wished he could see Sam's eyes, but all he could see was his own image in those dark glasses.

"Maybe I just wanted the chance to talk to another of my kind. It's not every day that an angel falls."

No. Some angels didn't even survive the fall. Their bodies just weren't ready for the onslaught of pain.

"So you were trying to save 'her,' huh?" Sam's head cocked. "Would that 'her' be that sexy little piece with that sweet Southern drawl?"

Keenan lunged forward and grabbed Sam by the front of his shirt. "*Where is she?*"

Sam didn't flinch. "She's really why you fell? You traded your wings, all your power . . . just for a human's life?"

"*Where is—*"

"Of course, she's not really human anymore, is she?" His brows rose. "Was that part of your plan? 'Cause her turning into a vamp must have really pissed off the guys upstairs."

Keenan shoved him back. Sam slammed into the front of an SUV parked in the motel's lot. The metal screamed and dented beneath the Fallen's weight.

Keenan shook his head in disgust. "You don't know anything. You're just trying to mess with my head." Everyone knew about Sam. The angel who'd been meant to fall. They'd all known it was coming long before he told the powers that be to screw off. He'd always had a darkness inside. Not fully good, too many whispers of evil had lurked within Sam.

Sam wasn't the only angel like that. When you had so much power, the darkness could easily get into your blood.

Keenan understood that pull so much better now.

He turned away from Sam.

"Does she know that you were the angel sent to take her soul?"

Keenan kept walking. He'd get on the bike and—

"No answer. That means you *can't* answer because you can't tell a lie."

And Sam was in front of him. Just like that, as fast as a blink. "You didn't have to fall," Sam said, "in order to get a piece of ass."

Keenan went for his throat.

But he touched nothing. Sam had already moved. Already shot five feet away.

"Got to be faster than that," Sam taunted.

Keenan launched forward.

Sam's fist slammed into his chest, a hit right above his heart, and this time, Keenan stumbled back.

"You've got to be faster," Sam repeated, voice rumbling. "And *stronger.*" Then it was Sam's turn to spin away. "When you're ready for some real power, come find me."

What?

Sam glanced back over his shoulder. "They never let

souls escape. You should know that. You *do* know that. I'm betting that's why you high-tailed it after your piece of ass once you regained your sanity."

Sanity.

Keenan's fingers began to smoke as the fire of his fury burned through him.

"Ah . . . got the firepower now, do you? That's a good step. But you'll need more than fire to keep your vamp alive." He gave a little salute. "When you want to play, find me."

"You fucking asshole, where is—"

"Now is that any way for an angel to talk?"

His back teeth clenched. "I'm not an angel any-more."

The sunglasses tossed back his stark reflection. "No. You're not." Sam pointed at Keenan. "But you've still got the power of an angel in there. Just waiting to come out. And you're gonna be wanting that magic and power back."

One touch to kill. His breath heaved out. No, he didn't want that back. "You didn't see Nicole."

Sam's shoulders rolled. "I'll give you a free one this time. Because, well . . . you don't have much time. Or rather, she doesn't."

Humans were close by. He could almost feel their eyes. It was all he could do to pull the rage back and control the fire that wanted to shoot from him.

"The last time I saw your lady, she was on the ground. Jerking. Her eyes were rolling back into her head."

"What did you do to her?" He'd rip Sammael apart and send the Fallen back to hell for keeps this time.

"Not me." Sam shook his head. "The good guys have her, and since your girl ain't exactly good . . . don't expect her to survive until sunset."

What?

But Sam was gone. Vanished. Only his scent remained. Not the light, flowery scent of an angel.

Brimstone. The scent of hell.

She woke up in a cage. Nicole opened her eyes, jumped up, and found herself trapped in a ten-by-twelve-foot jail cell.

Just freaking perfect.

She ran forward and grabbed the bars. "Hello!"

The place seemed deserted. It looked like some kind of holding cell, and she was the only one being held.

Uh oh.

"*Hey!*" She shouted. A cop had to be around someplace. "You can't do this! You can't just Tase a woman on the street and—"

Metal groaned as a door opened. She sucked in a breath and stopped talking. A cop was coming toward her. Not the one who'd Tased her. A woman this time. She looked to be in her early thirties. The cop had short black hair and glaring brown eyes.

"You're not just any woman, Ms. St. James," she said, Texas drawling beneath her words. "You're a wanted felon. A criminal who nearly killed a police officer."

Nicole's fingers tightened around the bars. "That was . . . I didn't mean to hurt him."

The door clanged shut behind the cop. "Of course. You were just hungry, right?"

Nicole stepped away from the bars.

"Hungry, and Officer Greg Hatten looked like the perfect snack."

"You . . . know what I am."

A slow nod. The woman—her ID read Jennifer Connelly—pulled out her service weapon. "I know what you are, and I know how to kill you."

She couldn't break through the bars, not while the sun was still up. The lethargy coursing through her body told her that the sun was most definitely up. "Then why am I still alive? If you want me dead—"

A black brow rose. "You already are dead."

People just had to throw that up to her. "I didn't ask for this. I didn't want to be a vamp, I didn't mean to hurt that cop—"

"Save the sob story."

Nicole blinked.

"Let me guess . . ." the cop continued with a smirk. "If you had it to do all over again, you'd go back to being human, right?"

Not exactly. Being human meant being dead.

But Connelly didn't give her a chance to answer. She said, "Whatever. Here's the deal. I'm gonna open your cage. You're gonna try to get out."

Yes, that was a good plan. Because staying trapped in there wasn't an option.

Connelly lifted her gun. "You're gonna come at me, and I'm gonna shoot you."

Nicole's breath whispered out. Not such a good plan.

"And because I'm such a fine shot, you're gonna bleed to death, right here, where I can watch." Connelly's weapon was aimed at Nicole's heart. "You see, I don't much care for vamps. The dead should be in the ground, not on the streets, feeding."

"You don't think someone else is going to notice when you shoot me? They'll wonder what the hell happened in here!"

"You attacked a cop." Connelly gave a careless shrug of her shoulders. "No one here will give a shit what happens to you." She approached the bars. Her eyes narrowed on Nicole. "I thought you'd be out a little longer."

"And I thought cops were supposed to *help* people." This sucked. Seriously sucked. Her fangs were burning, pushing out thanks to the adrenaline rush that pumped through her. Her claws were growing and if that cop came closer, she'd give Connelly a scratch the cop wouldn't soon forget.

"We do help people." The cop glanced over her shoulder. Probably to make sure no one else was seeing or hearing any of this. "*I* kill monsters."

"I'm not a monster! Six months ago, I was as human as you! I'm not—"

"Vampires lie. They trick. Deceive. One promised my sister she'd live forever."

Oh, crap. This wasn't going to end well.

"You know what he did?"

She could guess.

"He ripped her throat open, and I had to find what was left of her body." Connelly opened the cage and came inside. The gun barrel never wavered. "I know about *you,*" the cop said. "You play innocent now, but you attacked that sheriff just over the county line."

That punch would've come back to bite her. "I didn't kill him." Pointing that out seemed rather useless.

"Probably because you didn't get the chance." Connelly's eyes narrowed. "Tom called me and gave me a heads-up that you might be in the area. He was there when they found my sister's body. He knew I'd understand just how to deal with someone like you."

She could not win with this cop. "Listen, I—"

"But what about Jeff Quint?"

A fist squeezed her heart.

"Sam Bentley?"

Dammit. "I didn't want to kill them." They haunted her now. She'd never forget their faces. *Never.*

"Right." The cop's voice easily called bullshit. "You just got *thirsty* and you had to rip out their throats." Her voice thickened with fury. "*Just like that bastard did to my sister.* He tore her open from one ear to the other."

Nicole kept her hands loose at her sides. "I don't want to hurt you." She understood the other woman's pain and fury.

"Really? Too bad. I can't wait to hurt you."

Crap. "The cop who Tased me—he knows I'm in here." He had to. "He could come and check and—"

"No one's checking on you. No one gives a damn if you live or die. As far as they're concerned, you're a cop killer—"

Connelly was just steps away. *Kill or be killed.*

Nicole lunged forward. Connelly didn't have time to shoot. Nicole caught her wrist, twisted it, and heard the snap of bones. When the cop cried out, Nicole plowed back with her elbow, driving it right into the cop's nose. Cartilage crunched, and blood spurted as the woman went down.

Nicole kicked the gun out of the way. Her breath heaved out as she stared at the unconscious woman. "Lucky for you, I'm *not* a cop killer." Though that blood was tempting. Good thing Connor had taught her a few tricks out of the bedroom. Maybe she did owe that SOB a bit after all. Her eyes narrowed as she stared at the cop. "And lucky for me . . ." She knelt next to the other woman. "I think we're about the same size."

That meant the uniform might be a perfect fit.

So for the big question . . . how did a vamp go about exiting a police station? Well, if she was *really* lucky, she just walked right past the cops, her head down, and her body covered in a cop's uniform.

"I'm afraid you'll have to get cozy in here for a while," Nicole told the unconscious woman as she studied her. Right size. Right hair color.

She yanked off the cop's shoes. Too small, but they'd have to do.

Two minutes later, "Officer Jennifer Connelly" walked out of the holding cell. Her steps were sure, her head was down, and her heart thundered in her chest.

Behind her, the prisoner sat hunched near the back wall. Her dark hair covered her face.

As she marched down the long corridor out of the holding cell, Nicole felt the sweat slide down her back. She tossed her hand up to a few cops when she passed the bullpen, deliberately waving in such a way that her hand blocked her face.

Then she could see the exit door just steps away. The place was packed with people up front and it was easy to blend with the crowd now. Easy to slip past and walk right out.

She kept her pace nice and easy when she headed down the stone steps outside of the station. Nicole wanted to break and run, yet she couldn't take the chance of eyes being on her. At the same time, she couldn't move too slowly. If someone found Jennifer Connelly in her cell . . .

A motorcycle's engine roared and she glanced up. Her breath shuddered out when she saw Keenan pulling up to the curb. *Escape*. Nicole pivoted on her heel and headed toward him.

His head whipped to the right and his eyes locked on her. *Immediately*. Kinda creepy the way he could zero in on her.

"Nicole?"

She shook her head. Then jumped on the back of the motorcycle.

"I was . . . coming to save you," he told her, his voice a bit hesitant.

She laughed at that, had to, as she wrapped her arms around him. "This time, I saved myself." Barely. "Now haul ass, angel, before the cops realize I'm not back in that cell." The sun beat down on her, and she just wanted to slump over and sleep . . .

Soon.

He revved the engine. "Yes, ma'am."

Then he hauled ass and got her the hell away from that station—and the cops who wanted her dead. She figured getting her to safety was the least the guy owed her then.

It looked like she couldn't count on the good guys for help anymore.

I was . . . coming to save you.

Sweet.

What would he do when he realized that she was too far gone, that she'd never be saved? Officer Connelly had been right. She'd killed. More than once. She'd liked that wild rush of power that came from taking so much blood.

They were right to try and put her down. Unfortunately for them, she wasn't in the mood to die.

Nicole closed her eyes and held on to her angel. Tight. And they rode away as if hell really was at their heels.

Sam stepped deeper into the shadows near the police station. Rather impressive. Nicole St. James had managed to save herself. No fallen angel needed.

His lips curved.

If she hadn't saved herself, Keenan would have rushed inside to find a dead vamp. What would the

Fallen have done then? Would his rage have broken through?

Now that would have been a sight to behold.

But a time for rage would come, soon enough.

Because Keenan could run with his little vampire, but he wouldn't be able to hide her. Not for long.

You couldn't hide from fate, and Nicole's fate had been decided long ago.

Death.

Even a fallen angel wouldn't be able to save her.

CHAPTER SEVEN

Nicole's arms wrapped tightly around him, her breasts crushed against his back, and her scent surrounded him.

Safe.

He'd figured out Sam's riddle too late. He'd gone rushing to that station, and then *she'd* come rushing to him. Wearing, of all things, a cop's uniform. Not that she didn't make that uniform look good . . .

But he wanted to hear the story behind that outfit.

Keenan kept driving until the lights of the city were a distant memory. The truckstop he pulled into was more a bar than anything else. Run-down, with loud country music blasting into the night, the stop didn't look particularly inviting. The bike was sputtering though, and he knew the stop was as far as they'd get.

Until he got them other transportation.

He killed the engine and for a moment, he listened to the someone-done-me-wrong lyrics.

Nicole didn't ease her grip even though they weren't moving anymore. He rather liked that.

"I can't go in," she whispered, and the words feathered against his ear. His cock jerked at her voice. Sexy, husky. His whole body tensed.

Why did he react this way to her? Only her?

Temptation. Everyone had a dark challenge to face.

He turned to look at her.

She swiped her tongue over her lips. "We're trying to fade into the background, right? No one in that joint will forget a female cop."

He bent, pulled out the clothes he'd purchased earlier, and pushed them into her hands.

"What's—where did you get these?"

He shrugged. "I got them while I was out today."

Her delicate jaw hardened. "Oh, that's right. You would've had plenty of time to *shop* while I was getting threatened by *your friend*, Tased, and thrown into a cage." She jumped off the motorcycle and hugged those clothes to her chest. "So don't even think this makes us close to even again, got me?"

He stilled, his attention caught by her words. "What friend." Not a question.

She glanced to the left. The right. The lot was dark and he'd made sure to park in the deepest shadows. She jerked off her shirt and gave him a fast glimpse of her breasts. Her sexy bra cupped them nicely. Oh, how he'd like another taste . . .

Then she yanked on the new shirt, a tight T-shirt that clung just right to her curves.

"Nicole." His voice was a rumble and his eyes were straining to see her breasts. He cleared his throat and tried again. "Tell me what friend you're talking about"

She ditched her pants. Her legs really were perfect. Long, sleek. He'd been so close to learning every detail of her body—inside and out.

Would she ever let him close again?

Doubtful.

"*Eyes up.*" And she zipped the jeans he'd bought for

her. She'd even put on the new panties. Well, the scrap that was supposed to be panties.

The lady had done a full-on strip in the parking lot. The handlebars bent beneath his grip. When the metal groaned, her head snapped toward him. "What are you—"

He bounded off the motorcycle and grabbed her arms. "What damn friend?" Keenan bit out because he didn't have any friends who'd be walking the earth.

"The big guy with eyes the same blue as yours. He had black hair and black clothes to match because he's all goth."

"*Sam.*"

"Yeah, that's what he said—"

He lifted her onto her toes. His gaze bored into hers. "What did he say to you?"

"Ease up on the grip!"

He immediately eased his hold but didn't let her go. *Sam had gone after her.* "He could've killed you."

"Why does everyone seem to think I'm so easy to kill? I'm still here, still walking around, I'm—"

"For someone like Sam, you *are* easy to kill." But then, most people were—humans and *Other.*

She shook her head. "That guy was bullshitting. He was a demon who wanted to mess with my head."

"Sam isn't a demon."

Her eyes widened. "Then what is he?"

"He's like me."

"Fallen."

Not a question, but he nodded anyway. "Only Sam has been walking this earth for a whole lot longer than you can ever imagine." His fingers were stroking her skin. Reflex. "And he's stronger, so much stronger, than any level-ten demon living now."

"And why's he coming after me?" That was fear making her voice rise and break.

He clenched his teeth. "Because of me."

Her breath caught. "He said . . . I thought he was lying but he said you fell—"

Damn him.

"For me."

A big rig pulled into the lot with its tires rolling and its brakes groaning. Keenan pushed Nicole back, moving quickly, and in seconds they were up against the side of the building. Not the best place, but at least they had cover in case any trouble came looking for them.

"Is it true?" Nicole wanted to know, her voice dipping to rub right over his skin. "Am I the reason you fell?"

"No." Not a lie. "I fell . . . because of what *I* did."

"Oh." She sounded disappointed.

Nicole pulled her hands away. "He seemed so sure it was because of me."

Keenan had perfect vision—day or night—and he could see the way her gaze flickered away from his as if she were embarrassed.

"But you were my—my guardian," she said, "so I just figured—"

"I wasn't your guardian angel." Time for more truth. No, this moment, he'd tell her everything because she deserved no less.

A door slammed. He glanced to the left. The trucker was heading inside the stop. Keenan waited for him to leave the lot.

Then . . .

"There are a lot of angels. So many different kinds. More than even the theologians realize." Thousands. All with different jobs and duties.

"Some guard," he admitted. The stories had that part right. "Others punish."

Her chin lifted a bit at that.

"Some kill."

She blinked.

"That night, in that alley . . ." He forced himself to take a step back. "You were supposed to die."

"I did—"

"No." A rough laugh broke from him. "You were supposed to *die*. Not to wake as a vampire. The vamp was supposed to drain you, to rip your throat out, and to leave your broken body in the alley."

"Don't worry about sugarcoating," she muttered, and he saw her flinch. "I can get the visual on my own."

His fingers slipped down her cheek. "I couldn't let it happen. I . . . hesitated."

She stilled at his touch. "You were there to kill me."

"I was there to take your soul to the next life." He glanced down at his hand. "One touch. That's all it would have taken. That's all it ever took. One touch and death came."

Now she reached for him and curled her fingers tight around his hand.

"Instead of touching you," he said, voice hardening, "I touched him."

"Keenan . . ."

"I broke the rules. I took a life that wasn't mine to claim. *I* disobeyed, and they tossed my ass into hell."

"Hell?" Her nails bit into his skin. "Oh, Keenan . . ."

"My wings were burned away when I fell. Fire blazed through my whole body, and when I hit, when I finally landed . . ." he rasped out a breath and let his gaze scan the lot before coming back to her. "I didn't even know who I was. *What* I was. I woke up, in the middle of an empty field, the earth scorched around me, and when a farmer ran to help me . . . I just knew that I-I shouldn't touch him."

One touch had always meant death.

She didn't speak. Nicole just watched him in the darkness, and he knew she saw too much with her vampire eyes. "After heaven, trust me, this . . . it was hell to me." The emotions. The pain. The hunger. The thirst. The need. He hadn't understood any of them. He'd been lashed with agony, again and again, and hadn't realized why.

Because when he'd first woken, he'd known nothing but pain and rage.

Until he'd slowly started to remember . . . her.

Heaven.

Hell.

Falling.

"It took a little while, but I finally remembered." Not everything. There was some time lost between his fall and the moment he'd woken up in that field. When he tried to recall those days, he heard the whispers of fire and the echoes of screams.

"I remembered," he said quietly, "and then I came after you."

A tear tracked down her cheek.

He caught the tear on his fingers. "Don't cry for me."

Another tear slipped down her cheek.

"Don't cry for me, sweet." *I'm not worth it.* Because he'd almost taken her that night. She'd been right, he'd just stood there, and *watched*.

Never again.

His lips took hers. He tasted the salt from her tears on his tongue. Pain. Angels didn't know pain. They also didn't know passion or lust.

Now he knew it all, and he didn't think the emotions put him in hell anymore. The feelings didn't rage inside of him and threaten to rip him apart.

Now . . . they made him feel alive. *Human.*

Her lips opened beneath his. He kissed her deeper, harder, and let her feel the need that drove through him.

It was a need only she could satisfy.

His hands slid down her body, found her waist, curled tight and pulled her closer. Whenever he was around her, he was aroused, hungry for her. Desperate.

The lust beat through his blood. His cock ached, and he *wanted* her.

Naked. Open.

His.

But not against the side of a dirty building. Not with too many eyes that could see too much. When he had her—and he would—he wasn't going to share.

His tongue tasted her as he let the kiss linger. He'd never be able to get enough of her taste. Sweet and wild—a combination that could be deadly.

Not that he was too worried about death.

Slowly, savoring her, he lifted his head.

"What happens next?" She whispered.

The scent came then, teasing his nose. Flowers. Faint. Fresh.

"We get the hell out of here." He glanced at the lot. There. A pickup truck sat parked near the left. Big wheels. Shiny coat of paint. Probably with a motor that knew how to howl. "And we get out of here *now*." The instant they were safe, he'd take her because he couldn't wait much longer.

His control wasn't that strong.

But finding a place to keep them away from the prying eyes of an angel . . . that wasn't going to be easy.

The pickup's driver-side door was locked, so he just shoved his elbow through the window and broke the glass. A quick flick of his fingers on the lock had the door opening.

"You know how to hot-wire this thing?" Nicole asked.

"What the hell are you doin', you fuckin' asshole?"

Keenan turned at the snarl and saw a tall human male with blond hair racing toward him.

"That's my fuckin' truck!"

"Yes." Unfortunate but . . . "Sorry. We're going to need it."

"The hell you are!" The guy swung at Keenan with a hard roundhouse punch.

The punch missed.

The floral scent in the air deepened. *The last thing I need now.*

Keenan's right hand clenched into a fist. "You should have stayed in the bar."

"I'll fuck you up, asshole." Spittle flew from the blond's mouth, and the human pulled out a knife from his boot. *"No one messes with Betty."*

Betty?

"I think he means the truck," Nicole murmured.

The human screamed and came at him, that knife up.

He waited, waited . . . then Keenan just punched the guy in the face. Down he went. Keenan shook his head. Would it have killed the guy to stay inside and get just one more drink?

Nicole walked around and crouched next to the man. Her hands went to his chest.

"What are you doing?" Keenan asked, voice hard. If she was planning on grabbing a drink . . .

She can drink from me.

Her hand lifted. She tossed him a set of keys. "No hot-wiring required."

His fingers closed around the keys. Nice.

The doors of the truckstop banged open. Ah . . . more company was heading their way. "Get in," he said as his eyes narrowed.

She jumped into the truck. Nicole slid right over the broken glass and settled in the passenger seat. He shot in behind her. Keenan revved the engine, and even before the approaching truckers called out, obviously catching sight of the blond's slumped form, he and Nicole were racing out of the lot.

Nicole glanced behind them. "We can't keep doing this. I want to stop and find a place to rest."

Because it had been a hell of a day for both of them. He still didn't know what had happened to her at that police station. She'd mentioned a Taser . . .

Her fingers slipped down his arm as she shifted closer to him. "Where can we go? Tell me you know a safe house around here."

Safe from angels? And demons?

Was there such a place?

His gaze slipped to her. He'd *find* a place like that. She'd be safe. He'd make sure of it.

"I'm just . . . spooked." Her admission was soft. "That Sam . . . he said I'd suffer."

No, she wouldn't. Not while he was there.

But I wasn't there when the cops took her.

He yanked his gaze from her and looked ahead at the road—just in time to see an angel fall from the sky. No, not fall, *fly.*

Strong black wings flapped in the night, coming closer, closer to the ground. And when the man—*angel*—landed in front of the truck, the highway seemed to buckle beneath his weight.

Keenan slammed on the brakes. The brakes squealed, and the truck fishtailed.

The angel's knees had bent just a bit when he landed, and his head was bowed. As the truck flew toward him, he slowly lifted his head.

Bright blue eyes stared back at Keenan. Eyes that

had seen everything the world had to offer—and found it lacking. Azrael had never been impressed with the humans and their lives.

Azrael. Az. Heaven's big gun was down on earth—*not good*.

Az's face was cold and hard. No emotion appeared on that stony visage. There was never any emotion from their kind.

The truck finally stopped less than two feet from Az. His wings stretched behind him as he straightened fully.

"Keenan!" Nicole grabbed his arm. "What's happening? Why are we stopping?"

He knew she wouldn't see the angel. Couldn't. Not unless she was close to death. "We have company." He didn't take his gaze off the road. *"Angel."*

"Those guys sure seem to drop in a lot." The words were light, but her nails dug into him, and the hard rasp of her breath filled the car.

"More than they should," he agreed darkly as his hand grabbed the door handle.

But she didn't let go of him. Her hold tightened. "What kind of angel?" Fear had trickled into her words. Smart woman. Angels weren't always the good guys, not even close. No matter what the stories said, they could spill just as much blood as demons any day of the week.

He didn't want to tell her this but . . . "He's a death angel." It was the wings that always gave them away. Guardians had white wings. Only death angels and Punishers had wings of black because they dealt in despair.

He killed the engine and glanced at Nicole. Her narrowed eyes were on the road as she fought to see what she couldn't. His stare followed hers. Az stared straight at the truck. No, he stared straight at Nicole, and there was no mistaking the intent in the angel's eyes.

No.

Keenan jumped out of the truck. He raced for his old mentor. "*Stay away from her!*" He yelled.

Az didn't move. Not much had ever moved Azrael. Not pity. Not fear.

No emotion. *Ever.* He was the perfect death angel. While Keenan knew he'd been . . . lacking.

"I didn't think you'd find your charge so quickly," Az said, cocking his head slowly to the side. His voice was a strong rumble that filled the night.

Keenan tossed a fast glance over his shoulder. Nicole had started to edge out of the truck. "Stay back there!" He barked. "Don't let him touch you!"

One touch was all that death needed. Since Nicole couldn't see Az coming, she'd be helpless against that simple touch.

Keenan put his body between Az and Nicole. He didn't want the guy so much as looking at her. "What are you doing here?"

Az blinked. "You know why I'm here." He shrugged. "You know why I'm always here."

"Death." It's what they were. All they knew.

"Relax. Just because I'm here, it doesn't mean she's dying tonight."

"No, she's *not*."

Az gazed at him with those glittering eyes. "But a soul will pass soon."

Nicole's soul. Fury had him stepping closer to Az. "*Why?*"

"The job was never finished." Said simply. Az wore clothes any mortal would possess—jeans, a white shirt. He could have passed for a human . . . if those giant black wings hadn't been bursting right through the back of his conjured shirt. An angel could always conjure any clothing to fit over his wings.

"The job is over," Keenan told him as he braced his body for attack.

Az didn't move. "You know she's marked for death."

Keenan shook his head. "No. She lived that night. Fate *changed*." He'd made it change.

"It's not that easy, and you know it. You can't just switch one soul for another. That's not the way it works."

"I didn't fall . . ." *Just to lose her.*

Az watched him in silence. Then, after a moment, Az told him, "Her name's in the book."

Az's famous book. Once a scroll, now a Who's Who List of the To-Be-Dead. The book included the names of both those deemed blessed and those deemed damned.

Once the name was in the book, there was no going back. So the stories said.

"How long does she have?" Keenan asked, voice rough. If her name had just come up, she'd have forty days. After forty days, the soul had to be taken from the charge's body.

Only he hadn't taken her soul before.

And it won't be taken now.

"Ten days."

What?

"Maybe less." Az shrugged. "I truly thought it would take you longer to find her."

"You mean you wanted her to already be *dead* before I found her."

"She *is* dead." Az raised his hand and pointed behind Keenan. "She's already marked. Her fate was sealed. There's no changing it."

"Bullshit."

Az's brows rose at that. No, he wouldn't be used to one of his soldiers cursing.

Bullshit. One of Nicole's favorite words. Nicole. She'd hear everything he said, but no word that Az spoke. "Fate changed before, it can change again."

"Why?" Az showed the barest hint of an emotion. Curiosity. "Let her go. What does it matter if she lives or dies?"

Keenan wouldn't take his gaze off the angel to look back at her. "It matters to me." That was all Az needed to know.

Az sighed. "You're wrong, you know." His wings brushed against the pavement. "I didn't want you to arrive and find her dead. That would have served no purpose for me."

His gut clenched. "What is it that you want, Az?"

"She doesn't matter to me. She's just another charge. There are thousands, millions more just like her. They'll die, *just like her.*"

Nicole's soft gasp filled his ears.

Why would she gasp? Why would—

"Angels shouldn't fall," Az continued, his voice coming faster. "Angels shouldn't burn. Angels shouldn't suffer." Now he was the one to step closer. "We're better than the humans. Stronger. So much more powerful."

But the angels weren't the favorites. No, the humans were the ones who'd been given the gifts. Hope. Love.

"Angels *shouldn't* fall," Az said again.

"I did." *And thanks for the heads-up, Az.* That whole "*I've heard it's the fire that makes you scream the loudest*" line really hadn't helped.

"You fell . . . and you can rise."

Those words seemed to cut through him. He'd never heard of an angel going back, not after—

"It's simple, Keenan. I know she's your temptation.

We all have our trials. Prove you *are* stronger. Finish your job. Do what you were meant to do . . ."

Kill her. No, he wouldn't say it. Not with Nicole close enough to hear his words.

"Kill her and come home." Az didn't have a problem saying the words.

Keenan straightened his shoulders. "*No.*"

"If you don't, someone else will."

He knew it wasn't an idle threat. "Who?" Keenan demanded. "Is it you? Are you the one coming after her?"

Az just stared back at him.

"I don't want to die." Nicole's clear words had Keenan whirling to face her.

She stood in front of the truck, silhouetted against the headlights. Her gaze wasn't on him, but on Az.

Could she *see* him?

Then Az moved, shifting slightly to the left. Nicole's gaze didn't follow him. *Can't see him.*

"No one ever wants to die," Az said.

Now her gaze tracked to the left—to the angel who wanted her death.

"That's the problem," Az continued. "But it doesn't matter what you want, vampire. You *will* die within ten days. The only question is . . . by whose touch?"

Not mine. Keenan lunged for Az.

But with a flap of wings, the angel was gone. The headlights shone on the road, the light stabbing into the empty darkness.

"Keenan?"

He whirled to face her once more, terrified that Az had tricked him and circled in for the kill. *Can't be so unguarded. Not ever again.*

But she stood, alone, in front of the truck. Nicole appeared so small and vulnerable in that moment.

Then he caught a glimpse of fang.

Perhaps not so vulnerable.

He hurried to her side. Her eyes watched him—deep and dark and big.

"Are you going to kill me?" She asked him the same way another woman might have asked if he were going to kiss her. Quiet, husky.

He caught her arms and pulled her closer.

"Are you?" She whispered.

He crushed his mouth to hers, and he kissed her hard and deep and he didn't care that Az's scent lingered in the air. Let the angel watch. Let him see where Keenan's true loyalties were.

She wouldn't die by his hands.

And any angel who came close would find out that his fury was ten times hotter than hell's.

He hadn't fallen to lose her.

He'd fallen to fight for her.

Ten days.

No.

He knew it was time to make a deal with the devil.

The voices were louder. The whispers in Elijah's mind were seductive calls now, tempting him.

Stop them from seeing.

Elijah knew the humans could see right through his mask. They saw the monster inside, and they were mocking him.

He pushed through the crowd at the bar, snarling.

They can see.

His head throbbed, his heart raced, and still that voice in his mind taunted.

He needed the drugs. Needed them to quiet the voice so that he could breathe again—and hunt like he wanted. Hunt and kill without the eyes on him.

See.

He shoved open the door and the hot night air hit him in the face. He sucked in a breath, another, and stumbled away. His body shook and every step was pain.

That voice . . . so loud now . . . *They see.*

He doubled over as the pain sliced right through him.

"Hey, wait . . . are you okay?"

A woman's voice. High. Worried.

Footsteps raced toward him. He opened his eyes and saw small feet. White sandals. Tanned legs.

"You sick?" The owner of those legs asked. "Want me to call someone for you?"

He glanced up, slowly, and looked straight into her dark eyes.

She can see you. The voice taunted.

Those eyes of hers widened, and he smiled. Then he lunged for her.

The bitch ran, screaming, as she jumped away from him. But he had his knife out and he was gonna make sure that she didn't see him again. That she didn't see anything.

Then the voice would stop.

Can't see now.

He grabbed her hair and shoved her down.

"*Hey, demon* . . ."

Elijah's gaze whipped up in time to see a board come swinging at his face. He tried to stumble back, but the wood slammed right into his head.

Then he didn't see anything at all.

CHAPTER EIGHT

Keenan and Nicole made it to New Orleans a few hours after dawn. Nicole hadn't slept during the drive. She'd been too scared to let down her guard for sleep.

After all, it wasn't every day that an angel said you were marked for death.

And she'd *heard* him. His dark, deep voice had filled her ears as he'd asked Keenan to kill her.

Her eyes squeezed shut. If Keenan killed her, he'd rise. Okay, she figured that meant he'd get a free ride back up to the clouds.

But what happened to her? After what she'd done over the last few months, there'd be no comfy cloud ride waiting on her.

I don't want to die.

"I can't go back to the Quarter," she told him as she felt her nails bite into her palms. "I can't go back to my place." The cops might be watching.

"You don't have a place there anymore."

That had her eyes opening.

The vehicle slowed. "Someone else lives in your apartment. He took it over about a month ago."

Right. Of course. She cleared her throat. "Then where are we going?" He'd been adamant that they travel back to New Orleans, but New Orleans was not the place she wanted to see again. Too much pain waited in the city.

"I've got a place just outside of town."

Keenan had a place? How did he even have money?

He glanced toward her and his lips kicked up a bit. He must have read the thoughts on her face. "You keep forgetting, sweet . . . I know just about every secret the humans and the *Other* have. I know where all the bodies are buried."

Yes, she bet he did.

"And I had some *Other* who owed me. The house was payment."

"Payment for what, exactly?"

"You don't want to know."

Probably not.

Her heart squeezed as they drove past the city she'd loved so much. They rode in a different car now, a non-descript Ford. They'd switched vehicles just outside of Texas, the better to keep the vampire-killing cops off their backs.

Soon the streets thinned. Oak trees and moss swept past her.

Then . . .

"Here we are," Keenan said quietly as he pulled to a stop.

She gazed out the window and saw an old antebellum. The place had been fixed up, but it wasn't one of the too-fancy, too-rich houses she'd seen before. This house was half-hidden by the trees, yet standing strong against the swamp.

Waiting.

"Will we be safe here?" Nicole asked as she climbed out of the car.

He didn't answer.

She guessed that was a no. The sun beat down on her as she walked toward the house, and she felt its pull on her strength.

Keenan opened the doors and the smell of the house hit her. Not the closed-in, old smell that some places could get when they were left alone too long. Instead, the scent was light, soft, welcoming.

The furniture was sparse, but after six months of cheap motels, who was she to complain? The place looked like the Ritz to her.

"You should sleep." Keenan's deep voice rumbled from behind her. He locked the door. "Go get some rest. Get your strength back."

Her hand curved around the banister. Her palm was sweating. "What did the angel mean about trading one soul for another?" She hadn't asked her questions during the car ride. Hell, for most of that ride, she'd just been numb with fear. *Ten days left to live.*

She'd been on a countdown before, and she'd never wanted to be on one again.

Ten days.

A deep furrow appeared between Keenan's brows. "You heard that part?"

"I heard every part." *Including the part where he asked you to kill me.*

He shook his head. "You shouldn't have. Most folks can't ever see or hear angels, all they can do is just catch their scents every now and then."

Flowers.

Goose bumps rose on her arms. Six months ago, she'd caught that sweet scent a few times in her classroom and in her home. The scent—she realized now it had been Keenan. Watching.

But they'd get to that soon enough. First . . . "You didn't answer me, Keenan." She'd noticed he was very good at avoiding answers to her questions.

The furrow smoothed away. "Instead of you dying that night, the vampire died."

"You went against orders." Now she could think past the rage and pain that had consumed her at the motel.

He gave a slight inclination of his head.

Nicole swiped her tongue over her lower lip. "The vamp was supposed to walk away, but he was the one who bit the dust." *Help me.* She hadn't realized it but . . . he had.

In the only way he could.

Keenan stared back at her.

"Thank you," she told him softly.

Now he blinked. "Nicole . . ."

"This whole thing—it's a little much for me, okay?" She let go of the banister and faced him. "I mean, you're an *angel*. I've heard stories about angels all my life, but—" Her laugh sounded broken even to her ears, "I never thought I'd actually meet one."

"Most people don't think they'll ever meet vampires, either."

Right.

"You killed him . . ." Her focus centered totally on Keenan. "You killed that vampire so I'd live."

"Yes."

She stalked toward him and pressed her hands on his chest. "Thank you for saving me." He hadn't just stood by. No matter what he'd said—she was alive because of him.

But he pulled away. "I didn't save you."

She was there, breathing, fighting bloodlust, because he had.

"The angels are coming after you. Azrael—Az, he's coming. Nothing will stop him."

Don't think about that. Don't. "Then let him come." *Don't think about what happens after death.* "Right now, I don't care about him or what might happen in ten days."

"You're lying." His head cocked. "Humans lie so much, and usually so easily."

She stepped forward and closed that distance again. "I'm alive right now. I might not be alive much longer, but I'm *alive* now." Alive and with one of the sexiest men—*the* sexiest—she'd ever met.

He'd saved her. Suffered for her.

Protected her.

Definitely the sexiest.

She stretched up onto her toes and let her mouth hover near his. "Thank you." She breathed the words against his lips and then her mouth pressed against his. A hot, open-mouthed kiss. When his tongue touched hers, a lick of lust shot straight through her body.

But the fierce burn was so good.

His hands clamped around her arms, and he pushed her back.

What? *Back?*

"I won't stop this time." The words were a dark promise.

Oh, nice. She licked her lips and tasted him. Rich, like chocolate. Except better. So much better. "I don't want you to." But he needed to be warned. "Sex with me . . ." *Be careful.* "It won't be like with other women."

His mouth claimed hers. His tongue drove deep, and she moaned. Her nipples tightened. Her legs shifted as she fought to widen her stance and *feel* him.

Just when she was getting desperate, his mouth lifted. "I don't care about other women."

Very good to know. "It's just that vampires . . ." She swallowed and still tasted him. "For us, sex and blood-lust . . . it's not like when you—"

"I haven't been with another woman."

Now that stopped her. "What?" Not like she'd had oodles of experience. A few lovers, sure, but . . . *none?* And he wanted to start with her?

"Humans and most of the *Other* can't even see us." His lips quirked. "So sex isn't a big option."

But . . . "You've never—"

"I didn't want to. Angels don't feel emotions—no human needs."

Like love. Lust.

But he'd lost his wings, and right then, she could sure *feel* his arousal pressing against her. "I don't want to hurt you." She'd try to hold on to her control. The sun was up, so she'd be weaker, but . . .

"You won't." His lips skimmed her jaw. "You can't."

But he didn't understand what it was like when a vampire's bloodlust combined with the physical desire. Control could be so very thin. She'd learned that lesson the hard way with Connor.

"I think I wanted you," Keenan told her as he wrapped his arms around her waist and lifted her up against him, "since the first moment I saw you." His lips pressed against her neck.

Her fingers dug into his hair. Such thick, soft hair. "I'm not the same woman I was then."

His tongue licked over her skin. She shivered. "You're the woman I want."

She'd try to stay in control, for him. Try to keep the bloodlust back and enjoy the pleasure.

Just a man and a woman. She could do that.

His first time.

She didn't want to screw this up.

His warm hands slipped under her shirt. Inch by inch, they eased up her stomach, rising until they rested just under her bra. "You'll have to tell me . . ." His teeth grazed her throat. "What you like."

Her breath rasped in her throat. "You're, ah . . . doing pretty good."

But he eased away from her. "I can do better."

Then he lifted her into his arms and carried her through the house. Not up the stairs, but down the twisting hallway. Sunlight rained through the windows, chasing out the shadows. He took her inside the last room on the right. A bedroom. No dresser. No chest. Just a bed.

He laid her down, then pulled away, his gaze watching her as he began to strip.

Oh, yes. His shirt hit the floor and she had one awesome view of his chest. Muscled. So very muscled. Way more than a six-pack on her angel. Sun-kissed skin. Flesh that was so delectable she wanted to bite.

Then he dropped his jeans.

Her sex clenched.

Keenan's body was perfect. Absolutely *perfect*. And she wanted to touch every inch of him. Taste every inch.

His cock, full, thick, and long, stretched toward her and she rose up, reaching for him.

"No, sweet, I want to—"

Her fingers curled around him and he stopped talking. "Let me," she said because it was important that this be good for him.

She bent forward and nipped the hard plane of his stomach. Couldn't help that. Sometimes a girl needed a bite, but she didn't break the skin.

She licked the small wound, and her hair fell for-

ward, sliding against his body. He hissed out a breath
and his hands locked around her shoulders—not to
push her away but to bring her closer.

"You sure?" he gritted. "Am I . . . what you want?"

Her answer was to dip down and run her tongue
over the top of his cock.

His fingers dug into her skin.

She opened her mouth wider, and being very, very
careful with her teeth, she began to suck him. The flesh
was warm beneath her tongue, the skin soft, but
arousal had his cock taut and hard. Her tongue licked
over the head of his erection, and she tasted the salty
tang that coated him.

"*Nicole*." No mistaking the raw hunger in that
voice.

But she wasn't done with him. Not yet.

Death was coming too close to her. Right then, she
wanted to grab life.

And taste it.

So she used her mouth and her tongue, and she caressed his flesh. Nicole took him in deeper as she
sucked him, and she enjoyed the rough hunger in his
voice and the hard grasp of his hands on her.

But too soon, he pulled away and held her back with
a steely grip. "This time, I'll be inside you."

That was where she wanted him.

Keeping her eyes on his, she rose onto her knees.
Nicole yanked off her shirt and tossed it to the floor.
Her bra followed seconds later. Her breasts pointed
toward him, the peaks tight and aching.

She wanted his mouth on her.

Wanted him, *in* her.

He moved quickly, coming down on the bed in a
rush and caging her with his body. His legs pushed between hers. His mouth took her breast.

When Nicole felt the edge of his teeth on her nipple,

her panties got even wetter. She arched up against him, hating the jeans and the thin cotton that kept her from him. Her nails raked down his back as she pushed closer to him.

His fingers fumbled with her jeans, then he jerked the clasp open. He shoved down the rough fabric, and she helped him, lifting her hips, kicking off her boots, and when the jeans hit the floor, her panties were with them.

Yes.

Flesh to flesh now. His mouth was on her. Licking. Kissing. Stroking her and making her *crazy.*

Her fangs were burning as they stretched in her mouth. Even in the daytime, she wouldn't be able to hold the instincts and the changes back. Sex brought out the bloodlust too much.

Bite.

His fingers were at her sex—parting the folds and finding the center of her need. He stroked her and the sensual touch had her shaking beneath him. "Keenan . . . *more.*" She wouldn't be able to wait. She needed the pleasure *now.* Just as much as she needed air. Blood.

Him.

"You're hot and wet." His voice surrounded her, and the rough need she heard in his words had a dark thrill racing through her body. "I've thought about you . . ." The tip of his erection pressed against her, lodging at the entrance to her sex. "Dreamed about you, so many nights . . ."

The admission had her eyes widening. "You—"

His hands caught hers. He pushed them back on the mattress, holding them with ease. "Then I'd wake, and you *weren't there.*"

His eyes looked as black as hers. *Because they were.* The blue was gone. Only darkness remained.

He drove into her then, a long, plunging thrust that stole her breath. "You won't leave me . . . again."

Nicole locked her legs around him. She wasn't planning on going anywhere.

He pulled back, thrust, slamming balls-deep inside her, and they both gasped.

Pleasure ripped through her in a white-hot wave. Pulsing, cresting . . . The bed groaned beneath them as their movements became harder, wilder.

She licked her lips—*want more*.

He thrust deep.

Her sex clamped greedily around him. Her body was stretching, yearning. The tension built inside of her, and the promised release waited just beyond her grasp.

As he thrust, his head tilted back and his throat—his throat was right at her mouth. Her lips pressed against him as she tasted Keenan's skin. The pulse beat so fast beneath his flesh.

Thrust.

Her heels dug into his back as she pushed up to meet him, thrust for thrust.

Her teeth scraped against his neck. *Control.* She didn't have much control left. She wanted his blood, wanted his body, wanted everything he had.

Her mouth opened wider. Her teeth scraped harder.

"Do it." His order. "Nicole . . ." His hips flexed as he plunged into her. When he withdrew, his cock glided right over her clit. Glided—

Thrust.

She bit him when she came. Her teeth plunged into his neck even as his cock drove into her. The tension exploded in a firestorm—pleasure, hunger, need, *blood.*

Her body shook, every muscle trembling, and she drank from him as her sex contracted around his cock.

He kept thrusting. Keenan surged inside her, filling every inch of her sex. "Yes . . . good . . . *so* . . ." His voice rumbled around her, then he stiffened, his muscles locking, and the hot tide of his release filled her.

She licked his throat and caught the drop of blood that slipped down his neck. Her hands were free—when had that happened?—and she wrapped her arms around him.

His body shuddered against her as his hips pushed forward. Keenan's head lifted. He stared down at her with glittering eyes.

I didn't mean to bite. I tried to hold back.

But sometimes, there was just no fighting what you were.

She stared up at him, and, for an instant, the light seemed to dim around him. Dark shadows spread behind him, stretching out, up. Strong, thick shadows of black that curved from his back.

Like wings.

Fear whispered through her even as she pulled him closer. Her hands slid down his back, over the rough ridge of scars where wings had once been.

No more.

Because she didn't see those shadows anymore. They must have just been a trick of the light.

You will die within ten days. The only question is . . . by whose touch? The angel's voice pushed into her mind.

By whose touch . . .

Keenan's strong hands were on her. Stroking. Caressing.

It only took one touch to kill.

And it only took one touch to bring pleasure. This time, Keenan had brought pleasure.

But what about next time?

She closed her eyes and pressed closer to him.

* * *

Carlos Guerro stared at the demon before him. The bastard had tried to kill his cousin. He was so tired of the supernaturals thinking they could destroy his kind.

First his mother. That damn vampire had seduced her, then ripped her throat wide open as he drained her.

Then Carlos had watched his pack fall.

Now, for this asshole to come hunting in his part of Mexico, so soon after that bitch vampire and her boyfriend had killed two of his men . . .

You'll suffer. This one wouldn't die easily. Carlos would make sure of it.

The demon was begging now. Crying. Pleading. That was the way it always was for them at the end.

No one wanted to die.

Too fucking bad.

Carlos smiled at the demon. "You really thought you could hunt here . . . that you could come after a coyote shifter—"

The demon's head jerked up and horror filled his eyes. "I-I didn't know—"

Didn't really matter. The coyote shifters weren't the bitches of the paranormal world, and it was time people started to learn that lesson.

The members of his pack—those still alive after that last slaughter by the wolves in LA—had come home to re-group. And to start hunting. They'd been busy killing anything and everything that came at them.

Proving our strength. They weren't going to wait to be hunted. They *were* the hunters.

The demon's hands dug into the dirt. They'd made him dig his own grave. Easier to clean up that way. "I didn't want her!" The demon screamed out. "I was supposed to kill the fucking vampire!"

Carlos pulled back the shovel he'd been about to slam into the demon's stomach. "What vampire?" An image flashed in his mind. The woman with the devil-black hair and the too-pale skin. The woman who'd whispered so temptingly in the bar, then taken him outside.

He'd known what she was, of course. And he'd been planning to rip *her* throat wide open . . .

Then her lover had arrived.

The demon—he'd said his name was Elijah— glanced up, blinking bleary eyes. Getting the demon to make sense was hard. He seemed more than half out of his head. Probably from drugs. Some demons screwed around too much with them. If he was lucky, they'd all OD and head straight back to hell one day soon.

If he was lucky.

Elijah's jaw had gone slack.

"What. Vampire." Carlos lifted the shovel to the demon's throat. The weapon's placement was just a threat. He wouldn't make the killing blow this way. Carlos liked to be far more hands-on.

Behind him, his cousin whispered his name.

He ignored Julia. This wasn't her call. She'd just been the bait.

"W-woman . . . with black hair . . ." Elijah's body weaved. "Sh-she was h-here . . . before . . . supposed to kill her . . ."

Same vamp? Different? Did it even matter?

No.

Time was up for the demon.

"She took up with . . . f-fucking *angel* . . ." The demon laughed and blood dripped down his chin. "*Angel* and a bl-bloodsucker . . ."

Carlos dropped the shovel. "What?"

"He could see me," Elijah muttered, scratching his

eyes. "I knew it—one look . . . *he could see every-thing* . . . Can't let 'em s-*see* . . ."

Fucking lunatic. "There's no angel." *Mierda*. If only there was . . . In LA, he'd stumbled onto an *Other* secret. A very, very powerful poison.

Angel's Dust. A potent mix that, when ingested, de-stroyed demons. It didn't matter how powerful the demons were. Even level tens would die when the poi-son worked through them. No cure—just death.

Only one problem . . . Angel's Dust had to be made from pure angel blood, and there weren't a whole hell lot of angels walking around these days.

Those smart bastards knew to stay to the skies.

His claws ripped through his fingertips as Carlos got ready to have his fun.

"*Guardian* . . ." Blood leaked from the cuts Elijah had made on his own face. "Said h-he was the bitch's guardian . . ."

What if the demon was telling the truth?

"What did he look like?" Julia asked as she pressed closer. His cousin had always had trouble staying in the background.

At her voice, Elijah stilled. His head turned toward her, slowly, like a snake, and he smiled. "I *see* you."

She tossed back her long hair and sauntered to the edge of the hole. Julia wouldn't be scared of the de-mon. She'd just been pretending before—baiting their trap. Carlos had never seen her actually be scared of anything. "I see you, too, *cabron*," she said.

Elijah's smile grew.

"And you think you saw an angel, *si*?" Her claws were out.

The demon nodded as his gaze bored into her. His blond hair hung in thick chunks around his face.

"So this angel . . . what . . . he just flew down from *cielo*, from heaven?" Julia's voice taunted him.

Elijah edged closer to the edge of his grave. "Black wings . . . like shadows behind him . . ."

Carlos tensed. Okay, *this* he had heard before. When angels fell, they lost their wings.

"*Fell* . . . bastard fell . . ." Elijah licked his lips. "So he could fuck a vampire . . ."

Julia laughed. "So angels are that hard up?"

"If an angel was walking around," Carlos said, his voice cutting over her. "I think word would've spread by now." But . . . *what if?* His heart thundered with rising excitement.

Angel blood. If he got hold of angel blood, he'd be able to wipe out the strongest demons who got in his way. He'd be able to use that blood to buy allegiance with any paranormal he wanted. Everyone always wanted to kill demons. He could just provide folks with the means, and in return, he'd get . . .

Power.

Finally, power would come back to the coyotes. No more getting screwed over for them. *No more.*

Elijah didn't look away from Julia. "Most can't . . . see him." He spat out a mouthful of blood. "Can't see his w-wings . . . only those with demon blood."

Ah, now that was another story he'd heard. Legend or truth? "Describe him," Carlos snapped.

"Big, blond bastard, tails her like a . . . second skin."

Carlos remembered the fool who'd interrupted his games. The *gringo* who had struck out with too much power and killed his men. No, he hadn't killed them . . .

He'd moved so fast the bullets hadn't hit him. They'd hit Jo and Ruben.

And that man had been defending the vampire. No, surely it wouldn't be that easy. "He's fucking her?"

Elijah's gaze swept down Julia's body. "Her scent was . . . all over h-him."

"Where are they now?"

The demon's eyes were so big. The blood still dripped down his face. "Lost 'em . . . after they left Mexico."

Unfortunate. But still . . . very, very interesting. Because if the angel had fallen—*for a vampire, so sad*—then he'd have a weakness.

Carlos was good at using weaknesses.

"You take him, Julia," he said with a wave of his claws because she was all but salivating and Elijah had told him what that he needed to know. "*Mátelo*." Kill him.

There was no point in wasting more time. Especially not when there was new prey to hunt.

Julia crouched near the edge of the grave. "You were right, before, demon. I do see you."

He blinked and looked a little lost.

"I see the fucking monster inside, and I'm gonna rip him out." She lunged at him.

Elijah's screams filled the night.

Carlos turned away from them, his mind already on the vampire. Tracking her would be easy enough. Her kind always left a trail of blood in their wake.

There was no fighting the bloodlust for them. They couldn't fight what they really were.

He glanced down at his claws. When it came to the *Other*, humanity was only skin deep.

Elijah screamed again.

And that skin could rip so easily.

CHAPTER NINE

His heart thundered in his ears, and the wild beat shook his chest. Keenan pushed up onto his elbows and stared down at Nicole. Pleasure still hummed through his blood. The orgasm had pounded through him—and he wanted more.

No wonder humans had sex so much. Sex was . . . addictive.

Not as messy as it had seemed. Hot. Wild.

So much better than his dreams.

Her hands were on his back, sliding down over his skin, and his cock thickened again inside her.

Once wouldn't be nearly enough to sate the hunger that had been growing within him.

"Was that . . ." She stopped and licked her lips. "For a first time, you sure seemed to know what you were doing."

He leaned forward and pressed a kiss to the curve of her shoulder. *I've seen plenty of sex.* There wasn't a move he didn't understand. Mentally, he knew it all.

But the actual physical experience was something

that he'd gotten only with her. And there was so much more he wanted to do.

"Ah . . . Keenan . . ." Her hands slipped forward and pushed on his shoulders. "Again?"

Surprise lifted her voice. Why? What had she expected? He smiled down at her. "We're just getting started."

Her eyes had eased back to green but as he pulled back and began to thrust again, he saw the emerald slowly bleed away.

The edge of her sharpened teeth peeked out from behind her lips—the fangs she'd sunk into his flesh.

Her bite hadn't brought pain. Not even close.

Just pleasure. A sensual kick so powerful he'd shuddered.

He wanted her bite again.

He thrust harder, deeper. Her sex was slick from her climax, his, and so tight—a hot, clinging clasp that stroked over every inch of his cock.

This time, though, he wanted to watch her. Wanted to watch every flicker of emotion on her face.

In. Deeper.

His spine tightened.

Her legs squeezed him, so tight. Her sex—*incredible*.

"Harder this time," she whispered, those fangs peeking at him. "You don't have to be careful with me."

But he felt like he should be. She was small. Delicate, and—

Nicole laughed and pushed up, a fast, *strong* move and Keenan found himself on his back, staring up at her.

"You keep forgetting . . ." A different note had entered her voice now. Darker, sadder. "I'm not the same woman you watched before."

His cock still lodged within her and she straddled his thighs. She caught his hands, brought them up to cup her breasts, then she started to move. Lifting up, gliding down. The rhythm built. Faster. Harder.

Her breath heaved out as her gaze bored into him. "I can take anything . . . you've . . . got."

She was the sexiest thing he'd ever seen.

Keenan shot up as the thread of his control broke away. He caught her head and pushed her mouth to his neck. "Bite me." Because he wanted, needed that wild surge that came when she—

Bit.

Her teeth pierced him. His hands clamped on her waist and he yanked her up, down, thrusting, driving deep, and a groan tore from his throat.

His hands were too hard. His thrusts too strong. Her mouth just right. Her body . . .

Yes.

Deeper, harder. Her nails raked him. She licked his throat, and his cock jerked inside her.

Then he felt the ripples of her release, the hard squeeze of her sex around him as she came.

He exploded inside of her. Keenan's body stiffened, and the drumming of his heartbeat echoed in his ears as he climaxed. And as he came, she tilted back her head and stared up at him.

Dark, dark eyes . . .

His right hand curled around her chin, and his lips pressed against hers.

Pleasure hummed through him, so much pleasure, but at that simple touch of lips—*such a light touch*—he saw . . .

Death.

The vision came to him, as had a thousand others over the years. Death angels always had a vision of their charges' last moment . . . the better to know when to give the touch.

This time, he once again saw his charge's death. *Her* death.

Nicole lay in a pool of blood. A wooden stake pierced her chest. Blood trickled from her lips. "It's . . . okay . . ." Her voice was broken, just like her body.

And he was there. His fingers closed around the stake as she tried to pull it out.

"This time you can't save her."

He spun and saw Az.

"No one can save her."

"Keenan?" Nicole squeezed his shoulders. "Keenan, are you okay?"

The vision vanished. It was just him and Nicole again. In bed. In each other's arms.

He forced a smile to his lips.

But she shook her head. "What happened? You left me . . ."

"No." Said instantly. "I won't." Az was wrong. The vision was wrong.

But the visions were never wrong. And Az couldn't lie.

He shoved back the fear and fury as he pulled Nicole down onto the bed and held her tight. Her heart raced beneath his hands, the beat reassuring him. For now, she lived.

He just had to make sure she stayed alive. In order for her to keep living, he'd have to fight the angels.

His gaze drifted around the room. No telltale scent of flowers teased his nose, but that vision had come from somewhere. Since he'd fallen, he shouldn't see the images anymore. If he couldn't see them on his own, then that meant *someone* had sent that death picture to him. Someone who was one serious asshole.

Az.

Keenan's stare centered on the ceiling. *Want to play rough, Az? Then let's play, angel. Let's play.*

* * *

When Nicole opened her eyes, Keenan was gone. She blinked, rose quickly, and pulled the sheet with her. "Keenan?"

"We don't have much time."

His voice came from the darkness on the left. Night had fallen, once more cloaking the house in its shadows. Nicole turned her head and found him unerringly. Sometimes vampire vision could be a good thing. "Wh-what do you mean?"

"You're going to die."

Not what a woman wanted to hear moments after rising. She licked her lips. "The sex was good," she told him quietly. *Way better than good. More, please.* "But we've really got to work on your pillow talk."

He pounced. No other word for it. He caught her arms and pulled her against him. "I'm not making a joke here. You're *going* to die. I saw it."

Goose bumps rose on her arms.

"Death angels always see the end coming for their charges. We know exactly what it will look like."

"I-I didn't think you had those powers anymore."

She saw the sad twist of his lips. "Not sure it is my power."

That didn't sound good. She stared at his face, that perfect, sculpted face, and saw the rage lurking in the tightness near his mouth and the darkness of his gaze. "I don't understand." And she didn't. There was still so much about this *Other* world that she didn't know.

"Az is jerking me around. He sent the image because he wants me to know what's coming."

My death. She had to swallow to ease the lump in her throat. "Maybe there's no escaping what will come." She'd tried. Twice. But if death was just going to keep coming after her . . .

"You got out of that alley." His fingers tightened on her.

Yes. Part of her had gotten out.

"Nothing is written in stone. Humans have choices, and now, so do angels. Az can take his fucking rules and screw off."

Not very angel-like. But then, angels weren't exactly cute little cherubs carrying harps.

They were big, dangerous men who could burn an enemy to dust with a thought.

"Get dressed." His hands dropped. "We're going back to the Quarter."

"Why?" She'd already told him—

"Because if we're fighting Az, we'll need help." He turned to leave.

She grabbed his hand. "This fight isn't yours." Did he think he needed to do some kind of penance because of what happened before?

"It is," Keenan gritted out. He looked over his shoulder. His gaze seemed to burn her. "Because you are."

Her breath froze in her lungs. "We aren't—" Okay, they'd had sex. Great sex. But . . .

But she was a vampire and he kept thinking she was just a woman. If he knew the things she'd done, he'd be the one sending her to the afterlife.

And what's to say he won't? When he finds out that you're not sweet Nicole any more, maybe he'll change his mind. He'll be the one to give you that Death Touch and then he'll go back to the life he had.

While she—what? Got the death she deserved?

"You were my charge. *Mine*. Your life was mine to take or to spare. No one else's."

Oh, okay. He hadn't meant that whole *you're mine* thing in a sexual kind of way. Got it. Awkward.

Not as awkward as dying, of course. A close second.

Her fingers dug into the sheet.

"You lived in that alley. All the rules changed when you survived. *Everything* changed." His hands fisted. "The angels have been acting like we're the ultimate power for too long. Just because we *can* kill, it doesn't mean we have to."

"And you really think we can stop that guy, that Az—"

"Azrael."

Oh, damn. She knew that name. "He's not just another death angel."

"No. He's *the* Angel of Death. The strongest. The one we all reported to." He shrugged with a little ripple of movement and her gaze went to his back. Again, she had the quick impression of darkness surrounding him, of shadowy black wings spreading high, but she blinked, and they were gone. "Az is the one who's after us."

Not really "us." Just her. From what she'd heard, Az hadn't wanted to kill Keenan. He'd wanted to give the guy the secret key—*her*—back into heaven.

"Lucky for us . . ."

Again with the "us."

"Az has a powerful enemy."

And what? The enemy of my enemy . . . "Who?" Her voice came out too rough.

His lips tightened.

Nicole knew she wasn't going to like this even before he said—

"Sam."

Damn.

Sam stared at the brightly lit stage. He watched the new girl as she came out to the driving beat of the music.

Tall, a little too thin, but she had nice breasts. She didn't really look like a stripper though, and she didn't move like one with that dancer's grace, either, but—

She turned to face him and her eyes, dark and deep, pinned him to the chair.

Power.

He sat up and automatically leaned a bit toward the stage. The strip club was his place. *Temptation.* A fitting name for a fallen angel's hell.

But her . . . the new girl he hadn't tried out . . . something was very, very off with her.

She began to dance. Her moves weren't overtly sensual. They should have been.

She danced slowly, but still . . . the movement of her hips, the slow twist and roll. *Oh, yes, sexy.*

He realized the catcalls had stopped. No voices shouted and not even any whispers filled the room.

Every eye was on her. No one could look away.

Just like I can't. Trapped.

Power.

He grabbed Ron, the low-level demon he kept in charge. "Who is she?"

Ron blinked. "Ah . . . she just started, I didn't—"

"Name."

"Seline. Seline O'Shaw."

His gaze pulled back to her, almost helplessly. And he hadn't been helpless in . . .

A thousand years.

"She's not human." Absolutely certain. He didn't feel any glamour around her, but he'd bet a chunk of his power the woman on that stage wasn't your average Southern girl.

She sure as shit wasn't a stripper.

Because she wasn't stripping—not all the way. A teasing dance, yes. But her movements were too deliberate. Every time she revealed something, she concealed it instantly with a toss of her blond hair or a turn of her body.

The woman was good.

Demon?

Witch?

He'd find out.

Then she looked at him once more. Her gaze met his, and there was fury in her dark stare.

The music stopped. After one more glance from his dancer, she disappeared behind the black curtain.

He rose, blood heating. Finally, someone worth the—

"You've got company, boss," Ron said.

Slowly, he turned his head and glared at the demon. "Not now." He pushed ahead. The dancer would be backstage. He'd find her and discover just what she was.

The night had gotten much, much more interesting for him.

But Ron—with his high forehead sweating—stepped in front of him. "He—he said his name's Keenan . . . that you'd be looking for him."

Ah, yes, his other prey. Actually, Keenan was the reason he'd come back to New Orleans. Why keep hunting on the road when he knew Keenan would be coming home?

But . . . "Let him wait," he told Ron, and the demon's already wide eyes seemed to bulge.

The Fallen would have to cool his heels. Sam had other prey to catch.

Besides, the angel might enjoy the view in Temptation.

After the storm, it had taken a while for life to return to normal in her city, but this night, Nicole saw that

New Orleans was back. The streets were full, voices filled the air, and the city seemed to pulse with life.

Her angel took her to the last place she expected. A strip club. The bouncer didn't even raise a brow when they walked inside, but Nicole's grasp on Keenan was so tight she worried she might break his hand. "Why are we here?" She wasn't a prude, okay, maybe she'd been *before* her change. When he'd said they were getting ready to fight, she'd expected a visit to a magic shop. Or maybe even a trip to a nearby graveyard to summon a spirit.

Not *this* place.

"If the stories are true," he told her, voice deep, "this place is one of Sam's favorite hangouts."

A place named Temptation? Packed with breasty strippers? Yes, she could buy it as a hangout for a fallen angel. Especially that Sam jerk.

Her gaze slipped to the stage. A woman was walking away, a woman with long blond hair and a confident, can't-get-me stride. The men were staring after her in open-mouthed lust, but she didn't look back.

Keenan pushed through the crowd. "There he is."

Her head turned to the right. Yes, like she'd forget *that* guy. Sam was headed to the back, and he paused only long enough to yank open a "Staff" door.

Keenan caught her hand and hauled her with him. They were moving quickly, pushing through the crowd and—

"What's your rush, sweet thing?" A tall, muscled biker grabbed her left hand. "Why don't you just stop to—"

She had stopped. He'd yanked her to a stop. "I'm not part of the entertainment," she snapped. Did she look like one of the half-dressed chicks strolling around?

His hot gaze swept her. "You could be."

"No," Keenan said very definitely. "She couldn't be. Now get your hand off her or—"

But the biker wasn't letting go and the guys sitting at his table all looked nice and pissed and ready to rumble.

"Or what?" The biker taunted. "You gonna make me let her—"

Keenan's left hand shot up and shoved against the biker's chest. The guy flew back, about ten feet, and crashed into the side of the stage. The stripper on the stage screamed, but the DJ kept right on playing.

"Yeah," Keenan murmured. "I am."

The guy's buddies scrambled to their feet.

"You really don't want to mess with me." Keenan's voice was flat. "But if you want to try . . ." He shrugged. "Let's go."

They didn't go. They didn't move.

Keenan inclined his head in a nod. "Then stay the hell away from us." Then he was pulling her again as they headed for that closed door.

Hurrying, Nicole had to point out, "I could have taken him, you know." *Stop thinking I'm human.*

His hand pushed against the wood, but he spared her a hard glance. "I know."

"Then why—"

"I was just in the mood to kick some ass."

She shook her head. "You know, you just don't *sound* like an angel."

"Maybe I was never a good angel." His eyes went flat and hard. "But then, humans have most of the lore wrong anyway. Most of us were created to punish and to kill."

"And to protect?" She whispered. Because Keenan *was* protecting her.

He didn't answer. He shoved open the door and stalked down the narrow hallway. Half-dressed women filled the space. Some called out invitations as they glanced Keenan's way. Nicole glared at them. Maybe she was in the mood to kick some ass, too.

"Sam!" Keenan's voice boomed. "Get out here!"

But Sam wasn't appearing.

A small guy with bright red hair and dark eyes eased from a shadowy corner. He was the same guy Keenan had spoken with when they first came into Temptation. His name had been Ray or Ro—

Keenan grabbed the man by the shirt-front. "Where is he?"

A trembling finger pointed to the left.

"Playing games. Should have known." Keenan dropped their helper and then he kicked in the door.

Nicole saw Sam whirl to face them. A woman stood behind him, but Nicole couldn't see much of her because Sam's body blocked her view. Deliberately, she was sure.

"Your timing is shit," Sam said, crossing his arms and raising one dark brow.

"*You knew.*" Keenan launched across the room and grabbed Sam. In a heartbeat, he tossed Sam into the air. The Fallen's body slammed into a mirror and the glass shattered.

Nicole glanced over her shoulder. *Ron*—that was his name—watched with bulging eyes. "You should probably keep everyone away," she advised and flashed some fang.

He stumbled back.

Huh. Not very protective of his boss. Sometimes, it was just hard to find good help.

"You knew that Az would come, you *knew*—" Keenan snarled and lunged forward.

"*Don't.*" From the woman. The blonde. It wasn't a scream or a desperate threat. Just a flat order.

Nicole took a good look at her. The woman wore jeans and a loose white shirt. Her brown eyes were wide, and filled with cold determination.

And she had a gun. One that was aimed at Keenan.

"If you come at him again," the blonde said clearly to Keenan, "I'll have to shoot you."

Sam laughed at that. A deep, rumbling laugh. Then he said, "You can try, but a bullet won't keep him down."

Good to know.

"And you'd do better to be aiming at *her*, anyway," Sam added, pointing his index finger right at Nicole.

Asshole. This was the guy they were turning to for help? "A bullet won't keep me down either," Nicole felt obliged to point out.

But the woman's aim didn't falter. "*She* hasn't done anything," the lady said, voice clear and arctic. "You two are the ones with the fight, and I'm not looking to be collateral damage."

Because being collateral damage sucked.

"Does the fact that she's a vampire matter?" Sam asked, with mild curiosity flavoring his words.

"Doesn't matter. Neither does the fact that you two"—now the gun swung between Sam and Keenan—"are demons."

"Now that's just insulting." Sam brushed off the broken mirror shards and rose slowly. "Just because you're in hell, it doesn't mean we're demons."

Her arm lifted, and she pointed the gun at his heart. "Don't move."

He stilled.

"Good boy." Her voice mocked him, but her eyes turned back to Nicole. "I'd advise you to leave with me. Whatever these two are doing, you don't want to be part of it."

"Too late," Sam murmured. "It's all about her."

Nicole wet her lips. "Thanks, but . . ." She stepped closer to Keenan. "I'm not going anywhere."

The woman's jaw clenched. "Your funeral."

"She's already had one." Sam couldn't seem to keep quiet, and—judging by the expression on his face—he seemed to be *enjoying* this.

The blonde with the gun shook her head and backed toward the door, never lowering her weapon.

"I'll see you again, right?" Sam called. "Seline, you will be back to dance again tomorrow." The guy made the last part sound like an order.

Seline didn't speak. She kept her gun up, took a few more steps back, and disappeared through the open doorway.

Because she was watching Sam so closely, Nicole saw the flicker of his eyelids and the fleeting expression of . . . disappointment on his face. Interesting. She filed that little flash away for later.

Sam brushed off more glass shards and sighed. "There a reason you came slumming tonight, Fallen? Or were you just looking to get tempted?"

Keenan's hands fisted. "Az wants her."

Sam didn't blink. "Really." No surprise there, but then, he'd all but told her this would be happening.

You'll suffer.

"Guess you can't cheat death," Sam murmured, not sounding the least bit ruffled to hear that she'd be dead, again, soon.

Not his problem.

They'd made a mistake coming there.

"Sucks for you." Sam stalked forward. "But what the hell do you think I'm going to do? Why do I care if another vamp bites the dust?"

She winced. "Keenan, let's go." She wasn't going to

beg this bastard for anything, not even her for her life. *He won't help me.*

"Right." Sam nodded. "Go, Keenan. Go screw your little vamp while you have the chance. And when Az comes for her, and you try to stop him—well, then you'll find out just what death is like for a Fallen." His lips twisted into a cruel grin. "Think you're heading upstairs again?" He paused for a beat of time. "Think again."

Someone punched her in the chest. No, it just felt like that. The thought of Keenan dying . . . *it hurt.* No. "He's not dying for me," she said. She wouldn't let him.

"He fell for you." Sam shrugged his broad shoulders. "Dying's the next step."

"*Sam.*" Keenan's voice snapped out, and the room seemed to tremble.

No, the room *did* tremble, and a smile curved Sam's lips. "Getting some of your bite back, are you? Not being a demon-wannabe anymore?"

What?

Pieces of mirror crunched beneath Sam's boots. He stopped pacing right in front of Keenan. Her gaze darted between them. Same height, same build. One dark, one light. Power seemed to crackle in the air around them.

"What would you do . . . for her?" Sam wanted to know. "To save her, would you fall again?"

Keenan's eyes cut to her.

Oh, damn. He really did it. He fell . . . for me.

She swallowed the lump that was trying to choke her. He'd fallen for the woman she'd been before her change. When he found out about all that she'd done since becoming a vampire . . .

Tell him.

If he found out, he'd turn away and she wouldn't have to worry about him risking his life for her.

"I'm not letting her die," Keenan said flatly. "She lived before, that means she should get a new shot. Az—the bastard's making this personal."

Now that had her eyes snapping up to his face. She caught the flex of his strong jaw.

"Ah . . ." Sam sighed. "You don't buy that her name's on that big, magical list of death, huh? You think Az is trying to make an example of you? Trying to show all the other angels that if they fuck up, they won't get rewarded—no falling and pleasure for them—just another nightmare?"

"You tell me." Fury vibrated in Keenan's voice. "You've known him a lot longer than me."

"True." Sam's smile faded. "I know him well enough to say he'd do anything to keep his good little soldiers in line." His stare, black now and so cold, flickered to Nicole. "Killing you wouldn't give him a moment's hesitation."

Great. Nice to be so special—or rather, so insignificant. "Can we fight him?" she asked.

"*You* can't. You're just a vamp. You don't have the power."

Again with the making-her-feel-great talk.

"But you . . ." Sam nodded as he focused on Keenan. "If you got your powers back, there'd be no stopping you."

"My powers are *gone*."

"Really? Then how'd you throw fire the other night?"

"How did you know—"

Sam laughed. "There's little in this world I *don't* know about. Pay people enough, and they'll tell you anything. A vamp, Connor, came running to tell me about your visit to the blood room."

Connor. He'd always been willing to trade almost anything—even a life—for money.

"Tell me, Fallen," Sam continued, "If your powers are gone, then how'd you make the room shake just a moment ago? And how . . ." His voice dropped, became taunting, "did you see your sweet vamp's death . . . if your powers weren't coming back?"

Her teeth were burning, her claws pushing out. Sam was a threat to her, and her body responded instinctively. He was playing some kind of game with them; she felt like *everything* was a game, and she wanted it to stop.

Keenan's gaze flew to her. "You mean *all* the powers will be coming back?"

Sam laughed. "Bit of a bitch, isn't it? You can save her, but the cost will be hell."

"What are you talking about?" Nicole demanded, sick of being in the dark. "If we can stop this Az, tell me *how*."

"Fury's the key." Sam flashed his teeth in a grin that chilled. "You got to let the rage take you, and then you can take *him*."

"Why don't *you* just take him out?" Nicole snapped as she grabbed Sam's arm and jerked him toward her.

An electric shot flew through her fingertips. Not pain, not yet. But . . .

"Interesting," Sam said as he looked down at her hand. "Very, *very* interesting."

Keenan swore and pulled her away from Sam.

But Sam's stare had locked on her now. "Maybe you're not so insignificant after all."

Well, wasn't that grand.

Sam's tongue swiped over his bottom lip. "I'll help you, for a price."

"I thought you just said I could take him out—" Keenan snarled.

"I said you *could*, not that you *would*." Sam rocked back on his heels. "There's a difference you know."

"And just what's your price?" Nicole asked him.

His eyes glinted. "For fighting an angel bent on vengeance? Because it is vengeance. Your name's not on any list. Az just wants to take you out to prove that no one screws with his guard."

"You're sure?" Keenan's fingers squeezed hers, the grip just shy of actual pain. "He said—"

"He can twist the truth as well as any of our kind." Sam crossed his arms over his chest. "Az isn't the lily-white angel he wants to be. He's been tempted, he's broken the rules, and now, he thinks he *is* the power when it comes to death."

"You want to take him out." Keenan dropped the words easily, but his body was tight against hers. "You've been fighting with him—"

"Since before you took your first soul. Right." Now Sam looked bored. "Az owes me. Payback can be a bitch." His eyes narrowed. "Or in this case, a vampire."

The guy was weird.

A faint odor began to fill the room. Metallic, harsh—*gasoline*.

A soft *whoosh* hit her ears and she spun back toward the door. *Fire*.

"Huh. I didn't expect that," Sam muttered. "Pity. I was so looking forward to tomorrow night's dance."

What?

The smoke seeped through the doorway.

"You got enemies, other than Az?" Sam asked as he headed for the nearest wall. He punched it with his fist and the bricks crumbled. "Cause it sure looks like someone is gunning for you—or your vamp."

Then he was pushing through the loose bricks and heading into the dark.

"Dammit, Sam!" Keenan yelled. "*Wait!*"

But waiting in a burning building wasn't a good

idea. Especially when you knew you were living on borrowed time anyway. Nicole locked her fingers with Keenan's. *"Come on!"*

They'd just reached that broken wall when she heard—

"Help me!"

The smoke was already filling her lungs and trying to choke her. The smoke wouldn't kill her, it couldn't. But the fire sure could.

Keenan hesitated. His gaze met hers.

"Keenan . . ."

Another desperate scream rose above that crackling fire. A woman's scream.

Nicole turned back to the doorway. She wouldn't leave—

Keenan grabbed her and *threw* her out of the building. As she flew through that rough opening, the bricks scraped over her arms and legs. She hit the cement outside hard enough to make her whole body shudder. When she looked up, Keenan wasn't there.

Because he'd gone back into the flames.

"Some angels . . ." Sam's voice floated to her, rising easily above the fire and the shouts from those fleeing the building. "They just never learn."

She pushed to her feet.

"Can't save everyone." Sam wasn't moving. He was just standing there and staring at the fire. "Sometimes, you can't even save yourself."

Screw him. Sometimes, you *could* save someone.

Her hands slapped against the brick wall.

"You'll burn if you go in there." His quiet warning.

"I'm not leaving Keenan on his own." He hadn't left her. And that woman in there—screaming—*been there, done that*. She knew too well what it was like to be screaming for help that didn't come.

Help's coming.

"Nice sentiment." And somehow, he was right beside her now. No, behind her. His hand stroked down her arm and sent goose bumps over her flesh as that weird little electric shock vibrated through her. "But I can't let you save him."

The electric shock became a painful burn . . . one that fired right to her heart.

She opened her mouth to scream.

"Don't worry, this won't kill you."

The scream never passed her lips because her voice was gone. Nicole fell and hit the ground. She stared up at the fallen angel who looked—

Sad?

"It won't kill you, and maybe . . . maybe it won't kill him either."

Darkness coated her vision. No, not darkness. Smoke.

Keenan.

"He needs to learn . . . he can't save everyone."

The fire raged.

"Let's see just how far we can push him . . ." Sam's dark voice drifted with the smoke. "Until he breaks."

That bastard was supposed to help them!

She didn't want Keenan to break. She wanted him out of the fire.

Keenan!

She couldn't scream his name. Couldn't breathe. Couldn't move.

She could only lie there as Sam slipped away and the fire burned higher.

CHAPTER TEN

The flames crackled around him, flaring high, golden and red, seeming to strike out like snakes as he followed the broken screams.

Keenan kept his head down, moving quickly, jumping and darting through the fire. Nicole was safe, he'd seen to it; now he just had to—

There.

He saw her through the flames. The woman who'd pulled the gun on Sam. She was behind the bar. Trapped by the fire. Her hand was over her mouth, and she was coughing.

Behind the bar. Great. Right next to the wall with the alcohol. The last place you wanted to be when flames were so close.

Her head turned. Her wild eyes met his. The flames swarmed higher, and he knew time was running out.

Then the bar ignited.

Damning the flames, he ran through the fire.

* * *

Nicole sucked in a deep gulp of air. One. Two. Her starving lungs filled greedily and her fingers began to move.

Damn that Sam. He *wasn't* helping them.

Breaking us.

She pushed up slowly as her chest heaved. The air was bitter with smoke and it stung her throat, but she wasn't about to be choosy then. She'd take what she could get.

Her gaze flew around the area. Cops were on the scene now, swarming in their patrol cars. They were holding a crowd back. A fire truck roared up the street.

No sign of Sam.

Or Keenan.

Still in there.

She stared at the gaping hole in the wall. Smoke billowed. The crackle of flames taunted her.

If Keenan had come out, he wouldn't have just left her on the ground. She was sure of it.

Her knees shook a bit when she stood. Whatever Sam had hit her with, it had been strong.

Thirst had her throat drying up. Or maybe that was the smoke. Or the fear.

"Hey! Hey, lady!"

Her head whipped around at the call. A uniformed cop waved at her, his round face tense.

"Get away from there, lady! The fire crew's comin'! Get back!"

Could a fire kill a Fallen? Fire killed nearly everything—everyone—else. Witches. Vampires.

"Sorry," she muttered to the cop and dove for that opening, "but he needs me."

She wouldn't let Keenan break. Sam could go screw himself.

Keenan wouldn't break.

* * *

The vampire went into the flames.

Unexpected.

She should have run. Covered her own ass.

Not gone back for her lover.

But Sam smiled as she disappeared. He'd hoped she'd risk her safety for the Fallen. Hoped—but hope was such a weak thing.

Fleeting.

Human.

The fire could fry her skin off in moments. Vamps burned just as quickly as witches.

The light scent of flowers teased his nose and his smile vanished.

Someone *would* be dying that night.

Keenan. His vampire. Or the helpless humans inside.

The scent grew stronger. The wind pressed against his body.

Someone would die.

Someone always did.

The ceiling was collapsing. The groans and creaks of the wood and beams above Keenan blended with the crackles of the flames. He hoisted his burden, being careful to keep her limbs from the fire. The woman—Seline—had screamed when he jumped through the flames. She'd tried to stumble back, but had smacked her head into the glass counter behind the bar.

He'd barely caught her before she fell into the fire.

He glanced around and held her tight. The fire had caught him on his arms and his legs. The pain throbbed, making his gut churn.

Nicole had taught him of pleasure.

Now pleasure's evil bitch of a sister was back—and he didn't like her much.

The fire closed in.

Keenan lifted his right hand. He'd conjured fire before, so that meant that he *should* be able to control the flames. He'd already tried, over and over, but so far, no luck.

"*Keenan!*"

Now the flames seemed to be calling his name. Taunting him to walk through that hot kiss once more.

"*Keenan! This way!*"

No, that wasn't the fire calling. *Nicole*. She was inside. Surrounded by that burning hell when she should be safe, outside, protected.

No.

He wasn't aware he'd shouted the word, not until he heard the echo of his voice.

Then the flames before him, the fire that separated him from Nicole, began to flicker.

The fire would destroy her. Boil the skin off her flesh.

"*No!*" The building shook and the fire between them sputtered out in a blink. The rage stirred in his gut, and he ran to Nicole.

She grabbed his hand and he barely felt the pain, such was the pleasure of her touch.

But she was coughing and tears streaked from her eyes. "We've . . . got to . . . get out . . ."

So much fire still burned. The blaze was deliberate, he knew it. Someone had set this trap.

His fist slammed into the wall. The bricks cracked. They didn't break, not like when Sam had—

The bricks exploded and thick chunks flew out into the air. And Sam was there. He shoved his way inside and reached for the woman Keenan carried. "Give her to me!"

For an instant, Keenan wondered if Sam would throw the woman back into the fire. She barely seemed to breathe and blood matted her hair.

But Sam pulled her close and tucked her head against his chest. "*Weak human . . .*"

All humans were weak. It was just how they'd been designed.

Sam spun away with the woman, and Keenan grabbed Nicole. "You shouldn't have . . ."

The flames snapped and snarled around them.

" . . . come after me!"

Her fingers locked with his. "Later! Let's get—"

The ceiling collapsed with a shriek of boards and metal. Nicole slammed into him and pushed Keenan through that broken wall. She tumbled out right after him.

The *whoosh* of fire filled his ears, then he hit the concrete. The flesh scraped from his arms and hands. He rolled and caught Nicole when she landed on top of him. Ash stained her right cheek and her eyes were wide and dark. Her breath eased out on a sigh. The fire still raged behind her.

He kissed her. Keenan grabbed the back of her head, tangled his fingers in the thickness of her hair, and crashed his mouth down onto hers.

Too close. That fire had been *too* close to her.

Death comes.

The scent of flowers fought with the ash, choking him.

Death comes.

His tongue drove into her mouth. Her nipples pushed against his chest.

Not right now, you don't! You're not taking her.

He wouldn't let Az win. He hadn't fallen just to lose her. He'd do whatever it took to face off against his ex-boss.

Even slipping into the dark.

"Get 'em out of there!" A voice thundered, and then hands were grabbing at him, her, and yanking them apart. Keenan growled, ready to rip and tear and—

And he was staring at a firefighter. A young female with red cheeks who glared at him through a clear face mask.

"Get 'em to the EMTs!" She yelled, and her men pulled them clear of the building.

EMTs. He glanced down and saw the blisters on his flesh. The fire had tasted him.

His gaze darted to Nicole. No sign of any fire injuries, but she looked even paler than normal.

They loaded Nicole into the back of the ambulance. An EMT shoved an oxygen mask over her face.

Then they turned to him. A heavyset guy and a petite blonde cut off his shirt, and he saw the blonde wince at his wounds.

He could barely feel them now.

He glanced back at Nicole and saw that her fangs were peeking out. A sure sign of her desperate thirst.

"Oh my God." The loud exclamation came from the blonde at his side. His gaze whipped back to her. He found her staring at him, her eyes saucer-like in her elfin face.

The guy stared at him, too, only his face was quickly bleaching of color. *"What the hell?"*

Keenan felt the tightening of his skin. One quick look down showed him that the wounds were healing. They were shrinking and disappearing right before his eyes—*their eyes*.

"I don't need that!" Nicole snapped. "I don't— Keenan! Oh, crap!" She'd gotten a look at his chest. She lunged up and grabbed his arm. *"Let's go!"*

But she needed help. The EMTs could take her to the hospital. Get her some blood.

"*Come on.*" She jumped from the ambulance.

The little blonde lifted her hand toward him. "What are you?" She whispered.

He shook his head and leapt after Nicole.

"*Stop!*" The guy shouted. "You can't leave! We need—"

But he and Nicole were already running through the night, pushing through the crowd, and Keenan knew he'd made a fatal mistake.

He'd let the humans see what he really was.

By the time they stopped running, Nicole *hurt.* The thirst shook her body and her teeth burned. Whatever Sam had done to her, it had knocked out her reserve energy and she needed blood. Badly.

"*Nicole . . .*"

She spun to face Keenan. They were in an alley, a too-thin slice between buildings that would give them a bit of protection from prying eyes. "Did you know that would happen?"

He blinked at her, looking sexy and strong, and—

Her breath rasped out. "They *saw* you heal, Keenan."

His gaze held hers. "I didn't realize I'd heal that fast. I hadn't been hurt before."

He hadn't been— "What? Run that by me again. Nice and slow."

His shoulders rolled. "Angels don't feel pain. Not death angels. We collect souls."

She knew—

"Only the dying can even see us. And if you're dying, there's no need to fight back. No need to suffer."

Uh, right. "So you didn't even know what pain was . . . until you fell?" Unlike him, she knew all about pain. About how it ripped you apart and tormented your mind.

The fire.

She'd never forget the lick of flames.

"Didn't know about pain or pleasure." His gaze caressed her face. "Until you."

That was sweet. No, no, it wasn't. She'd taught him about *pain?* Pain wasn't some nice hallmark card. Pain was a nightmare. "Keenan . . ."

His fingers skimmed down her face. A sensual touch so at odds with the aches in her flesh. He crept closer and caged her against the wall with the strength of his body. "Do you need blood, sweet?"

"Yes." It was all she could do not to sink her teeth into his throat. *He was just in a fire. Hold back. Hold back!*

His lips skimmed her jaw. "You shouldn't have come into that building after me."

Her laugh was weak. "Did you really think I'd let you face the fire alone?" She shook her head, and he leaned in close. His lips slid down her and pressed right over her pulse. She shivered. "We're a . . . ah . . . team . . ." *Us against the angels.*

Hopefully, they wouldn't be the losing team.

"If Sam hadn't frozen me," she said, "I'd have been there sooner." *Damn Sam.*

His head whipped up. "What?"

She licked her lips. When he touched her, she didn't hurt as much and his fingers were currently sliding down her side and curving over her hips. "He got me as soon as you left. One touch, and I couldn't move." *Helpless.*

"Bastard." His fingers were under the edge of her shirt. Pushing up and caressing her flesh. *In an alley.* For someone still new to the whole earthly temptation bit, he learned fast.

"I . . . don't . . . ah . . . think we can count on him," she managed, her heart thudding hard in her chest.

Her growing lust merged with the blood hunger and she wanted to *bite*. But she kept her teeth up and away from him as she said, "N-no matter what he said, we can't . . . He wanted you to break."

Keenan's gaze bored into hers. His lips parted, but before he could speak, the roar of motorcycles shook the night. Her head turned and bright headlights flashed out of the darkness and filled her sight.

"Well look what we have here . . ." A booming voice called out.

A familiar voice.

That biker jerk from the bar.

Keenan didn't move. He kept his hands on her, but his gaze was on the men closing in.

The biker. Shit. Nicole recognized the big, burly, bald biker from the club. About thirty, muscled, both arms tattooed. And he was heading right for them.

"Knew our fire would smoke you out." He smiled. "Vamps can never handle fire worth a shit."

Did *everyone* but her know the paranormal score in this world?

He pointed one leather-clad hand at Keenan. "I don't got a fight with you. Take my advice, buddy. Go find another screw tonight."

Her eyes slit. She needed blood badly right then, and that ass was begging for a bite.

"*Watch* what you say," Keenan ordered, voice flat.

"Fuck you."

Guess he wasn't into watching his mouth.

Now the guy pointed at her. "I know what you are, bitch, and I know *who* you are."

The more she stared at him, the more familiar he appeared to her. Something about the line of his jaw, the bulge of his nose . . .

"Knew as soon as you walked into that club . . ." The biker's hands dropped, only to rise up half a second later gripping a stake. *Definitely prepared.* "I been carrying this in my pack since I buried Jeff."

Oh, hell.

An image flashed in her mind. A big, burly guy with fists that had been thick and hard as he drove them into her face.

Then that body had fallen, sagged so quickly. When his head hit the cement, Jeff Quint's eyes had been wide open, and so had his throat.

She grabbed Keenan's arm and tried to shove him away. "I-I've got this. You go, I'll meet you back at—" *Our place.* Had she really almost said that? She swallowed and forced a smile. "I'll see you soon."

But Keenan wasn't moving. Not even an inch. "No way, sweet. I'm not leaving you alone to face—"

Laughter cut him off.

"You really think somebody like her needs protectin'?" That stake rose. "What she needs is a good killin'." Mutters of agreement came from the men behind him. "Hell, even death's too damn good for her. She needs to *suffer.*"

"Tell the bitch, Mike!" One of his buddies called out, and, of course, the buddy had a stake, too.

Not my night.

But then, she'd known this night would come for some time. A night of reckoning. They wanted her blood. It seemed only fair, considering she'd taken all of Jeff's.

"I didn't want to kill him." She said the words without looking at Keenan. She couldn't look at him then. *Time he found out the truth.* She stepped away from him and the alley wall and faced the vengeance that was coming.

"Right. You just tripped . . ." Mike closed in on her. "And your teeth landed in his throat." A snarl burst from his fat lips. "Jeff was my brother, the only fuckin' family I had. I knew vamps were after us, but I never expected a fresh-faced piece of ass like you . . . guess he didn't either."

No.

She could feel Keenan's stare on her. She glanced his way, just for an instant. "He doesn't have anything to do with this."

"Then *he* can damn well leave." Mike grabbed her shoulder, his fingers digging deep. "But you're only gettin' out of this alley in pieces."

The alley seemed to tremble. *"Get your hand off her."* Keenan's too-lethal voice.

But Mike only had eyes and bloodlust for her. "Jeff and me . . . you know how many vamps we killed?"

No, but all the vamp slaying would explain why she'd been sent after Jeff Quint. *He preys on us. Now we prey on him. Rip out his throat. Make him bleed. Make him beg.* How long had those words played through her mind? Over and over, until her will was gone and all she could do when Jeff came at her that night was . . . *attack.*

He hadn't even had the chance to get out his stake.

Not like his big brother.

Mike didn't take his hand off her. Those thick fingers just dug deeper as they seemed to squeeze right to the bone. Behind him, the guys—five of them, all big, leather-clad and with go-to-hell grins—began to close in.

"I gave you a chance to run," Mike snapped at Keenan. "Last call, dumbass. You stand with the vamp bitch or you save your own ass and get the hell out of here."

"Get out of here, Keenan," she whispered. She was going to fight, but this wasn't *his* fight. In case things didn't go her way—the odds were a bit heavy in old Mike's favor—she didn't want Keenan paying for her crimes.

"I'm not going anywhere." His gaze burned into Mike. "Get the hand off her, human, or *lose it.*"

She had the feeling he really, really meant those words. "Keenan . . ."

But Mike didn't drop his hold. He did bring up his stake, getting it too close to her heart for comfort.

Then Keenan shoved *his* hand against Mike's chest. Mike flew back into the air and slammed into two of his biker buddies.

"You had your chance," Keenan said. "*Dumbass,* you should have backed off while you could."

Mike sprang back to his feet and attacked, with all his men running right behind him. Six against two. Not bad odds. Actually kind of good considering the bikers were human and—

Keenan jumped in front of her, swinging out with his fist and sending two guys flying back. The men hit the walls of the alley and didn't get up.

Okay, four against two. Even better.

Keenan grabbed the next guy around the throat. The stake dropped from the blond's hand as he clawed at Keenan's hold, struggling to get free. His pale face began to purple.

She grabbed for Keenan's arm, afraid the guy was about to die right there. "Keenan, *no.*"

"Callin' back your dog?" Mike was there, charging by Keenan and coming for her. "Nothin' can save you, bitch, nothin'!"

He ran at her with the stake up. His buddies took Keenan, swarming him. Her teeth burned, her claws lengthened, and when Mike lunged at her with that stake—

She just ripped it out of his hands, broke it, and tossed the pieces behind her.

That didn't stop Mike. No, he swung at her and slammed his fist right into her face.

Definitely remember that.

The bloodlust rose but she stumbled back.

"That's right, run, get ready to *bleed*."

Um, no. She wouldn't be bleeding for him. His fist came at her again. She caught it in her left hand. Then *her* fist went at him, plowing into his cheek. Not the light hit of her pre-vamp days. Nicole swung with a blow strong enough to break Mike's jaw. When the bones crunched, she knew the punch *had* broken his jaw.

He kicked out, his booted heel aiming for her stomach, but she twisted and he missed her, and he fell to the ground.

"I'm sorry about your brother," she said the words between pants. "If I had it all to do again . . ." But there'd been no choice at the end. He'd fought her and if she hadn't killed him, he would have taken her head.

"*Fuckin' bitch* . . ." Mike shoved up and yanked a knife out of his boot. "He should've killed *you*." He shot off the ground and sliced with his knife.

The blade never touched her skin. Keenan grabbed Mike's hand, twisted, broke the guy's wrist, and the knife clattered to the ground.

"I said you'd lose this hand," Keenan reminded him.

Veins bulged along Mike's neck.

Behind them, she saw the scattered remains of Mike's crew. Still alive—she could see their chests moving—but out of commission. No backup for Mike.

Nicole stalked to the biker. She didn't touch him. Wouldn't.

"Gonna bite me now?" Blood dripped from his lips.

Oh, she wanted to. Even more, she needed that blood.

Keenan's shove had the guy sinking to his knees and staring up at her with his throat bared.

"Gonna kill me like you did Jeff?"

Her gaze swept to the unconscious men once more, and she held onto her control with all the strength she possessed. "Do you always hunt in a pack?" Wolves weren't the only ones smart enough to do that. Mike hunted vampires, but he was human. Humans against vamps—that equaled a serious disadvantage. One he'd tried to make up for with the numbers tonight.

"Not tellin' you a damn thing about how I hunt." Deep lines bracketed his mouth. Keenan still had a grip on Mike's hand and she could see the sweat that beaded Mike's upper lip. "Not talkin' so you might as well rip me open."

She shook her head. "I'm sorry about your brother." She could understand Mike wanting her blood. The other vamps he'd killed—maybe they'd deserved to be put down. But maybe they hadn't. *We're not all evil. Not when we have a choice.*

"Bull . . . shit . . . just a . . . damn . . . bloodsucker."

Right. She was. And he could see her fangs. But . . .

But she wasn't under the control of the Born Master anymore. Her gaze slipped to Keenan because what she had to say was for him as much as Mike. "You know—you know when vampires are *Taken* . . ." *Taken,* the term for vampires who were made through the blood exchange. Made, not *Born.* Only a very few were actually born as vampires. The Born Masters were the strongest, baddest, and hardest to kill vamps out there.

She took a breath and glanced back at Mike. "When they're Taken, they're linked to the vamps that changed them." Only the vamp who changed her had been dead. So she hadn't been told anything about vamp rules and powers. She'd had to find everything out the hard way.

"*I don't give a shit about—*"

"Vamps are linked, through the blood, back to the Born Master that started their line." She'd talk, he'd listen. Not like Mike had much of a choice. "We're linked, and the Born Master—he can control us, he can force his thoughts into our minds and—"

"*No fuckin' Born killed my brother! It was you!*"

Her shoulders sagged. He was right. The Born had been in her head, whispering, ordering, breaking her will, but in the end, *she'd* been the one to make the kill. Her teeth. His throat.

"*Kill me, kill me and get this damn mess over!*"

Nicole shook her head. "I'm not killing you." The voice in her head was long gone. The Born, Grim, was dead, courtesy of a female bounty hunter named Dee Daniels. There were no more whispers in her mind these days. No more hell.

Control. "I'm not a killer." Anymore. She drank to survive, that was all. Not to kill.

Because if she crossed the line and started killing, she knew that Dee would come after her, too. Dee had warned all those Taken by Grim . . . *kill and I'll come.*

Nicole wasn't particularly in the mood to face off against Dee or the Night Watch Bounty Hunting Agency.

"Let him go, Keenan," she said quietly.

Keenan dropped his hold.

Mike fell forward. His hands slapped against the concrete.

"Don't cross my path, I won't cross yours." They'd both just keep living. She eased back and her shoulder brushed Keenan's. "Let's get out of here."

They'd taken five steps when she heard the rustle of sound. Clothing. A scrape of wood.

She spun back around. Mike was on his feet, a stake in his left hand, and he was barreling for her again.

Crossing her path.

Keenan tried to shove her back. No way. She shoved *him*. Keenan went down. Her arm came up, and she blocked the blow. The stake hovered in the air. Mike strained, trying to shove down and impale her heart.

"I'm not a killer," she told him as the bloodlust burned and called her a liar. "But if you keep coming at me, I *will* fight back."

"Good," he spat. "Cause I'm not stoppin'. That was my brother, my flesh, *mine!* I'm not stoppin' 'til yer rottin' in the ground!"

Unfortunate. She really didn't want to kill him because she'd promised herself she wouldn't take another life.

But she wasn't in the mood to die, either. No matter what death angel might be circling her.

"Come at me again," her last warning to him, "and I'll drain you dry."

"Just like you did Jeff?"

Through gritted teeth, she managed, "Yes." She yanked the stake from him and drove it into his shoulder. He howled as his blood flew into the air.

Keenan drove his fist into Mike's face. That stopped the yelling and Mike joined his unconscious men on the ground.

Keenan met her stare, his eyes dark. "If you leave him alive, he'll just come after you again."

"Maybe." *Probably.* "But I have to give him the chance." *To walk away. Just walk away.*

Yet with blood involved, would the guy walk? This wasn't about pride, it was about family.

Vengeance.

He'll come after me again.

And she'd have to kill him. But not now. Not tonight. The scent of flowers that thickened the air—the angel that was close—he'd have to wait on her prey.

"Maybe he'll wake up smart." *I could have killed you. I gave you a chance.*

Give me one.

"We've got to get out of here," she said. Before the guys on the ground woke up and before those sirens she heard got any closer.

Coming home again—bad mistake. There too many dangers to her in New Orleans.

But then, these days, it seemed like someone was always after her.

Because I'm marked for death?

Time was running out for her.

"Come on," he said, and snagged her hand with his. She heard the crack of anger in his voice and hesitated. *He knows.* He knew about the darkness in her now. He'd realized she wasn't the woman he'd watched before. While he'd been away, her bad side had most definitely come out to play.

"Hurry, Nicole, *come on!*" Then they were running, streaking down the streets and darting through the alleys. Bourbon Street came and went, the crowd a blur around her. Voices, laughter. Bodies brushing. Faster, faster they went as they pushed into bars, darted outside, and cut through the city.

Then . . .

Silence.

They'd stopped outside a voodoo shop. The place was closed for the night. The windows and doors were covered with thick bars. The street was empty— everyone was busy partying a few blocks away. Nicole sagged, her breath heaving. Safe. For now.

"You killed." The anger was back in Keenan's voice. More reckoning time.

She brushed her hands against her thighs, sucked in more air, and managed a jerky nod.

"After what that vamp did to you in the alley . . ." He shook his head and stared at her with confusion clear in his gaze. "*You killed someone else?*"

More than one "someone else." She cleared her throat. "You know about the Borns." She'd fought, for as long and as hard as she could. But he'd broken her. "They take away your will." She'd been linked to Grim from the moment she took her first breath. She'd heard his whisper in her mind, taunting her, and as the days passed and she became weaker, that whisper had turned into a scream.

She paced away from Keenan. The heat of the night wrapped around her. The scent of the river teased her nose. "I didn't want to kill." She flung out the words. "Do you really think I could ever want that?"

She'd killed the vamp who attacked her, but that had been self-defense. No choice. And the others—

How long are you going to keep justifying?

She swallowed. "He put the compulsion to attack in my head. The men he sent me after—they'd been killing vamps." Right, like that was such a bad thing. Most of the vamps she'd met had lived to torture and slaughter.

Grim had made sure that his Taken were just like him.

"You'd never killed . . . not until that night." Now Keenan sounded sad and his voice made her heart ache. "I knew—the first time I saw you in Mexico, I knew you looked different."

Fangs. Claws. Seduction. Blood. Yes, she'd gotten some new features. Not exactly upgrades. "I had to change in order to survive." She wouldn't apologize for all that she'd done. The killings—yes, she regretted them and had vowed not to take another life, but the other things . . . Seduction, blood drinking—*I had to survive*.

His gaze raked her.

What did he see?

A monster? Or a woman?

"Wishing you'd touched me and let me die that night?" The question slipped from her lips, and, oh, damn, she hadn't meant to say that. She'd been thinking it—for days now—but she hadn't meant *to say it*.

His eyes narrowed into chips of blue ice.

She spun around and began marching, um, running, down the street. She didn't want to hear his answer. Didn't want to know that the man who'd had her back these last few days actually wished that she was dead.

Enough people were already wishing that.

Hard hands caught her and hauled her back against a muscled chest. "*Never say that*."

He whirled her around. His eyes didn't look like ice anymore. Black now, not blue, and burning.

"Keenan, I—"

His mouth took hers. Not soft. Not gentle. No hesitant lover. Hard. Rough. The kiss was wild with need.

The fear in her heart pushed her to be wild, too. She grabbed his arms and pulled him closer. They stumbled back and her shoulders rapped into the wood of the nearby building.

She opened her mouth wider, sucking on his tongue, and taking everything she could get from him. His taste filled her mouth, had her arching against him.

He still wanted her. He knew what she'd become, and he wasn't turning away. He was touching her, his hands greedy and possessive, stroking and caressing, and her angel wasn't running.

Neither was she. Not now.

Even through their clothes, the hard length of his cock pushed against her sex. Aroused. Thick and strong.

She wanted him in her. Nicole didn't care where they were. Didn't care about anything right then—but him.

Need him. Want him.

His body. His blood. Oh, a taste of his blood would be heaven right then.

His hand shoved under her shirt. His fingers pushed under her bra. His thumb scraped across her nipple.

Yes.

"The building's deserted."

He was right; she didn't hear any sounds from inside and—

Keenan stepped back, but kept a hold on her arm. "*I need you.*"

She was on fire for him.

He kicked open the door. One kick, and the wood flew inward. Then he pulled her inside. An empty space. No furniture, but walls, privacy and . . .

He pushed her against the nearest wall. Keenan drove his tongue in her mouth and took.

His hands went to her ass and he jerked her up, pressing her hard to the thick bulge of his arousal.

She held him tight. Nicole pushed the worries and fears from her mind and just held him.

His fingers were at the waist of her jeans, yanking at the snap, and then shoving down the zipper.

Her inexperienced Fallen had her jeans down around her ankles in about two seconds, then her panties were gone and his fingers were pushing between her legs. Pushing up, rubbing, stroking her.

Nicole rose onto her toes as her body tightened. *Yes.* She loved the way he touched her. He already knew her body. Knew just what she liked. How she needed to be touched.

He dropped to his knees before her.

"Keenan . . ."

He spread her thighs and she kicked the jeans away. His breath blew over her sex and she shivered.

Then his hands were pushing between her legs, and his long, broad fingers slid into her sex.

She jolted at the first touch, her body so sensitive that she almost climaxed.

"Not yet." His growled order.

His fingers stroked her, plunging harder and deeper now. His thumb brushed over her clit and sent a pulse of electricity right through her body.

"*Beautiful.*"

Her hands clamped down on his shoulders. "Keenan . . ." They shouldn't be there—where was *there*? She'd never had sex in public, before vamp life or after, and this still counted as public to her and—

His mouth was on her sex. His tongue drove inside and her knees would have buckled if he hadn't held her up with his tight grip.

She came quickly, a hard wave of release that whipped through her.

The aftershocks still trembled through her sex when he rose up and lifted her. His pants were open now. Oh, he moved fast. He caught her hips, lifted her against the wall, and drove his cock into her.

The pleasure pulsed.

His eyes were on hers as he thrust. Deep, driving thrusts. She licked her lips, fought back the hunger and clamped her inner muscles around him—the better to feel that slow, slick glide.

Her heart thudded in her chest, her breath heaved, and the tension rose again, higher, higher, as her body tightened.

Her hands were still on his shoulders, curling tightly around him, and she leaned forward, swiping her tongue over his throat. Her teeth scraped his neck, not breaking the skin, just—

He plunged deeper.

Her teeth pierced his flesh and the sweet drops of his blood spilled onto her tongue. Her control shattered.

Nicole climaxed again, drinking, taking his blood as she gulped that sweetness down greedily. He choked out her name as he drove faster, harder, even *wilder*.

This time, the climax wasn't a snap. Or a pop. It was a full-on eruption that had her whole body trembling as the pleasure lashed her.

He stiffened against her. Nicole's head lifted. His taste filled her mouth. His eyes—blacker than night— met hers. She felt the jet of his release inside her, the hot splash, and as she watched, she saw the shadow of black wings stretch behind him.

The air seemed to rustle around her as the wings moved. Her gasps filled the air, his fingers still cut into her hips, but as the pleasure faded, she could only stare at those wings.

Then she had to touch.

Slowly, her right hand eased down his shoulder. Her hand drifted down his back, and her fingertips stretched out.

She felt the lightest, softest silk. Just a whisper. Just—

Keenan shuddered against her. His head was bent now, and his mouth pressed to *her* throat. "What are you doing?" He rumbled, then his lips opened wider over her throat. His tongue stroked her flesh, and his cock began to thicken. "*Feels good*."

It did. Because her fingers were tingling. "I'm . . . touching your wings."

He tore away from her, pulling that thickening flesh from her—

No.

—as he stared at her with stunned eyes. "What?"

She could still see them—big, dark wings. They seemed to come right from his back. She tried to step forward but her knees were doing a jiggle. "Your wings, I—"

"*I don't have wings.*"

She hadn't thought so either, but she nodded.

He spun, showing her his back. "They were burned off when I fell."

She could see the angry red scars on his otherwise perfect back, but she could also see those dark shadows, rising up, covering him like a cloud. "I can *see* them."

He whirled back to face her. "No, they're *gone.*"

The scent of flowers hit her then. Light, sweet. Such a strange smell to mark someone who could destroy her so easily. Nicole grabbed her jeans and hauled them back up even as Keenan cocked his head to the side and stared hard at the broken front door. A breeze blew into the room, and then . . .

Wings. Black wings. Not shadows, but real, honest-to-God wings appeared as the angel approached. *Angel.* His face seemed carved from stone but made of beauty. He wore a white T-shirt, dark jeans. Strange, she'd expected—

Nicole swallowed. *I shouldn't be seeing him.* This was wrong. *Something* was wrong. You didn't see an angel of death unless you were dying. That's what Keenan had said. "I see your wings," she told Keenan. "And I see *him.*"

If she saw the angel of death, that meant . . .

Her time had come.

CHAPTER ELEVEN

As Keenan lunged forward, his arm swept out to make sure that Nicole stayed behind him.

She can see Az.

Fear and fury churned in Keenan. "You're not taking her!"

Az's eyes narrowed. "You really think you can stop me?"

"I can damn well try."

Az's eyes jerked at the curse. Right. Angels weren't supposed to curse.

Or to fuck.

Not an angel anymore. And Nicole was rubbing off on him.

"Get in my way," Az told him, voice deep and dark and promising, "you'll die."

"*No!*" Nicole shouted as she shoved past the arm Keenan was trying to use to shield her. Her clothes were wrinkled, her face flushed, her lips red and swollen—and she was so beautiful.

And she was running toward Death.

"Don't even think about hurting Keenan!" She yelled at Az.

Az blinked, then his light brows pulled low over his eyes. "You can truly see me." Now he sounded surprised.

What? An emotion? From Az?

No time to dissect that now. *"You aren't taking her."*

"No." Az cocked his head to the side and studied Nicole. Then he took one step inside the abandoned building. Another. The floral scent deepened, but Az wrinkled his nose, obviously smelling something else. *"Sex."* His nostrils flared. "That's why you came in here?" His eyes judged Keenan. Found him lacking. "How very human of you."

Keenan knew the words were supposed to be an insult. "Thank you." He'd always thought humans got the better end of the deal. Pleasure, passion. Sure, pain was thrown into the mix, too. But you could live through pain.

No expression crossed Az's face.

Nicole stood between the two men now. Her hair fell over her shoulders and tension held her small body tight. "I thought I had ten days."

"Um . . ." Az took another step inside. A step that put him closer to Nicole.

Don't touch her.

One touch would be all it took.

Keenan caught Nicole's arm and forced her back. She tried to fight, he just pulled harder. "He touches you, you die." Flat.

That stopped her struggles. Her eyes widened and she looked back at Az. "Why do I see him?"

Only the dying should see Az. Only the dying or—

"Been drinking angel blood, have you?" Az asked.

The mark on Keenan's neck seemed to burn. But he hadn't minded her bite. He'd craved it.

Az shook his head slowly. "We're not meant to be prey, Keenan."

"He's not," she snapped, and Keenan felt a spurt of pride. Even with death close, she wasn't weakening.

But Nicole's words had Az's eyes zeroing in on her. "I know about you."

"Good." She barred her sharp teeth in a cold smile. "He"—her hand tightened on Keenan's—"knows, too."

Az measured her with his gaze. "With all that you've done, are you worried about what the afterlife will hold for you, vampire?" He offered her a smile in return, and it wasn't pretty.

"I know why you were on the church steps that night . . ." He whispered the words. "You would have gotten a free pass that night. Straight upstairs then, but now . . . now fate will be different for you."

"Get out of here, Az!" Keenan snarled, his control fragmenting.

Az didn't move.

"You wanted another chance, didn't you?" Az asked. "But that's not what you got, you got—"

Keenan raced across the room and plowed his fist into the angel's jaw. The smash of bones and flesh felt *good.* Az flew back. The angel crashed through the door frame and stumbled outside.

"Guess what that is, buddy?" Keenan followed him out, and Nicole ran at their heels. "It's called *pain.*" Time for the angel to start learning how humans lived.

Az picked himself up slowly. He lifted a hand to his jaw. His eyes narrowed. "No—you can't—"

"I can see you." Keenan stalked closer. "I can touch you. And if you try to come at me again—or send any of the others after us—I will kick your ass."

Az's jaw clenched. "You can't."

"Yes, well, until about five seconds ago, I'm guessing

you didn't even think I could deck you—think again."
His hands clenched into fists. "The rules in this game
are changing."

"Because *you* say so? Who are you to judge?" Fire
there, cracking through the ice of Az's words. "You're
an angel whose wings burned. You were cast down to
live in this hell . . ."

"Watch it," Nicole warned. "I rather like this place."

Az's lips tightened.

"How does it feel?" Keenan pressed.

That blue stare cut to him.

Keenan smiled. "The anger is better than never
feeling anything, isn't it?"

Az's wings folded down behind his back. Ah, his
control was coming back as that slight break in emotion vanished. "You don't want me as an enemy."

"No, Az, you don't want *me* as one." He shrugged
and opened his arms. "I've already fallen. What do I
have to lose now?"

Wrong words.

Az's stare immediately shifted to Nicole. "What indeed."

Keenan lunged forward.

But he moved too late. Wind whipped against his
face as Az's words floated in the air, "I'll be seeing you,
Keenan."

The angel vanished.

But Keenan knew Az would be back. After all, angels never lied. They could twist the truth, confuse and
beguile, but they couldn't *lie*.

Neither could the Fallen.

*If you try to come at me again—or send any of the
others after us—I will kick your ass.*

His words to Az had been a promise.

* * *

The sun beat down on Carlos Guerro as he sauntered down the New Orleans street. Sweat trickled down his face, but he didn't care. He'd long grown used to the heat.

He was alone on this hunt. That was the way he wanted to be. The day he couldn't kill a gang of humans on his own . . .

He turned the corner and found the old bar, just off Bourbon Street. The place was open now, of course, even though it was barely one o'clock in the afternoon.

His eyes narrowed as he went inside. Dim interior. They probably kept the lights that way so the folks didn't notice how worn the furniture was or see how the cracked mirror in the back hung haphazardly. The darker a place was, the better it tended to look.

His prey waited to the left. Six men slumped in chairs. Bruises covered the men, and blood stained their clothes. He inhaled, a nice, deep pull, and caught the scent he needed—*vampire*. Not just any vamp though. *Her.*

Following her hadn't been easy, even with the speed of the private plane he'd chartered. But then, he didn't really like the easy hunts. He'd found a sheriff just over the state line who'd survived her attack. Then he met a female cop in San Antonio who'd been pissed to hell and back about the prisoner who'd escaped.

The San Antonio cop hadn't been as guarded as the sheriff, so he'd known he could push her. Carlos had flashed his own badge. It paid to keep a fake one, he'd learned that long ago. Once she'd realized she was talking to a brother in blue, the cop had opened up and revealed all about the escapee.

Nicole St. James. Age twenty-nine. Ex-school teacher who'd snapped one night and killed a man in a New Orleans alley. Minutes after that kill, she'd attacked a cop.

Since that night, Nicole St. James had turned full-on psychotic killer. Two more men met her, then bled for her. The female cop had said St. James was a serial killer. One who got off on slicing the throats of her victims and drinking their blood.

Good story, but he knew it was bullshit. The serial killer story was often used to cover *Other* crimes.

Carlos motioned to the bartender. "Whiskey."

Voices rumbled around him as the glass slid across the table. He took a deep breath, inhaling more of that elusive scent. Then he drained the glass and the fire of the liquid burned his throat. Oh, but it was a good burn. His eyes narrowed as he studied his whispering prey. The group of bikers looked pissed—and in pain. He wondered about them. Did they pretend the world was normal, too, or did they screw the rules?

"What the fuck are you looking at?" The big one snarled. But, to be honest, there were a few big ones.

Big—thick with fat and muscle.

And they'd still gotten their asses kicked. He knew a vamp's work when he saw it.

"Did you hear me?" The guy shouted again as he jumped to his feet. The table shoved forward and his beer bottle crashed to the floor. His face mottled as he pointed at Carlos. "You been starin' at me the whole damn time you've been in here! What do you—"

Carefully, slowly, he put his empty glass on the bar. "I was just wondering . . . who beat the shit out of you and your crew?"

Ah, *not* the right thing to say. Now they were all on their feet and storming for him. Good.

He'd been right. They were all big. Had to be over six foot three. Except for that one scrawny guy who was hanging back, nursing two black eyes.

"Boy, you picked the wrong bar." The leader—a

bald guy with snake tattoos curving down both arms—smiled.

Huh. He'd never really liked snakes. Carlos lifted one brow. "That a broken hand you got there?" *Si.* It was. "Guess you touched something . . . or someone you couldn't handle, *hombre*."

The leader lunged for him.

Carlos sidestepped and caught the guy's broken hand. "Now, Mike, you really need to control that temper." *Mike.* That was the name the helpful stripper had given him. She'd seen the guy set the fire at Temptation, and then she'd seen the biker corner a woman and her lover in the alley.

The stripper hadn't helped the couple. Tina wasn't real big into helping others, but she'd given *him* the information, for a price.

Finding prey is always the best part.

"How do you . . . know me?"

For fun, he squeezed Mike's broken hand. When big Mike hissed in pain, his men swore and came at Carlos.

"*Don't.*" His snapped order. He dropped Mike's hand and faced them all, his back to the bar. Carlos lifted his hands, palms out, and made sure that his claws weren't showing. "I'm not here to fight you." *Yet.*

His gaze met Mike's fuming stare. "I'm looking for the woman who broke that hand."

Surprise flashed on Mike's face. Then he smiled. A twisted, broken smile. "Hoss, there's no way you could handle her."

Carlos let his gaze sweep the bar. Only a few other stragglers remained, and they were high-tailing it out because they thought a fight was coming.

Maybe.

"Let me be the judge of that," he murmured.

"Dumbass, you don't get it." Big Mike stabbed a thick finger—one from his left hand, not that swollen right—into Carlos's chest. His voice dropped as he said, "That bitch ain't even human."

So what? Was he supposed to act surprised? No, not his way. Carlos nodded. "*Si,* I know. That's why I want to take her out. She killed *mi hermano*—my brother in Mexico."

The men around him all glanced at Big Mike.

Mike swallowed. "Mine, too."

What? Really? Carlos almost smiled. Talk about a fucking perfect cover story! He couldn't have planned that one better.

"I want her to pay," Carlos said and let his voice vibrate with fury. "I want her to hurt, I want her to beg, and I want her to *pay.*"

"Good luck." Mike rubbed the stubbly line of his jaw. "That vamp's got some kind of guard dog—bastard won't let anyone close."

Carlos tried very hard not to let his excitement show at that news.

"Probably uses him for fucking and sucking . . ." One of Mike's gang muttered.

Probably.

"*He's* the one who broke my hand, because I was touching his whore," Mike said.

"Gettin' ready to stake her . . ." This came from the same guy who'd spoken before, the one with a big red lump on his forehead.

Big Mike grunted. "He took us all out." He waved a hand toward his tight-jawed men. "If we couldn't take him, you damn sure ain't gonna have any better luck with the guy."

Maybe. "I will if you help me."

Now that had Mike looking interested.

"Your mistake was that you tried to take 'em down

when they were together." Huge mistake, especially for humans going up against supernaturals. "We need to separate them."

Mike started nodding.

"We want the vamp, right? She's our target." The idiot would believe anything he said then.

Mike licked his lips. There were murmurs from the men. A few "damns straights" and one "fuck, yeah." After a minute Big Mike said, "Yeah, that bitch is the one I want to stake."

"You'll get your chance." Eventually. "But first, we've got to break them apart. Break them apart, make them weak—then we attack."

Because Nicole St. James, killer and Taken vamp, wouldn't be nearly as fierce on her own. Not once she lost the angel on her shoulder.

"So how we gonna do it?" Mike wanted to know. "How the hell are we supposed to get her away from him?"

Now that was the hard part. But, luckily, he had a plan. "Leave that to me. You just get your men ready to jump her."

Lie. Lie.

Mike and his men *were* his plan. They were his bait and his distraction. Because Nicole and her angel would be so focused on them, well . . . the vamp wouldn't even realize the true danger until it was too late.

"We've got to act fast," he said. "We're gonna need to attack before the sun sets." No sense in going up against a stronger vamp. Not while there was still daylight left.

"You *know* where she is?"

Shifters had good noses for a reason. They were the best at tracking. Once he'd caught her scent at Temptation, he'd followed her all the way back home.

He'd always had the strongest nose in the pack. Blood, fire, and sex—it wasn't easy to miss that combination. Tracking Nicole had been fucking child's play.

"I know." He smiled. "Now let's go and drag that bitch into the sunlight."

Nicole woke, her heart racing, her body shaking as the nightmare still played in her mind.

The alley. The blood. The monster.

She sucked in a deep breath.

She'd been the monster.

"Nicole?"

Her head turned. Keenan lay beside her in bed, his chest naked, and the sheet loose around her hips. She swallowed. "Ah, it's nothing . . ." It was still daylight. She could see the sun trickling through the blinds, could feel the weakness in her body. He'd chosen to sleep in the day? With her?

The lump in her chest had nothing to do with her nightmare.

"Something scared you," he said.

Me. I scare myself. I have for a while now.

His fingers brushed down her arm and she shivered. "It—it's really nothing—"

"Liar." The word sounded like a caress. "Tell me about it."

The drumming of her heartbeat wasn't slowing down. She pulled the covers up and held them with tight hands. Right then, she needed some kind of shield, and it was the cover or nothing. "Before I was attacked, I-I didn't even know I could kill."

"Everyone *can* kill. People just have to be pushed hard enough," he said flatly. There was a lot of dark knowledge tinting his voice. But then, he'd probably seen everything humans had to offer. Good. Bad. All that waited in between.

Death.

Right. He'd know all about killing.

"You said you saw me . . . before." Before she'd gotten the stylish new fangs, the bad manicure, and the pretty much unquenchable thirst for blood.

"Yes."

"*She* never would have ripped a man's throat open. Not once." Her voice dropped. "Twice. I killed two humans." *And one vampire.*

"You were under compulsion, you didn't—"

"I-I . . . *liked the blood.*" This was the darkest part of her confession. Her gaze dropped to the hands that balled the sheets. "I liked the rush of blood, the power. I wanted to stop. I knew it was wrong. I knew I was killing them and that voice was in my head, pushing me . . . *but I liked the blood.*"

And that was her shame.

"You're a vampire."

Uh, yes, she knew that.

"Nicole . . ." He sighed out her name. "You're supposed to like it."

"Because vamps like the blood so much, that's why they kill." Why she'd had to fight her urges. "The schoolteacher I was . . . the woman who always got in by ten on a work night, she wouldn't have—"

His fingers curled over hers. "Why do you keep talking as if she's someone else?"

Her gaze lifted to his. Why couldn't he see? "She *was* someone else. She was someone *good.*" She'd tried to be, anyway. Volunteering her time in afterschool programs. Donating canned goods for the homeless. Recycling for goodness' sake. That woman had been *good.*

Not a killer.

Not a monster who lusted for blood. Who fought. Killed. Who licked her lips as she stood over a dead man and thought—

More.

No wonder the dreams wouldn't stop. "That woman died in an alley," she told him, holding his stare. Even if she hadn't died then, she wouldn't have made it through the year.

His hand skimmed down her arm. Slowly, his warm fingers rose to her chest and pressed over her heart. "If she's dead, then why do I feel her heart beating?"

"I'm not the same person anymore. The things I did—" Not just the killing. But with Connor . . .

Her eyes squeezed shut. "I'm not the same."

The warmth of his hand seeped into her skin. "You couldn't be the same and keep surviving."

She cracked open her eyes.

"The bloodlust is always strongest at first." He rose, pushing up to sit beside her now. "I've seen it drive some crazy. They'd lose control and turn on anyone who came near."

Nicole remembered that first, desperate hunger. The bite that she'd given the cop who'd come to her aid. "Yes." She'd felt crazy then.

"You didn't kill the cop you attacked."

She shook her head. "It was a near thing. I . . . couldn't stop." She never wanted to feel like that again. So hungry—the hunger an ache that burned her whole body.

"You did stop."

Her lashes lifted fully. "Barely." She wouldn't let him think she was something that she wasn't. "I didn't have the control. If I did, I wouldn't have ever bitten him. I wouldn't have listened to that voice in my head—*I wouldn't have killed.*"

She had to get away from him. His touch made her weak, and she was already weak enough. Nicole jumped from the bed, yanking the sheet with her. "Angels are real." She tossed that out at him and glanced back just in time to see him blink.

"Uh, yeah, we are."

This was the part that scared her. "I knew that—I always knew that." She'd been a good Catholic girl after all, *before*.

His head cocked as he watched her.

"Angels are real," she said again. "And demons are real. That means after this life . . ." *Already knew this. Always knew.* Her knees locked. "After this life, there isn't going to be any sunshine and paradise waiting for me." Maybe if Keenan had taken her soul that long-ago night, but now . . .

He stared back at her. Didn't deny her words.

No.

She choked down the very real fear in her throat. "I want a chance to make it up." She sounded crazy, so what else was new? "I don't want Az to take me, not until I've had a chance to *make it up*."

He climbed from the bed and didn't bother covering with a sheet. "You can't bring back the dead."

He'd know.

A muscle flexed along his jaw. "And Az isn't taking you anyplace."

Nicole could only shake her head. "Why?"

Keenan blinked at that. "Because you're not ready to go, you don't want—"

"No." Her head shook again, fast, as her hair whipped around her face. "Why does it matter to you? Why do you care what happens to me?"

He gave another slow blink, then said, "I don't know."

Well, great. She turned away from him and grabbed

for her clothes. Not like she'd expected some big declaration or anything. The guy didn't know her, he hadn't—

He fell for you.

Obviously, that was bull. She yanked on her panties and shoved into her bra.

"What I said . . . it angered you?"

Her lips pressed together as she snagged her jeans. Jeans *he'd* bought for her. "It confuses me." Okay, that was a lie. Half-lie. He confused her *and* he made her damn angry.

She spun back to him, her shirt gripped in her hands. "You lost everything, you gave it all up, and you don't even know why."

I wasn't worth it. The words just wouldn't come out of her mouth. She wanted to say them, but couldn't. She'd told him about her crimes, her needs. He should realize the truth for himself.

Maybe he did. Her shoulders slumped and her chin dipped. *Maybe* . . .

"For over two thousand years, I never felt anything."

That had her head whipping up.

His eyes stared right at her, but Keenan didn't actually seem to see her. "I saw babies born, parents die, wars, weddings, happiness, *life*. But I never felt a thing."

His words were so cold she shivered.

"I only knew touch . . ." He lifted his hand and stared at his palm. "When I killed. And then, there was no warmth in the bodies. I took the warmth away before I even touched them."

His hand fisted.

Silence.

What could she say? "Keenan . . ."

"I wanted more than that."

Seemed only fair.

"Humans had more. Even the *Other* had more—and they were supposed to be the *mistakes*."

Was that what she was now?

"Angels were created for a purpose. To protect. To guide. But not to feel." His fist fell. "No sorrow. No pain. And no happiness either. Just . . . duty. Just . . . nothing."

He stepped toward her. "I wanted more," he said again. "I didn't even realize it at first, but with every soul, I just—*wanted more*."

Wanting. Didn't he realize that was a form of feeling? Maybe the other angels hadn't felt any emotions, but he had, and they'd driven him to the edge.

No, they'd driven him to fall.

"With you, I decided to take more." His fingers curled around her chin, and he tipped her head back. "Silk," he whispered. "Smooth, soft, and *warm*."

She realized he was talking about her skin.

He lowered his head and pressed a kiss against her lips. "Just as soft here, but the taste . . ." His eyelashes lowered. "A little sweet, and a hint of spice."

Oh, he could seduce her so easily. Had, actually.

His knuckles slid down her neck. "And being inside you . . ." His lashes rose. "*Pleasure*."

She licked her lips and wanted his mouth again.

"I was tempted, and I fell." His knuckles were at her chest now, pushing against the edge of her bra. "Humans get to feel. They get to fuck. They get anything they want."

Not always. Sometimes, they got nightmares they didn't want.

"Try living with nothing for two thousand years, and then see just how hungry you are for *everything*."

His mouth took hers in a hot, hard kiss that she met

head-on. She knew about hunger, not just for blood, but for someone to hold you, to kiss you, *to want you,* no matter what.

Was she just a body for Keenan? Just a temptation? Maybe, but for her, he was becoming so much more.

A man who stayed with her through the good and bad. A man who didn't care about the monster inside of her. He'd known her before, but didn't judge her now.

She dropped the shirt. Her fingers lifted to wrap around his shoulders and hang on tight. The future wouldn't, *couldn't* matter. Now was all that mattered. Making a memory, having something to take with her when she went to the next life.

Hell.

Her mouth opened wider.

Then she heard the snarl and roar of engines. Motorcycle engines. Not too near. Not outside, not just yet.

But coming closer.

She held the kiss for a moment longer. *Why hadn't he just stayed away? I gave him a chance.*

Vengeance.

Keenan lifted his mouth. "Nicole." He breathed her name.

"Mike is coming for me." She hadn't wanted to kill.

"You knew he would."

She just hadn't expected him to find her so quickly. But a hunter like Mike would have connections, and probably eyes everywhere. "He's coming while I'm weak." She pressed her forehead against Keenan's shoulder. His arms were around her and even though death was coming, she felt safe right there.

"He won't touch you."

Because she had, what, eight days left? Seven? Less? Az hadn't actually said she had ten . . . *less than ten.*

Angels might not lie, but she had the feeling they might not always tell the full truth, either. Angel semantics.

"I killed his brother." Because Grim had thought Jeff was too much of a threat. The hunter had already taken out a dozen vamps. She'd been the bait to take down the big gun. "If I were him, I'd come after me, too." But she didn't want to kill Mike. Stop him from killing her, yes, but kill him?

I already have enough blood on my hands. Killing him won't get me any forgiveness.

Like there was a chance of that happening.

Mike wasn't coming alone. She heard the growls from the other bikes.

"They can't beat us both," Keenan said.

No. The humans would lose. They'd die. Because even though she was weak, Keenan wasn't.

But it wasn't his fight.

"They're not hurting you," he told her and edged away.

She bent and grabbed her shirt, yanking it on as he pulled up a pair of jeans. "I wanted him to walk away."

He laughed at that. "And you really think you're so different from the woman you were before the bite?" His blond head shook. "Sweet, a cold-blooded killer wouldn't care, human or no." He turned away. "I'll take care of them."

"What? No, you're an angel, your job is—"

"Death." He yanked open the door. "The last time I hesitated, an innocent woman became a vampire." He glanced back at her. "I won't make the same mistake."

Then he was gone—racing out to face the vampire hunters who didn't want his blood.

Mine.

She ran after him because Nicole had learned—the hard way—how to fight her own battles.

If she had to do it, she'd kill Mike because he wasn't sending her to hell.

Though it looked like she'd have to send him there.

CHAPTER TWELVE

"Still got your guard dog, bitch?" Mike shouted the minute he saw Nicole step onto the wooden porch.

Keenan locked his back teeth. The human had been given every chance, but still he sought death. *Humans*. Didn't they understand it really was all about free will?

Mike could have walked away . . .

Instead of coming straight for death.

"You gonna hide behind him again this time?" Mike stalked closer, and then his left hand came up—a hand holding a gun. "Do it. Cause I want to see just how strong that bastard is."

Keenan rolled his shoulders but Nicole jumped in front of him. "My fight," she whispered to him, then she raised her voice and called out to Mike, "This is your last chance. I don't want to kill you—"

"I want to kill you, bitch! I want to slice your throat open, rip out your heart, cut the skin right off—"

"*I don't want to,*" she yelled over his threats. "But I will." Absolute certainty. Then, voice dropping, turning mean and cold, she said, "Just like I killed your brother."

The five men on the bikes behind Mike didn't move. Mike's face hardened, twisting with hate.

"This time, I'm the one who's ready." Mike aimed the gun at Nicole. "Ready to die, vamp?"

"You mean *again?*" Nicole asked.

Keenan knew that even during the day, bullets wouldn't kill her.

She stalked toward Mike, the thud of her footsteps seeming to echo as she headed down the front stoop. "No, I'm not particularly ready to—"

He shot her.

She'd dodged to the side, so the bullet missed her chest, but Keenan heard it thud as the bullet went into her shoulder. She trembled a bit and slid back a step. But then she shook her head. "Try again."

Keenan's admiration for her kicked up a notch.

She glanced back and her gaze met Keenan's for an instant. "Stay back . . . my fight."

The others didn't get off their bikes. Didn't make a move for their weapons. Maybe they were just there to watch the show.

He'd be sure to give them a real fine show.

Her blood was dripping on the ground.

Did she really think he was just going to stand back and watch?

His fingers began to shake, so he balled them into fists. The wind kicked up and blew against his face.

"You're weak!" Mike snarled, that gun still up. "Can't take much more of this before you go down." He fired again. Missed her. Aimed. Fired.

Hit.

This one grazed her arm. Slowed her a bit. More blood flowed. She was halfway to her target.

Mike smiled. "*Now!*"

Then his buddies stopped watching. Their hands dove into their satchels, and they all came up with bottles.

"Burn the bitch!" Mike ordered.

They started throwing the bottles right at Nicole. She swatted them away. More bottles flew, some with burning rags in them.

No!

Not just her fight—*theirs*.

Keenan flew off the porch. He grabbed her in his arms and turned so that when the Molotov cocktails hit, they crashed into his back. The bottles rained down and a fire sprang at their feet.

Nicole screamed, and he saw the fire eating at her shirt.

The hunters *had* been prepared this time.

"Special brew, bitch! Somethin' I picked up from a voodoo shop down here! Somethin' to burn a vamp right to ash!"

Keenan held her tight and raced forward, shoving through the fire that circled them. Once they made it past that line of flames, they crashed onto the ground. The fire was on him, eating at his flesh, but he barely felt the pain.

Not like when I fell.

Nothing would be like that fire.

He rolled Nicole and slapped at the flames on her clothes. She was crying, thick tears rolling down her cheeks. Angry red blisters were all over her.

But his skin was already healing.

"It's okay," he whispered, the rage making his voice lethal. "I've got them."

He'd always known some humans deserved death. Deserved to scream and beg for mercy.

He wouldn't give mercy this time.

He kissed her cheek. Tasted her tears. The scent of blood and fire filled his nose.

"Nicole?" Fear had his gut clenching.

But she nodded. "I-I'm . . . okay." Bleeding, bloody, burning, but alive.

Until the next attack. With Az breathing down her neck, she wouldn't survive many more hunter attacks.

And the bastards were *laughing* as she bled and ached.

"I'll kill them for you." A simple promise. Right, wrong. It didn't matter anymore. He brushed a shaking fingertip over her cheek. "*I'll kill them.*" He was on his feet. He ran toward Mike and the bastards with him.

Mike and his men were already on their bikes, revving their engines. Trying to get away.

Mike's motorcycle flew away in a hail of gravel. Two others followed him.

No, they wouldn't get away.

Keenan lunged forward and caught one bastard around the neck and yanked him off the bike. The man's head—minus helmet—slammed into the ground.

Keenan jumped on the bike. He locked his hands around the handlebars and leaned in low as the motorcycle leapt forward.

You're not escaping.

He'd hunt the bastards down. He'd take them out. Nicole *would* be safe.

The roar of his rage was the only sound he heard. *Death.*

"*Keenan, no!*" Nicole was on her feet, her arm throbbing, her side aching, her clothes—*still smoking*—and she shouted as loud as she could.

But Keenan didn't stop.

She knew he wouldn't, not until . . .

I'll kill them for you.

Was this really what she'd done? Turned an angel into an assassin?

Her breath hissed out at the pain as she hurried to the man on the ground. She needed blood. She'd have to take his. Donating was the least the guy could do for her—he'd tried to burn her alive.

She dropped to her knees, reached for him, and realized, too late, that he was dead.

His horror-filled eyes stared up at her. His mouth was wide open while his face was frozen in a mask of pain and terror.

Her hands ran over him. No broken neck. No broken bones at all. No wounds, no blood, nothing.

But still very, very dead.

As she stared at him, trying to understand what had happened, a new scent teased her nose. Wild, musky, like an animal.

"You really are just a baby to this game, aren't you?" A male voice asked, one with a hint of Mexico purring beneath the words. "*Querida,* you don't even know what I am, do you?"

Slowly, carefully, she turned her head to the right. A man walked from the woods. His shoulders were pushed back, his pace slow and steady, and a wide grin stretched across his handsome face.

Dark hair. Dark eyes. Square jaw. Cruel lips.

A face she'd seen before.

Mexico. Carlos.

Prey that had become hunter. Nicole jumped to her feet and felt the lash of pain sweep over her. "What . . . what are you doing here?" Dumb question. Like the others, he was there to kill her.

Because of what she was.

He smile widened even as his gaze raked her. "That looks like it hurts."

It did. She wouldn't stop hurting until she drank and healed.

"Off to stop them, isn't he? Off to kill them . . . for you."

She needed a weapon stronger than her claws. "I wasn't going to hurt you that night. I was just—"

"Thirsty." He smiled and his teeth looked far too sharp to be human.

Vampire? No, a vamp wouldn't care if she got a little hungry.

He lifted his hand and his claws were out. Not sharpened, razor-sharp fingernails like she had but actual, *real* claws. The kind an animal would have.

Oh, shit.

That scent, the claws . . .

"Figuring it out, eh? Took you long enough." He sauntered closer.

Weapon!

The fire sputtered on the ground but there was a broken bottle nearby. She grabbed it and held the jagged glass toward him. Glass had worked for her once before.

"Did you think that since you're undead, you're at the top of the food chain now?" His teeth snapped together. "Not even close."

"Y-you're a shifter." She should have realized that fact sooner. But she'd been so hungry in Mexico. She'd noticed the scent was off, but . . . bad mistake.

"Um. Guess I am." He shrugged. "That glass isn't goin' to hurt me. Unlike you, I'm not weak during the day." His dark gaze dropped to her neck. "If I wanted, I could rip out your throat right now."

As weak as she felt, that might be a possibility.

Ten days. Nine, eight . . . who knew what was left?

Her nostrils flared. Was that flowers in the air? Did the smell come from the woods or from . . .

Time's counting down.

"But I don't want to kill you. Not yet, anyway." Carlos leapt at her. He grabbed the broken bottle and yanked it from her hands. He hauled her close to him, and the slam of his body against her burned flesh had her screaming in agonized pain. He caught her hair and wrenched her head back. "I fucking hate vamps!"

Who didn't? She bit her lip to hold back another cry.

"You're a screamer. Ah, I like that." His claws slipped down her cheek. "Before we're done, I'll make sure you scream plenty."

Her own claws were lengthening as the rage and fear built. Her fangs burned and if she had the chance, she'd—

"What?" He wrenched back her head. "You want my throat?"

Yes.

"You wanted it that night in Mexico, too, didn't you?"

She'd wanted blood. "Not like . . ." she gritted, "I can stop the thirst."

His brows lowered at that. "No, I don't guess you can." He shrugged. "You still smell fresh, not like the decomposing piles of shit vamps usually are."

Well, great for her.

"Didn't introduce myself formally before," he murmured and finally lifted those rip-me-open claws away from her. "Name's Carlos Guerro."

"I don't care who you are!"

"No, you never did. That was part of the problem." The faint lines around his eyes tightened. "You just wanted to drain me."

She swallowed. The pain was making her nauseous

and the throbs from the blisters wouldn't stop. "He'll be back," she whispered. Keenan hadn't deserted her. She'd seen the fierce rage in him. He'd gone after the hunters, but *he'd be back*.

"Good." His smile flashed once more. "I'm rather counting on that, *querida*."

Keenan's entire focus centered on the hunter, Mike. Keenan's motorcycle sped up as the bike ate up the road. He drove faster, faster.

As the group roared down the road, two of the men lost control of their bikes. They crashed and their bikes slid right off the road.

Mike didn't slow at the crash. Just revved his engine, and drove faster.

Not fast enough.

Keenan had the bastard's scent. Fear and fury and fire. Mike wouldn't get away.

Keenan could still see Nicole's tears.

His front wheel pushed into Mike's bike. With a scream of metal, the hunter's motorcycle flipped, sending that jerk flying through the air.

Mike's two surviving men kept racing away. Keenan didn't go after them. He'd get to them later.

The fire of his vision centered only on Mike, only on the man who was scrambling across the road, moving like a crab and laughing as blood poured from his nose.

"B-bitch is dead!"

Keenan's fists were at his sides. "She didn't plan to kill your brother. Another vampire forced her to attack him." If this Mike was really a vampire hunter, he would *know* all about mind control and compulsions.

Mike lifted his gun. Aimed and fired.

The bullet never broke Keenan's skin.

"*What the fuck?*"

"She gave you the chance to walk away." Everything around him was red. The fury nearly blinded him. "Then you came back, and you *burned her.*" He shook his head. "It's ending. You're not hurting her again, you're not—"

Mike's laughter stopped him.

"Left . . . her . . ." Mike spat blood and what looked like a tooth onto the ground. "Fool . . . did just what he . . . said."

The wind seemed to chill. "Who? Who said?"

More laughter. "Left her . . . dead before you get back."

No, her attackers had been gone. She'd still been conscious, and he'd stopped the fire. She'd said . . .

I-I'm okay.

The breath burned in his lungs.

She'd been alive and . . . he'd left her. The fury had been so strong and the need to punish driving him—

To kill.

"Bitch will . . . s-suffer."

His breath heaving out, Keenan stalked across the road. "No, she won't."

"She is!" Mike's wild laughter tossed on the wind that shouldn't be there. "She's . . . sufferin' now." His lips were curved wide, showing that bloody grin. "Justice."

Keenan shook his head. Bull. No one was left to hurt Nicole. She was—

"He said you'd . . . leave her."

"He?" *Get back to Nicole.* The whisper filled in his mind and had his body tensing.

"He'll kill her." Mike's laughter choked in his chest. "When you find . . . her . . . Vamp will be ripped open—"

Keenan lunged forward and grabbed Mike, yanking him up. "Who? *Who's* after—"

Mike's eyes widened. His breath rasped. Pain and fear tightened his face. "W-wings . . ."

And he died.

He *died*.

Keenan stared down at his hands. Hands that had grabbed Mike.

One touch.

Death.

Keenan's hands lifted. Mike's body dropped to the ground, as hard as stone. Frozen in death.

Sam had been right. All the powers were coming back, and he'd just gotten the power he'd dreaded the most.

"No." Keenan stumbled back and then stared up at the perfect blue sky. "*No!*"

If his touch could kill, then he couldn't touch Nicole again. Couldn't—

Vamp will be . . . ripped open—

He couldn't let her die. Keenan shoved back the rage and trapped it deep inside his body. He spun and ran back for the motorcycle. He'd stop whoever was after Nicole, stop him, kill him—with a touch.

Because the angel of death was back.

He could almost feel the beat of his wings as he raced down the highway.

When Sam came upon the battered motorcycles on the old highway, he smiled.

And knew that his plan was working.

He braked his truck—he rather enjoyed that truck—and climbed out to survey the wreckage. Two men, still alive. Groaning and twitching on the ground. One man . . .

Sam walked closer, his booted feet thudding on the concrete.

One dead.

Sam's head cocked as he crouched and studied the body. Big Mike. A semi-legend in vampire-killing circles. Mike and his brother Jeff had followed the motto that the only good vamp was a dead one. So they'd staked every vamp they could find.

At least, they had until old Jeff had gotten good and drunk one night and let a sweet little newbie vamp with a good ass and a bad bite get too close.

The urge to fuck could blind even the smartest hunters.

Sam's gaze tracked over the dead man. No wound that he could see. Not on the outside, anyway. But if Big Mike had died the way he suspected, the marks would be on the inside.

Smiling, Sam rose. So the Fallen had come into more of his old powers. Good. Keenan would probably be afraid now, and worried that every person he touched he'd kill.

Sam sauntered back to his truck.

Keenan should be afraid. Very afraid.

That was why Keenan would be so glad to see him. Ah, yes, the Fallen was just where he wanted him to be.

My game, my rules.

"*Nicole!*" Keenan yelled her name as he jumped from the motorcycle. Smoke rose, curling in the air above the dying fire. Blood stained the ground, but Nicole wasn't there.

"*Nicole!*" His voice thundered out as he ran up the porch steps. Maybe she was inside. Maybe Mike had just been messing with his head.

Yes, she was inside. Probably cleaning her wounds or getting ready to rip into him for leaving her behind. She *was* inside. She had to be.

Two minutes later, he realized she was gone. All that remained was an empty house and a blood trail that led to the woods.

He stared at those woods. Had she gone chasing someone? He sucked in a breath and ran into the brush, trying to follow the light spray of blood that he saw on the ground. He shouted her name as he ran, afraid that he'd be too late.

Stay away from her, Az.

He hadn't fallen just to lose her.

The woods cleared up ahead. An old, red dirt road cut through the trees. Fresh tire tracks had sank into the dirt.

The blood trail disappeared.

Gone.

No, not gone. *Taken.*

And he'd killed the one man who could lead him to her. Mike had told him . . . *He'll kill her.*

Who the hell was "he"?

Nicole was strong. She wouldn't be easy prey.

But she'd been bleeding and covered in blisters and burns. His head tilted back as he glared up at the blue sky. The sunlight would work against her.

If she could just survive until night, until he found her . . .

Stay alive.

Because if she died, there would be hell to pay.

He whirled and began running back to the house. Mike might be dead, but two of those bastards in his gang had survived. He'd find them and they *would* talk—or they'd die, too.

His legs pumped as he ran faster, faster, and the trees passed him in a blur.

Is she hurting?

He burst out of the woods—and found Sam lounging against the side of a shiny black pickup truck.

Sam lifted a brow when he saw Keenan. "Everything okay?"

He didn't hesitate. He ran right for Sam. The Death Touch never worked on anyone with pure angel blood. So when he drove his fist into Sam's stomach, he didn't worry about killing the guy. It would take a lot more than a punch to kill Sam, but the jerk *could* be killed.

Sam took the punch and didn't even flinch. "Ah . . . good to see you, too, Keenan."

Keenan grabbed his shirt. "Where is she?"

Sam blinked at that. "Uh, which she?"

His back teeth ground together. "Nicole."

"Oh, yeah. Your little vamp." Now his brows lowered as his gaze darted toward the house. "I thought she was inside."

"No." If Sam didn't know where she was, Keenan was wasting his time. He thrust the guy back and jumped on the motorcycle.

But Sam was there beside him, moving with his enhanced speed, a speed that hadn't returned fully to Keenan, not yet.

"Got the touch back, don't you?" Sam asked and he was *smiling*.

Keenan revved the engine.

"I saw the little playdate you had with Big Mike out on the highway." Sam's appreciative whistle rose even over the howl of the motorcycle. "Playing rough, are you?"

Big Mike.

His head turned, slowly, and red began to flicker over his vision once more. "How did you know I was out here?"

Sam shrugged. His eyes didn't waver. "I knew the minute you bought this place. Little happens in New Orleans that I don't know about."

Time seemed to slow down. No—maybe *he* just

moved real fast. Because in the next second, the motorcycle was on the ground and he had his hands around Sam's throat.

Sam was still smiling. "Gettin' your speed back, too."

"Little happens that you don't know about?" His voice was a growl, all he could manage right then with the fury choking him. "You knew Big Mike, you knew where I was hiding with Nicole—you knew it all! *Dammit, where is she?"*

"Easy." Sam wasn't fighting back, yet. "I don't—"

"It was a trap! They came at her with bullets and fire while she was weak. When I went after them—"

Sam knocked his hands away. "You shouldn't have left your girl. You never leave her behind, not if you—"

"They tried to kill her! They weren't getting away!"

Sam nodded. "Still don't have control, do you? I thought . . . after six months . . . maybe you'd be used to the emotions by now." He rocked back on his heels. "Guess not."

"Where is she!"

Sam stabbed a finger in Keenan's chest. "Get control. Emotions are shit. They screw with your head. Fear. Anger. Need. Lust. Humans are born with those feelings, and they still drive them crazy. What do you think they do to beings who've been without 'em for centuries?"

They tear me apart.

Like Nicole's captor was tearing her apart?

The wind whipped against his face.

"Control," Sam snapped out. "If you lose it, you'll be no good to her."

"I have to find her!"

"Then let me help you." Sam's voice seemed so sincere. The guy was very good at controlling his image, Keenan knew that. "I know where Mike's men would run. I can show you where they went to lick their wounds."

"If she dies . . ."

"That will really suck, won't it? You fell to save her, and those bastards up there still take her from you." Sam's voice thickened. " 'Bout time someone showed those assholes that they aren't the only game in town. 'Bout time they realized even precious *angels* can suffer."

Keenan swallowed his rage. *Control.* "Take me to them."

"You'll owe me if I do," Sam said, his eyes watchful.

"Take. Me. To. Them."

"Then I guess we have a deal." Sam held out his hand. "I was coming out here to say I'd have your back, that you could count on me." He still sounded *so sincere,* but Sam's eyes showed no emotion. "I never expected to find . . . this."

Keenan couldn't believe him.

Sam's offered hand didn't drop. "Do we have a deal? I'll help you . . . and when the time comes, you help me."

Help you do what? Did it matter? He grabbed Sam's hand. "Deal."

Brimstone teased his nose.

"Then let's go find those hunters." Sam's smile was evil. "And make 'em beg to tell us everything they know."

Keenan nodded and finally realized just how far he had fallen.

Because the brimstone scent wasn't coming from Sam.

From me.

CHAPTER THIRTEEN

She wasn't dead. Why wasn't she dead? Nicole sat up, but didn't rise far. Her arms were chained to the floor. Thick, dark metal chains secured her.

Where was she? The last thing she remembered . . . Carlos had been—

Carlos.

He wasn't a human. Wasn't just prey. He was a shifter.

Which brought back the question . . . why was she still alive?

And not just alive. She tested those chains again. When she stretched her arms, she didn't feel the lash of pain. She was weak, yeah, but the blisters were gone, and the wounds in her shoulder and side were healed. Night had fallen, she could tell that instinctively, but the darkness wouldn't have healed her. She would have needed blood.

Blood she hadn't gotten.

A metal door groaned open and a musky scent teased her nose. "Awake, are you?" Carlos shuffled inside, then came to a quick stop.

It was dark in there, but her vamp senses were enhanced so that she could see him perfectly, and she saw the surprise that flashed across Carlos's face.

He didn't expect me to be healed, either.

So she'd *definitely* not gotten any blood. But she felt great. Why?

Keenan. The answer whispered through her mind. His blood was different, and it was starting to make her stronger.

"How the hell did you do that?" He sprang at her. His hands slid down her arms. His claws scratched her skin. "You were barely alive. How did you—"

She lunged for his neck.

He swore and dove back.

"Careful there, shifter," she taunted, "get close enough again, and I'll rip your throat open." And, oh, but she wished she had her silver bullets right then. But no, that gun she'd taken from the feeding room was back at Keenan's. She hadn't thought she'd need silver in order to fight off humans.

Carlos was on his ass now, and his eyes glittered at her. His claws scraped across the cement because, yeah, she was sitting on hard cement, in some kind of locked room.

No, wait. Her gaze darted to the left. That window—it was stained glass. Her nostrils twitched. She could smell the shifter now—*won't ever forget what that woodsy smell means again*—but she could also smell . . .

Death.

He laughed. "Figured it out, did you? Well, hell, I thought . . . what better place to store you?"

Than a cemetery.

She was in a mausoleum. One that had been altered to include her chains. At least he'd taken out the dead body.

But she suspected he had plans to leave another body, *hers*, in its place. "Why am I still breathing?"

"Because I need you to be." He rose and brushed off his hands. "When you stop being useful, I'll drive a stake into your heart."

She didn't see a stake on him. She pulled at her chains—no give.

"Your . . . friend. The man who was with you in Mexico . . ."

She stared at him, not letting her expression alter.

"He's your lover," Carlos said.

She didn't speak.

His nostrils flared. "I can smell him all over you! I know he's been fucking you."

"If you know, then why'd you ask?" *Bastard*.

"Because I'm still surprised an angel would fuck something like you."

He knew about Keenan. Oh, that couldn't be good. *I'm in chains—how can anything about this be good?* "Something like me?" She said carefully. "What, you mean compared to an *animal* like you? At least I don't grow fur and piss on the ground when I—"

Ah, now the stake was out. He'd had it tucked in his boot. His right hand gripped the stake as he bared *his* fangs at her. "Maybe your dead body would be just as useful to me."

The scent of flowers wafted to her nose.

She tilted her chin up. "Maybe."

He shook his head. "You're trying to push me, but that's not going to work, *querida*." He backed up a step. "You'll get death, but only when I'm ready to give it."

So why was he waiting?

"He'll come for you." His twisted lips mocked her. "As soon as he figures out where you are, anyway. If it takes too long, I'll just have to make sure he gets a tip."

"Why do you want Keenan?" If he knew Keenan was an angel, then Carlos had to realize that he didn't want to tangle with her lover.

"The angel has something I need." He gave a quick laugh. "Something you need, too."

Her eyes narrowed.

"When I'm done with him . . ." Carlos laughed. "Dust will be all that's left."

Angel's Dust. Fear shoved into her gut as she understood. She needed Keenan's blood to live. Hell, his blood was probably why she'd healed so quickly. *An angel's blood.* And that vamp in the feeding room, he'd said demons could be killed by Angel's Dust. But to make the Dust . . .

"Guess you've already learned how powerful the new lover is, huh, vamp?"

She didn't speak.

"I'll have to drain him dry to get enough for the mix." He lifted a brow. "Is he a bleeder? How long do you think it will take for him to—"

"Screw you!"

His gaze raked her. "Maybe. Later." His claws tapped against his chin. "You know, I just thought you were another walking parasite, and then I learned you were strolling around with one very precious gift."

Keenan.

"Do you know how many demons I'll be able to kill with his blood? Do you know how many *Other* will fucking bow to me?"

The chains dug deeper into her flesh. "The stories . . . they're wrong." *Can't let him get Keenan.* "Demons *came* from the Fallen, so Keenan's blood won't do anything to them!"

"His blood will kill them." Absolute certainty in his voice. "What creates—can destroy. You should know by now that's the way of the *Other* world."

She swallowed back that rising fear. "He'll kill you."

He tucked the stake back into his boot and sauntered toward the door. "I don't think he will. He'll be too worried about saving you."

"You won't be able to hurt him! You won't—"

Carlos's claws lifted, and they were wicked sharp. "Did you know that angels can't be injured by most weapons?" He nodded, not waiting for her to respond. "*Si*, they're like the ancient demons that way. But now I know your Keenan's weaknesses." He turned away from her. "*Both* of them."

Then he yanked open the door, that echoing groan filled the tomb, and after he stalked out, she was left with silence.

She pulled at the chains. *Nothing*. "What did he mean?" She whispered to the shadows. Shadows that were too dark near the left wall, right where the floral scent was strongest.

Silence.

She pulled harder. The thick metal dug deeper into her wrists and blood began to drip onto the floor. "*What did he mean?*" She shouted. "Dammit, I *know* you're there!"

The air shifted around her, as if a fan had been turned on. Or as if wings had flapped.

"*Answer me!*"

"He knows what can hurt Keenan," came the dark, cold voice. Az. Like she'd ever forget the sound of his voice.

"The gunshots didn't hurt him." Was the chain starting to give? She tugged harder, rising to her knees and straining as she stretched forward. "There weren't any bullet wounds, no—"

"Weapons forged by man can't hurt him." He'd moved. She couldn't see him. She just had the impression of dark shadows shifting. "And he controls fire,"

Az said, "fire can burn his flesh, but it can never *kill* him."

Fire's kiss could sure kill her. "Then what is it? What makes him—"

"*You* make him bleed easily enough."

She swallowed. "Yes." She did. Biting him was as easy as biting a human. A slice right through the flesh.

"Because your weapon wasn't forged by mortal hands."

Her weapon was her teeth.

Carlos's weapons would be his very, very big claws—and his teeth. Teeth that were sharper than hers. Not weapons forged by man. Shit.

"Get me out of here!" The chains wouldn't break. "Get me out!"

"I can't." Said flatly.

"You're just going to stand there?" Her eyes narrowed as she strained to see. Az seemed to *be* a shadow.

"I'm going to wait," he said. "My job is to wait and then to take."

Her soul.

"Do you fear death?" He asked her, and she could have sworn the guy sounded curious. Great.

"What *I* fear is what is going to happen to Keenan!" If Carlos got to him, he could take Keenan's head with a swipe of his razor-sharp claws.

No.

"You care." Again, the faintest hint of curiosity or . . . surprise? "I didn't expect that."

"Well, a year ago, I never expected I'd get turned into a vampire and I'd have an angel stand by and *refuse* to help me while I'm trapped in a crypt."

Silence.

But he was still there. She could feel him.

"Don't you ever get tired of watching people die?"

she gritted. The chain was just locked too tightly around her wrist. She'd always had too-sharp, too-big wrist bones.

"I do what I was born to do. Watch. Shepherd."

"Shepherd?" Yes, the bones were too big in her wrists and her hands . . . That was the problem.

"I take the souls when they are ready to leave this plane."

"And you're never tempted? Never once do you think, hey, maybe this woman wants to live longer with her daughter and not die from cancer when she's only twenty-eight . . ." *Her mother* and the pain still bled inside her. "Or maybe this guy wants to have a chance to see—"

"I know why you were at the church that night."

That shut her up. Figured he'd know. "I never made it inside the church." The doors had been barred to her. Talk about a big glowing sign of things to come.

"He watched you then."

Keenan.

"He watched too much, I knew it, but . . ."

"But *you* didn't stop him." Ah, sounded just like Mr. Hands Off. "You could have stopped him from falling!"

"If I had, you'd be dead."

Right. There was no win-win in this game.

"He's losing himself in you."

She wasn't sure what that meant. And the chains wouldn't break, so that meant there was only one—

"If he goes too far, there will be no saving him. Once the line is crossed, he's lost."

What line? "Keenan's not lost! He's had my back this whole time and, by damn, I will have his!" Once she got out of there.

"Carlos can kill him."

The chain wouldn't break.

"I can't see a Fallen's future, can't see what will be, so I don't know how quickly he'll die."

Screw this. She sucked in a deep breath and slammed her right hand and wrist into the concrete. Once. Twice.

The chain wouldn't break, but she could. Her wrist bones were twisted, mangled, but now she could get them out of the chain. One hand down. *It will heal.*

"Why?" His voice, showing more emotion. This time, there was no mistaking the confusion.

"Because he's not dying." She pounded her other wrist against the cement and ignored the waves of pain that rolled through her. She and pain were starting to become good friends. Tears slipped down her cheeks but she didn't realize she was crying until she tasted the salt on her lips. She rammed her hand into the ground. Once, twice more, and the bones shifted. Nicole slid that hand free. *"He's not dying."*

"How will you save him? You can't even fight now, you can't—"

"I'll just get a little bite first . . ." She rose, but almost staggered from the pain. "Then I'll be ready."

"Death *is* coming."

Her shoulders straightened. "Death . . . *you* . . . can wait." She made it to the door. Nicole didn't even bother trying to push it open. Her hands were a mess. She needed blood, fast, in order to get the strength to heal, and even then, she wouldn't fully recover until her next rising.

Carlos could be waiting right outside. He probably was.

Won't get Keenan.

She kicked open the vault's heavy metal door.

* * *

Sam had taken Keenan to a bar, one that looked like a dozen others. But this one was different—his prey waited inside.

"There." Sam's finger pointed to the right. The two bikers who'd escaped were at the bar, guzzling beers and acting like they didn't have a care in the world.

He'd make them care.

As Keenan stalked across the bar, smart people got out of his way. Maybe they could feel his rage. It sure burned him.

"Don't touch 'em, not yet," Sam muttered. "We need 'em alive to talk, remember?"

He jerked his head in agreement. The idiots must have sensed trouble because they both spun around. When they saw him, their eyes widened and fear slipped over their thick faces.

"Didn't think it was over, did you?" He braced his legs apart. The scrape of chairs filled the room. Folks were leaving as fast as they could. Guess they were used to trouble in this place, and they knew better than to stay around and watch the show.

The guy right in front of him, a burly guy with grizzled cheeks and a buzz cut, swallowed. "D-don't know you."

Keenan's hand lifted. Oh, to touch . . .

"*Keenan,*" Sam warned, "the dead can't talk."

The buzz-cut biker blanched.

His buddy, a tall, tattooed guy with a mop of curly red hair, startled to sidle away.

"I can kill you with less than a thought," Keenan said.

Both men froze.

"Where is she?" he demanded.

The red-haired guy shook his head.

Wrong answer. Keenan grabbed a beer bottle, shattered the glass and pressed the jagged edge to buzz-cut's throat. Since he wasn't touching the guy directly, the biker wouldn't die. Well, he wouldn't die until Keenan sliced his throat wide open with that glass. "I'll ask once more, then you'll start bleeding."

Sam reached for a glass of whiskey that had just been placed on the bar top. He drained it in one gulp, then swiped the back of his hand over his mouth. "Better tell him, he's *real* good at killing."

"Y-you talking about the vamp?" This came from the redhead.

"Shut up, Pete!" Buzz-cut snarled.

"They'll kill us, Bo! I ain't dying for—"

Ah, a weak link. Keenan kept his weapon on Bo, but turned his stare on Pete. "Are there a couple more members of your little gang still living? A member or two who took my vampire?"

Pete shook his head. "N-not us . . ."

"Bullshit." From Sam. "I think you should slice this one for lying. A long slice right down his cheek."

"*Pete, shut the hell up! The vamp bitch deserves to die after what she did—*"

"I'm not r-ready to d-die," Pete stammered. He was younger than Bo. He didn't have that hardened, been-to-hell look yet. Pete's breath whispered out. "The other one—he took her. It was all his idea, using the fire, coming to that house. *He's* the one who knew where you were."

Sam lunged forward and jerked Bo away from Keenan.

"What are you—" Keenan began.

Sam slammed Bo's head into the bar. Bo's eyes rolled back into his head and when Sam lifted his hands, Bo slid to the floor in a heap. "Now we only have to deal with one."

One who looked very, very scared.

"*Who* knew?" Keenan asked Pete, struggling for control. *Wasting time.* He needed to hurry.

"S-some Mexican. Car-Carlos . . . big guy, dark hair, said he'd been huntin' the v-vamp."

The thunder of Keenan's heartbeat filled his ears.

"H-heard him t-tell Big Mike . . . he'd t-take her to St. Louis Cemetery and leave her—leave h-her to rot."

"Ummm . . ." Sam lifted a brow. "I think that might be all he knows."

Keenan's fingers tightened around the bottle.

"Do we let him live?" Sam asked, eyeing the guy with a hard stare. "Or do we kill him?"

"*Please* . . ." Pete begged and the guy's eyes were filling with tears.

Keenan stared at him. "You burned her. Your gang attacked a woman. *You burned her.*"

"I-I didn't throw my bottle! I-I didn't—"

"But you didn't stop the others, did you?" Sam leaned in close. "You were right there for the party, and you didn't help her out."

Pete started to shake.

"If she's not in that cemetery, if she's not still *alive* in that cemetery . . ." Keenan ran the glass down Pete's cheek and let the blood flow. "Then I'll be back, and you *will* truly learn to beg."

The guy's face couldn't get whiter. And he was one fast bleeder.

Keenan dropped the bottle.

But Sam caught it before the glass could shatter. Quick as a flash, he turned, and drove that broken bottle into Pete's shoulder. Pete went down, screaming.

"That will teach you," Sam said with his eyes

slitting. "Next time, *don't just fucking watch while a woman burns.*"

Keenan turned away from the screams. He'd taken two steps when the angel scent hit him. His gaze zeroed in on the shadows near the bar's entrance. No, not near the entrance, *blocking* the entrance. "Don't get in my way, Az."

The shadows shifted. He glimpsed the wings. Az's stark face. "You're losing control," Az warned.

Losing? *Lost it.*

"Soon you'll be like him . . ."

Sam laughed behind Keenan. "Wouldn't that be damn great? Then you'd have two pissed off Fallen on your trail."

Keenan rushed for the door. "*Get out of my way.*" Because if he had to, he'd pound his way through the angel. He'd do anything to get to her.

"She's made you like this," Az said. But the shadows lightened as he pulled back. "She'll destroy you."

"No," Sam spoke with certainty behind him. "She's just making him stronger—and that scares you, Az."

The shadows vanished.

They screamed when Nicole kicked open the crypt door. A guy and his girlfriend, both dressed in goth black, whirled around, their cries filling her ears. They'd been leaning down, lighting candles near another crypt, leaving offerings—

Didn't they realize the voodoo queen wasn't even there anymore? Tourists.

"*Look at her teeth! Oh, Sean, look at—*"

Okay, the girl didn't sound scared. More like excited.

"*Bite me,*" Sean whispered. "*Please.*"

Well, if he was gonna be offering . . . She lunged

forward and sank her teeth into his throat. His blood spilled over her tongue and strength started to push back into her body.

"Sean?" A thread of fear entered the girl's voice, banking that excitement. "Sean . . . she's . . . really drinking your bl-blood." Then the girl let out a shriek. Her footsteps thudded as she ran away.

Nicole took more blood from her donor. Not too much. Just enough to survive. When she let him go, her savior slipped to the ground. Not dead, but unconscious.

She pushed her hands against the nearest crypt. The bones popped and snapped back into place as she reset them. Not perfect, not yet, but she'd make it through the night. She'd—

"I can't leave you alone for a minute, can I, *querida*?"

Nicole stiffened. *Carlos.* "No, I guess you can't." She licked the last of the blood away and turned toward him. "You should have used that stake when you had the chance."

He stood between two stone vaults, his claws scraping over them. "I'll take the chance now. Your angel can just mourn over your broken body."

No, he wouldn't.

"The bait's already set. I wager one of the bikers broke by now and told him where you were." He pulled out the stake. "Let's see how fast you can die."

He leapt at her.

But Nicole was ready for him. She jumped back and the stake missed her. She kicked out and caught his wrist with her foot. This time, the bone that snapped was his. When the stake flew from his hand, she scrambled after it, diving to her knees. Her fingers curled around the wood just as Carlos grabbed her legs and yanked her back.

"I'll cut off your fucking head—"

She had the stake. She twisted and came up ready. Nicole drove the stake right into his chest. "And I'll take your heart." Her whisper.

Another kill. Another death.

What was one more stain on her black soul?

He stared at her, mouth open, eyes gaping, then he sagged back, slipping onto the ground as blood began to pool beneath him.

Killing again hadn't been nearly as hard as she'd hoped.

Connor had been right. Perhaps she did have a talent for murder. Damn him.

She closed her eyes.

"Nicole!" A roar that was her name.

Keenan. Her eyes flew right back open. And it was just like Carlos had said. She could see Keenan now, running toward her, snaking through the vaults. He wasn't even checking around him for an attack—just running straight for her, his gaze locked *on* her.

He would have run right into Carlos and never seen the danger until the claws were at his throat.

"It's okay," she called out as she rose and hurried forward. "I—"

Bones snapped. Crunched. Still not hers. *Not. Hers.* Goose bumps rose on her arms. Nicole glanced back over her shoulder.

Carlos was shifting.

Fur sprang up over his flesh. Thick, brown fur. His hands had already turned into paws, his claws had lengthened, sharpening even more. His face contorted as she watched. Stretched. Elongated. Animal, not man.

An animal with really big teeth—and she knew all about big teeth.

I missed his heart.

Oh, damn.

He was a shifter. He didn't need blood to heal and kick ass. He just needed to transform.

"Run," Nicole whispered and then she whirled around to face Keenan as she shouted, "Run!"

Too late. Keenan was almost on her. He reached out to her, but then froze, his fingers inches away. She stumbled for him. "You've got to get—"

A coyote's high, quavering howl broke the air.

Then that guy, Sam, he was there. Sam yanked her into his arms and pulled her away from Keenan. "Oh, what the hell?" He huffed out a hard breath. "Now the dogs are in this?"

Not a dog. A coyote. A very big, very pissed-off coyote with bloodlust burning in his glowing eyes. "It's a trap," she whispered. "He's after Keenan. We can't let him get . . ."

"The sonofabitch figured it out." Sam shoved her behind him. She caught a glimpse of the coyote. *Way* bigger than your average coyote. The beast lunged into the air and leapt right for Keenan.

No!

But Sam was there. Moving with his super speed, he jumped in front of Keenan.

The coyote gave a choked bark and twisted in mid-air. The beast landed on the top of a shallow crypt.

"Didn't count on two of us, did you?" Keenan snarled.

Then another coyote's wailing cry echoed in the cemetery. Another, another . . .

If coyotes could smile, she knew that beast would be grinning.

Her head whipped to the right. She saw a black coyote stalking along the high stone wall. The coyote had its eyes locked on Keenan's back.

"Keenan, watch out!"

But her scream came too late. The coyote jumped from the wall and lunged for Keenan. The beast's mouth—wide with sharp teeth and dripping with saliva—went for Keenan's throat.

But Keenan shoved his forearm into the coyote's mouth. The beast stiffened. Its whole body froze and as Nicole watched, the fur began to melt away.

A rolling, mourning cry rumbled in Carlos's throat, but he didn't close in on Keenan. No, the coyote jumped back and fled toward the high walls.

And as for the black coyote that had attacked Keenan . . . it wasn't a coyote anymore. The fur was gone, the bones still reshaping, but now . . . yes, now that was a woman.

A dead woman.

Keenan rose and stared down at her body.

The cries from the coyotes became softer. They were all leaving. Retreating.

"Running away?" Sam taunted, voice dark and strong. "Didn't plan for that, did you, bastards? We're not as easy to kill as you thought. You want our blood? *Then you'll die for it.*"

Nicole crept closer to Keenan. He was still staring down at the woman. The wind lifted the woman's dark hair and blew it against her golden cheeks. Her eyes were open, staring with horror, and her lips were parted as if to scream.

Keenan's gaze shifted to his arm. Faint bite marks were already fading from his flesh.

"Keenan . . ." Nicole reached for him, but he pulled away. She took that snub, right in the heart. He'd killed—because of her. And now maybe he was finally seeing just what she was.

His jaw clenched. His gaze rose slowly to meet hers. "Are you . . . okay?"

She put her hands behind her back. "Fine."

Keenan's head moved in a jerky nod. "Coming back to New Orleans was a mistake."

She'd tried to tell him that. Coming home again really wasn't a good idea. No matter what the damn songs out there said.

"You need to get out of here as fast as you can," Keenan told her, but he wasn't looking directly at her. Just over her shoulder. "I'll take care of the coyotes. You just . . . run."

Nicole shook her head. "No way, I'm not leaving you to—"

"I want you to go." His gaze came back to her when he delivered that knife to her heart.

She realized he hadn't even touched her. Hadn't hugged her. Hadn't pulled her against his chest. She wanted him to. Needed him to pull her close.

Instead, he was backing away.

He knows what I am now.

She glanced at the still-unconscious college goth guy. "I didn't kill him."

"No, but I sure killed *her.*"

A beautiful stranger. A woman as still as stone now.

"Who do you think came for her?" Sam asked, closing in and crouching next to the naked woman.

The coyotes had left the dead female fast enough. Deserted one of their own.

"There are so many flowers out here . . ." Sam glanced at the vaults. "We never even would've smelled them coming."

But she'd scented an angel earlier. She'd known Az was there.

He's losing himself in you.

Keenan couldn't even look at her longer than a few moments now.

"Take Nicole out of here," Keenan said, turning his back on them. "Get her to someplace safe and just *take Nicole out of here.*"

The words hurt. She'd expected them to come eventually, once he realized exactly what she was, but she'd started to hope that—

He'd still see me as a woman.

Guess not. Her spine stiffened. "I'm not leaving you here alone." The coyotes could come back. Probably would. Or what about the members of that vamphunter group that had been after her? Some of those bikers had gotten away. They could try to make a run at her again. Or at him.

"I want you to *go.*"

Now that was like a slap. She even stumbled back.

"I saved you, Nicole. We're even now. I stood back before, but this time . . ." He still wasn't looking at her. "I saved you."

Her hands were clenched into fists behind her back, and the healing injuries burned. "I saved myself," she whispered. *And you.*

But he didn't want to hear that. He was telling her to go, to get the hell out of his life, and fine, she wouldn't beg.

He wouldn't look at her. Wouldn't touch her.

Guess he finally saw the monster.

She turned around and nearly ran into Sam. Her breath heaved out. The guy moved too fast. "I can find my way out on my own."

"No." His gaze drifted along the stone wall. "They know what you are."

A vamp. Right. Seemed like everyone knew.

"They'll use you against him. You can't be separated. Not now."

She glanced over her shoulder, her eyes drawn right back to Keenan, and she saw him turn at Sam's words.

Keenan clenched his jaw and gritted, "You know she can't stay with me."

"Control, Fallen. I keep tellin' you . . . you've got to have *control*."

A burst of wind shoved against Nicole and Sam. "Around her, I have no control."

Was that good or bad? Around him, she had no control, either.

Except she wasn't telling him to hit the road.

Carlos almost killed me. I hurt. Every part of her hurt. And she just wanted Keenan's arms around her. She wanted to feel him, strong, safe and alive against her.

He wanted her ass to walk away.

"Get the control," Sam warned him, voice snapping. "Get it or—"

"Or what?" Keenan fired back. "She dies?"

Whoa. Wait. This *she*—

"Yes." Soft but certain from Sam. "If you lose control, then Nicole dies."

Well, *damn*.

Carlos watched the bastards leave. The asshole who'd killed his cousin bent down, brushed back her hair, then yanked off his shirt and covered her body.

Carlos's muscles locked. He wanted that bastard's throat between his teeth, but he knew if he got too close to the Fallen, he'd wind up like Julia.

One touch, then death.

Killing the Fallen would be harder than he'd thought. He'd have to take the guy out without ever giving him a chance to strike back.

They were outside of the cemetery now. As he watched, the three loaded into a black pickup truck.

He inhaled, drawing their scents in with the blood and the death. Finding them again wouldn't be a problem.

Killing them would.

I underestimated my prey. It wasn't a mistake he made often, and one he wouldn't repeat.

When the truck's taillights disappeared down the road, he tossed back his head and howled. Another loss for his meager pack. Another body to bury.

His bones snapped, reshaped. The fur melted from his flesh, and he went to collect his dead in the form of a man. In death, Julia's pretty features were twisted. So misshapen.

She'd been terrified of what she saw in her last moment.

He bent and picked her up and held her gently. "It's okay now." Julia had never feared anything. Until she died.

"They'll pay." The other coyotes slunk out of the darkness. *"They'll pay!"* Carlos vowed. It wasn't just about getting an angel's blood anymore.

Vengeance. When the angel died, he'd fear, too. Fear, beg, and suffer.

Just like his precious vampire bitch would.

CHAPTER FOURTEEN

"**W**hy won't you look at me?"

Nicole's soft voice had Keenan's head turning toward her. She stood, her body pressed against the stark white wall in Sam's "safe" house.

No place was safe enough. Keenan knew the coyotes would come after them. Once a shifter got your scent, it was pretty impossible to shake him. Going back to the antebellum house he'd bought—*for her, everything had been for her*—wasn't an option. He might as well just paint a bull's eye on his back if he did that. There would be folks who'd come looking for vengeance on Big Mike's killer.

Those folks would have to get in line.

"Thank you," Nicole whispered.

He blinked, but was careful to keep his face expressionless. Sam, ever the sly one, had brought them to this place—an apartment in the Quarter. One with reinforced shutters and a perfect view of the outside. Once, the Quarter houses had been designed to keep out enemies. Shut the doors, bar them, and no one could get in from the street. The buildings were all lined next to each other—the better to keep intruding soldiers out.

The design still worked to their advantage. At least, this way they'd know when company came calling.

Nicole rubbed her arms. "So you're looking at me now, but you're not speaking? Fine. Okay. *Fine*. You didn't have to come after me, you know. You didn't have to—"

He stepped toward her. Her lips pressed together. He took a breath and could almost taste her. "Did you really think I wouldn't come for you?" Of course, he would. He'd do just about anything for her.

That sexy chin lifted as her eyes glittered. "No." Soft but certain. "I knew you'd hunt for me. What happened . . ." She cleared her throat. "What happened to the leader, Mike?"

One touch. "You don't have to worry about him anymore." He turned away from her and paced out onto the balcony. Jazz music drifted up to him, and he saw the people strolling down the street. A motorcycle raced below him. "That coyote, he's the one we have to worry about now. He wants you dead, and—"

"You're the one he wanted." The floor squeaked behind him. She was coming closer. Her scent reached him, wrapped around him. "Keenan . . ."

"Don't touch me."

He heard the sharp inhalation of her breath and knew she was hurt. Better to be hurt than dead. He grabbed the railing. "You need to get away from me. Get out of New Orleans and don't come back."

"You're the one who brought me back!"

"My mistake." So foolish. But he'd wanted her back in the city because *she'd been happy here*. She hadn't been happy the whole time he'd been with her in Mexico and Texas. He'd thought if she came home, he could keep her safe. *Make* her happy.

Make her laugh. She hadn't laughed once in all their time together, not laughed and actually meant it.

"I can't touch you." Anger snapped in her words. "You barely look at me . . . but you were screwing me yesterday."

More than screwing. "Things have changed."

"You don't want me anymore?" Pain darkened her voice.

"Wanting isn't an option."

"Dammit! What the hell is with you? You *never* give me a simple yes or no answer to any question I ask you!"

Because he couldn't. "Things are never simple."

"You want me." Certain and not so soft now.

He stared at the street below. The river was close, and the scent of the water drifted to his nose. "Lots of people in this world want what they can't have—or what they don't need."

"You fight for me, then tell me to get away." A choked laugh. *Not* the kind of laugh he'd wanted to hear from her. His fingers tightened on the balcony's railing and the wrought iron groaned. "You're giving me some seriously mixed messages, Keenan."

"Then let me be very clear." He took a breath. *Face her.* He turned slowly and looked right at her. She was pale. So very pale. Her eyes were big and dark. "I want you to get away from me, and I want you to get away now." *Truth.* He'd never spoken truer words.

And she realized that. He saw the words sink in as she took a step back. Her hands came up, as if she'd cover her mouth, but she caught herself. Nicole stiffened instead. Shoved back her shoulders and dropped her hands. *Bruised, bloody hands.* He frowned.

But she was the one turning away now. "Watch your ass, angel. That coyote wants you, and he knows how to kill *you.*"

It was his turn to laugh, and his laugh was as cloaked with bitterness as hers had been. "Killing me isn't easy." The female shifter had learned that.

"He knows how," she said and she didn't stop walking. "He won't stop until he has your blood and his Angel's Dust." Her hand reached for the bedroom doorknob. It looked like she'd battered that hand to pieces.

His jaw clenched and he had to ask, "What happened to you? What did he do?"

"Chained me in a crypt. Left me as bait." She threw a fast glance over her shoulder. "For you."

That had his brows rising.

"*Angel's Dust.* He wants to use your blood because he thinks getting it will make him the big badass in the *Other* world."

If Carlos could take out the level-ten demons with the Dust, he *would* be the badass that the Others feared.

"I told you," she murmured, "This time, it wasn't all about people wanting to take out the evil vamp. The coyote wanted your blood, not mine."

Carlos had been willing to sacrifice Nicole to get what he wanted. The coyote would pay. *Want blood? I'll make sure you bleed.* He pushed back the fury. Tried to. "What did he do to your hands?"

A ghost of a smile tugged at her lips. "Nothing. That was all me."

She'd done that?

"Vamps heal, you know. We heal from just about everything. Even the wounds that asshole angels give us." She opened the door and walked away.

Keenan knew she was right. She'd get over him. She'd get past the pain that he'd glimpsed in her eyes. She'd heal.

It was a pity he couldn't say the same thing.

His nostrils twitched. He hadn't just scented the river on that balcony. "Az, you bastard, I know you were watching . . . *hope you're happy now.*" Because he'd lost the fight against temptation.

He'd lost everything.

Keenan stepped forward and slammed his fist into the glass of the open balcony door.

"You're just going to walk away?"

The drawling voice stopped Nicole as she neared the bottom of the staircase. She looked up and saw Sam strolling toward her. Dressed all in black, again. Black T-shirt. Black pants and boots.

"He wants me gone," Nicole said without flinching and kept her gaze up. "So it's time for me to leave." She'd survive. She'd made it for the last six months. She'd make it six more.

Screw the angels waiting.

She brushed by him and felt a little jolt of electricity zing her as her shoulder pressed against his.

"He was desperate to save you."

Right. He'd looked desperate when she first saw him in that cemetery. Now he was just desperate to kick her butt out. *Why?*

Nicole forced her back to stay straight and tall as she walked. She wasn't about to show weakness in front of Sam.

"Don't you wonder . . . how he killed that shifter?"

Yes, she did. But Keenan hadn't exactly been the chatting type with her upstairs. "I thought . . . she must have broken her neck, the angle she attacked—"

"She didn't break her neck."

She stopped walking.

"You didn't think it through, did you? But then, I'm guessing you're still so thirsty for blood that you can't think very much at all right now, can you?"

She was thinking he was an ass. How was that for *thinking*?

Nicole took another step toward the door and freedom.

He was there, of course. Instantly blocking her path.

"How do you do that?" she asked, rubbing a tired hand over her neck. "Nobody is supposed to move like that."

"Different angels have different strengths." His gaze tracked down her body. "And different weaknesses." He caught her right wrist. She expected pain, a rough touch, but his hold was light. Almost . . . gentle.

"The chains bit into you here." His thumb slid over the dark red line that still marked her wrist. He caught her other hand and traced the similar mark. "And here."

Nicole swallowed. "Yes."

"He had you chained in one of those crypts. The juicy steak to bait the trap."

At least someone seemed to understand what Carlos had planned. "Keenan won't listen to me. He's the one in danger right now, and—"

"And here," he kept talking, seeming to roll right over her words. "This is where you made the first break in your wrist when you realized you had to get out . . . in order to save Keenan."

She inclined her head toward him. "The first break is always the hardest, right?" She tried to sound flippant.

His lips hitched up a bit. "Bet you damn near shattered your bones to break loose. That's why that college kid was sleeping near Laveau's vault, eh? You needed a drink." He still had her hands and didn't seem to be showing signs of letting go. "I'm guessing you still need a drink. It takes a lot to overcome fire *and* broken bones."

Yes, it did. "I'll find a snack."

"You sound so tough, but the words don't really suit you, schoolteacher."

What? He thought schoolteachers weren't tough? Had the guy ever *been* in a school?

"Maybe after you have your bite, you'll be able to think better. Then you'll realize what's really going on here."

Jerk. "Why don't you just *tell* me what's happening? If you know why Keenan's suddenly pushing me away, then just say—"

"He thinks he's keeping you safe."

"Bullshit." She'd call it just as she saw it. "I think it's more likely he decided to feed me to the wolves." Or to the coyotes.

Sam shook his head. "Think about the dead girl. *How did she die?*"

"I don't know! She came at Keenan. They hit. His hand shoved between her jaws, and she fell over." Dead.

"One touch," Sam murmured.

Her heart beat faster. "You're not saying . . ."

"He told you how it was for death angels, right? To take the soul, you just have to touch."

"He's touched me." *Plenty of times and in plenty of ways.* Sam was lying to her, had to be.

"There's something else you should know." He paused. "Angels, even fallen angels, can't lie. So when I tell you something, trust me."

She wouldn't trust the guy as far as she could throw his shadow-winged self. "Keenan lost his powers when he fell."

"No, he just forgot them."

Uh, what?

"Falling isn't easy." His thumbs stroked her wrists. She tried to yank away but he wouldn't let her go. "Once you get here, you're lucky if you can even remember your own name."

Keenan hadn't remembered, not at first. He'd told her that.

"Then the memories start to filter back. When they first come, you think you have to be batshit crazy. But then . . . then you start to *know*."

Right. He'd fallen. Been there, done that. So, of course, Sam could speak from experience.

"You start to know," he said again, "and then, slowly, the powers come back."

Her breath seemed to be freezing in her chest. "You're telling me that Keenan can kill with a touch." Her gaze fell to their hands. "That you can." *Then why are you touching me?*

"If killing that way was what I wanted . . ." His eyes glinted. "Yes."

Good thing he didn't seem to *want* it then.

"Sometimes the powers are locked deep inside, and you have to chip away at the locked box to get them out."

Her stomach started to knot.

"Sometimes, you just need the right key to open that box." His smile stretched. "You were a wonderful key."

If he weren't holding her hands in that unbreakable grip, she would have punched him then. Not the sweet move of a schoolteacher, but the hard right hook of a vamp who'd learned to fight dirty. "You've been using me." Her eyes narrowed. "Just how did Mike find out where we were hiding?"

His smile dimmed a bit. "You think I led him to you?"

The hard suspicion in her gut said yes. "Didn't you?"

His hold became harder. "I'm the one who helped Keenan find you in that cemetery."

She realized he hadn't answered her. Like Keenan, the guy couldn't say just yes or no. "Angels can't lie, but that doesn't mean they have to tell the complete truth, right?" Cause there was a difference. "They can avoid answering the question or they can—they can just twist their words, twist the truth."

He nodded. "I knew the first time I saw you that you'd be the key to making Keenan break."

He's getting lost in you. "I don't want him to break."

"Really? Don't you want a little vengeance? Come on . . ." His voice lowered. "It's just us. Keenan's upstairs, hating the world. He won't know what you say."

"Let go of my hands."

He didn't let go. "I mean, if he'd just moved faster, just touched that vamp who attacked you that night *faster*, you'd still have your nice, picket-fence life. Hell, maybe you'd even have met your prince charming and be getting ready to settle down."

Her claws were coming out.

"But he didn't move fast enough, did he? Because of him, you suffered and you changed and you lost everything you held dear."

She would have lost it anyway. No matter what Keenan had done, there wouldn't have been a prince charming or a picket fence for her. "I don't want vengeance."

He laughed. "Good thing vamps can lie, huh?" Finally, he dropped her hands, but he still stood between her and the door. "In order to stir his powers," he said, "Keenan needed to let his emotions go. Angels don't feel emotions, did you know that?"

She didn't answer.

"So when they fall, they get slapped with them. The emotions are what strengthens us here, and what weakens us." His head cocked. "To get Keenan to conjure and control his fire, he needed rage. He got that rage when your life was threatened."

And in order for him to kill . . .

"That's right." Sam's eyes gleamed. "He just had to feel the killing fury. He needed to *want* to kill. When Big Mike attacked you . . ." A soft laugh. "The *only* thing Keenan wanted was to kill."

"Good for you." She glared at the jerk. "You let the tiger out of his cage."

"No, I let the Fallen loose. Or, rather, you did."

"Because you set us up!" Everything—was it just a game to him? And why did it matter? "No wonder Keenan didn't want me close. If he touches me, he'll kill me."

That shouldn't have made her feel relieved. It should have terrified her. Made her shove Sam aside and haul ass for the door. But, no, she was there thinking . . . *He wants me to leave so he can't hurt me.*

Figured. That was her angel. No, her *Fallen.*

"He won't kill you."

She blinked. Sam sounded real sure of that.

"Didn't you hear me?" Sam exhaled on a hard sigh. "I said he kills because when he touches, he *wants* to give death. When he touches you . . ." One brow rose. "I bet death is the last thing he's thinking about."

Her teeth were burning. "I . . . have to go."

"To get blood?" He smiled at her. "Why go out? You can dine right here."

"Keenan wasn't exactly offering—"

"*I* am."

That shocked her. "You'd trust me? At your throat?" Oh, no, wait, this game she understood. "When I touch you, will you kill me?" Because he was Fallen, just like Keenan. Only maybe he could kill at will. He'd been on the human plane longer, so perhaps he'd gotten total control over all his powers.

He smiled at her. "I promise not to kill if you promise not to bite too hard."

Her eyes measured him. "Are you hitting on me?" Impossible. No way.

He moved in a blur—didn't he always?—and grabbed her hand once more. "You're still living."

Her heart slammed into her chest.

"Trouble's coming after us. Those coyotes will be howling at the door soon. If you're going to listen to Keenan and run out of here . . . which, by the way, I don't recommend because they'll just follow you and hunt you down eventually, so that idea pretty much fucking sucks . . ."

Uh, yeah, it did.

"Unless you're leaving tonight," he said, "you need to get strong, and you need to get strong *fast*."

His blood. She inhaled and caught his scent. She could hear the thunder of his blood. So close. Her tongue slipped over the edge of a fang. "Most *Other* . . . they think it's an insult to get bitten." Especially the shifters. She'd heard those guys would rather die than get bit.

"I'm not most *Other*." His gaze burned her. "Besides, I know there's pleasure as well as pain in the bite—that's a mix I rather like."

He was offering. She *needed* the blood. Nicole pushed up onto her toes and pressed her lips against his throat.

If the coyotes were coming, and she didn't doubt that part of his story, then she wouldn't have time to find other prey. Not that she'd even been particularly good at finding prey to begin with.

Her fangs scraped his skin.

"That's it," he whispered. "Have a taste."

Her teeth pressed—

"What the hell are you doing?"

She spun around, but didn't go far. Sam had her clasped tightly to him, his arm a steel band around her waist.

Keenan thundered down the stairs, his eyes flashing black, then blue, as he raced toward them. "Get your hands off her! What are you thinking? You could *kill* her!"

Sam didn't let her go. "Only if death was what I wanted." She felt his shrug. "I don't want death for her."

"Let her go."

"She's holding me."

Oh, crap, she was. Her hands were still on him. She dropped them instantly. "Keenan, it's okay, I was just going to—"

"Have a bite," Sam finished and Keenan jumped down to the landing. "After all, you left her weak, Fallen. Burned, broken, *weak*. What did you expect her to do?"

Keenan staggered to a stop less than a foot away. His hand lifted, then his fingers clenched into a fist. "Nicole, get away from him. You can't trust him. He'll turn on you in an instant."

Like that was something she didn't know.

"You want her, then take her." Sam's voice was mocking. "Touch her, take her, if you think you're strong enough."

Oh, so *that* was what this was about. Nicole jabbed out with her elbow, as hard as she could. Sam's grip loosened, just a bit, and she sprang away from him. She didn't hurry toward Keenan, but rather backed away from them both. "*She* doesn't need taking by anyone," Nicole said clearly.

But the two fallen angels were too busy glaring at each other to listen to her.

"Don't ever touch her again," Keenan ordered.

"I don't touch her . . . you don't touch her . . . that's gonna be one lonely vampire."

Keenan growled.

"Just back off," she snapped right back at him. "You're the one who told me to leave, remember?"

His head inclined in a tight nod.

"Dammit, she *needs* blood." Sam threw his hands into the air. "Look at her. *Look*."

Keenan's gaze darted to her. She saw the hunger in his eyes. The need. The fear.

"If you're not gonna help her, I will." Sam reached for her.

"No," Nicole said, her voice firm. She'd been planning to pull back even before Keenan came flying down those stairs. "I'll find another source."

Keenan's jaw tightened and she caught the flash of fury in his gaze.

So did Sam. "Don't like that, do you? Makes you jealous." His voice lowered. "Those damn emotions. They're real bitches, aren't they?"

Keenan ignored him. "I *won't* kill you," he told her.

Sam laughed. "Isn't that what this whole mess has always been about? You . . . killing her."

Keenan didn't glance back at him. "If you leave now, you'll have a good headstart, sweet. I'll make sure the coyotes don't follow you."

"Because it's okay to kill them," Sam said, "but not her?"

Keenan's eyes narrowed. "Go, Nicole."

The guy was really throwing her out the door. Fine. She spun away, took two steps and locked her fingers around the doorknob.

"Thank you."

His whisper stopped her cold. "For what? Leaving you?" So that he'd have to fight a vicious battle without her?

But Keenan didn't say anything else. Damn him. Nicole looked over her shoulder, glaring. "*For what?*"

"Life." He inclined his head. "Now I understand why you fought so hard."

No, no, he was not bringing that up to her—

"Some things are worth fighting for."

He turned away and began to march back up the stairs.

"He *can't* kill you." Intensity hardened Sam's voice.

Nicole's tongue swiped over her lips even as her fingers tightened around that doorknob. "Th-that's not what Az said."

"Az is a dick."

So was he. "Az said that if . . . if Keenan killed me . . ." And Keenan was halfway up the stairs now. His shoulders up. His head high. Couldn't he have looked a little depressed? "Az said if Keenan killed me, he could go back."

She turned the knob and opened the door.

Sam slammed it closed instantly. "*What?*" Lethally soft and vibrating with fury.

"You heard me." Nicole didn't doubt that for a moment. "Keenan can go back. He can get his *life* back. I just have to die."

"There are *no* do-overs. Az knows that. He can't bullshit his way through—"

"I don't think he was bullshitting." She wasn't going to run after Keenan even though it *hurt* to watch him walk away. "Now get out of my way, Sam."

He blinked.

"*Out of my way.*"

"You'd leave him?" He edged away but watched

her with curiosity in his eyes. "I . . . didn't count on that."

She bared her fangs. "Maybe I finally realized it was time to save my own skin." She yanked open the door. The night waited for her. Dark and heavy.

She wouldn't look back. Death was the only thing that waited behind her. She'd never wanted death.

Not when the doctor told her that the same cancer that had killer her mother was slowly destroying her own body.

Not when that vamp had slammed her onto the ground in that alley.

No, she'd never wanted death.

But she sure wanted her angel. She could almost feel his touch.

A touch that would kill.

"You're a fucking idiot."

Keenan didn't turn when Sam burst into the room. His gaze was on the street below him. On Nicole. She moved so quickly through the shadows that he could barely keep track of her. "If she stayed here, she would've been dead by dawn." Because he was a greedy bastard, and he wanted to touch. *So badly.*

"So you send her out alone? That was your genius plan?"

"No. My genius plan . . ." Nicole was turning the corner, heading out of sight now. He swallowed. "My plan is to track the coyotes before they track us and to kill them. Then Nicole won't have to worry." He'd thought she'd stay safe if he was with her, watching her back every moment.

But that plan was too risky. Because when he was close . . .

Touch. Take.

Human needs and emotions were, indeed, a bitch.

"It's all because you think you can't touch her, right?"

The question didn't need answering.

Sam sighed. "I *told* you. You have to want to kill. When you touch her, you're just gonna be wanting to screw."

The always eloquent Sam.

"You don't believe me? You know we can't lie!"

Such a crock. Now Keenan did look Sam's way. "Why bother to lie when the truth can be just as deceiving?" Sure, pretty it up, make the truth look righteous, but in the end, it was just as twisted.

"Fine. You don't believe me. Then go find some human. Touch away. See if you kill or not."

Keenan allowed himself a smile. "Actually, that's exactly what I'm planning to do." Then he leapt off the balcony. For an instant, he felt the whip of the wind, the roll of wings, then his feet slammed into the ground. His knees barely buckled.

He began to walk slowly down the street. No rush— he knew just where to find his prey.

The wind pushed around him. "You're bullshitting me, right?" Sam wanted to know as he stepped to Keenan's side.

"No."

"You're just gonna pick some random mortal—"

"Not random." Not random at all, but then, he'd long ago learned that nothing in this world was random. There was always a plan in place.

Sam whistled and kept perfect pace with him. "Going for some revenge, are you?"

He slanted a hard look Sam's way. "Worried?"

The faint lines around Sam's eyes tightened. "Sometimes when folks get a touch of power, it's a little too much for them to handle. Too much temptation."

"I've had that." Far too much. He rounded the corner, caught Nicole's scent, and stumbled, just a moment.

But then he strode faster. The streets were crowded here, thick with humans already drunk and with *Other* hiding in plain sight. And his prey.

Pete. Tattooed, redheaded, and still alive. For now.

"Get lost, Sam."

But the other Fallen just grabbed his arm. "No."

So now the Fallen had a conscience?

"The guy told you everything he knew." A line appeared between Sam's brows. "Why go after him again?"

"Because if I don't stop him, he'll be coming after me."

"What?"

Keenan brushed him aside. "I'm not the only one who wants vengeance." Sometimes, it was easy to understand the motives of men. Perhaps he was finally getting a handle on these emotions after all.

But then Pete shifted his stance and Keenan saw the prey that he was actually seeking. Pete was simply a means to an end. A wannabe without the hard-core spirit.

Buzz-cut Bo was the real threat—and the man was currently heading for the voodoo shop on the right corner. Doubtful that the guy was going inside just for protection. More likely, he was heading in there to get some magic that he thought might work on a vamp.

Vengeance.

Keenan lunged forward. The crowd seemed to pass him in a blur. He made sure not to touch anyone. He didn't want an innocent's death on his hands. *Don't want to kill. Don't want to kill.* Just in case Sam wasn't bullshitting, he kept that little mantra running through his head. And he didn't want to kill Pete, but Bo . . . that was a different story.

He'd seen Bo before. Seen him at death scenes in the past. Bo liked to hurt his victims, vamps *and* humans. If anyone deserved getting put out of his misery, it would be Bo.

Keenan's hand reached out. His fingers stretched. Bo spun around, finally seeming to sense the threat.

Pete let out a high-pitched yell.

But then someone blocked his prey. Someone with pale skin and midnight-black hair. The last person he'd expected to find on his hunt.

And Nicole was blocking his prey.

"I don't know what you're doing," she whispered as he froze. "But attacking humans . . . this *isn't* you."

It was now.

"Get away from them, Nicole." Maybe she didn't realize just who it was that she was protecting. She'd been on the ground, burning, so she might not have seen their faces so well. "They're the ones who tried to kill you."

"I'm not worried about them." Her chin lifted. "I only care about you."

His hand was still up and just inches from her face.

Sam cursed. The wind rushed against Keenan, and Sam vanished. Figured.

Behind Nicole, Bo bent down, grabbed at his boot—and came back up with his fingers clenched around a wooden stake.

"*You should be worried, bitch!*" Bo screamed, spittle flying from his mouth. "*I been waitin' a long time to kill you!*"

Nicole spun toward him, but Bo was already plunging that stake down, and when she turned, it gave him perfect aim at her heart.

Death.

Here. *Now*.

Keenan leapt forward and shoved Nicole out of the way, and his hand caught the stake and Bo's hand. He caught them—then he crushed both the wood and the hand.

Bo screamed, the cry high and pain-filled, but the shriek ended mid-breath as Bo collapsed.

Dead.

"Keenan . . ."

His head whipped to the right. Nicole was on the ground, pushing to her feet. She was still too pale and weaving just a little. Probably because she hadn't taken a drink before tracking after him.

"You touched me," she told him and he wondered if she hadn't just set him up, with herself as bait. "*You touched me.*"

"I had to." If he hadn't, she would have died. *No choice.*

Her gaze held his. *I didn't kill her.* He wanted to pull her close. But . . .

She pulled him close instead. Around them, the crowd continued, not even noticing the dead man. Or maybe not caring.

"You're touching me, and I'm not dying," she seemed to breathe the words.

Thudding footsteps raced away. He glanced up in time to see Pete fleeing. Smart man.

Nicole's fingers dug into his arms. "Sam was telling the truth."

Just not all of it.

"It's about what *you* want," she said, her eyes searching his. "And no matter what Az may say, you don't want to kill me."

His forehead pressed against hers. "No." He'd kill to protect her, had, and would again. But kill *her*?

Not his plan. Not now, not damn well ever. "If you'd been wrong . . . if Sam had been wrong . . ."

"According to the angels, I'm on borrowed time." Her voice was flat. "Besides, I figured it was time I started trusting someone."

A surprised rasp of a laugh escaped Keenan at that as he pulled her away from Bo's body. Pretty soon, someone would notice the guy wasn't just passed out from booze. "You decided to trust?" He led her into the thin alleyway between the buildings. The noise immediately dimmed. "And you figured you'd start by trusting Sam?"

"No." Her fingers were curled around his. Holding tight. "You're the one I trust."

He stopped and turned slowly to face her. "Are you sure about that?"

"You could have your old life back, could have had it for a while now." Her head tilted as she studied him. "But the way I see it, you want something else more."

You. He'd never tried to hide his desire, not even when he pushed her away.

"You're not facing the coyotes alone." Her hands lifted and pressed against his chest. "You're not facing Az alone. From now on, we're a package deal, got it?"

He wanted to get it. His body was hot, heavy, aching for her. He wanted her there, against the broken brick wall. Wanted her any place he could get her because time wasn't on their side. "And if you die?"

Her lips curved the faintest bit. "Haven't you noticed yet? I'm a little hard to kill."

He kissed her. Had to. He didn't crush his lips down on hers like he craved. He just caressed with his mouth and his tongue and he tasted her.

She moaned into his mouth, a breathy, hungry little sound that made him want her all the more.

But not there. Not with the stench of the alley around them. Not with onlookers so close. This time, it would be right.

He caught her hand once more. "Come with me." They'd go back to Sam's. He'd strip her and taste her and savor the time they had left.

Because he knew . . . that time wouldn't last long.

But I won't kill her. His darkest fear and the reason he'd tried to force her away. One touch . . . but for her, his touch only brought pleasure. He'd make sure that pleasure was all she ever knew from him.

For the others who came after her . . . he'd make sure they would only know pain.

Az stared down at the still body of Bobby "Bo" Reynolds. Reynolds hadn't been a particularly nice or remarkable human. Sure, he'd had a few good moments, but Bo had let bitterness lead him to vicious acts.

Now, he was just dead.

Az had been the one to shuttle Bo's soul. He'd seen Bo's last moments. Az had known that Bo would try to go out fighting, and he had.

Az turned away from the body. Just a shell now. Keenan was already gone with his vampire—running away from the scene of his crime without looking back once. No remorse. No guilt. Killing was becoming easier for him.

Keenan was changing. Adapting. Evolving?

Soon there would be no stopping him.

Az wouldn't be able to ignore Keenan's threat much longer. If he did, Az knew it could prove to be a fatal mistake.

So he flew away from the crowd. He let his wings brush through the air in powerful arcs as he sought the ones who would aid him. The coyotes were done mourning their dead. And at least they'd mourned— some *Other* didn't care about those who passed.

He landed near the coyotes and touched ground close to the alpha. The alpha—Carlos was his name— tensed as his nostrils flared. The coyotes wouldn't be able to see him, but with their enhanced sense of smell, he knew they might pick up on his presence.

He was *counting* on their enhanced senses to help him. Because projecting his voice and energy for too long would be a dangerous drain on his strength.

"Find Sam." To him, his voice boomed, but to the coyotes, it was probably little more than a whisper.

Carlos tensed, then spun around in the next breath. His gaze swept the clearing.

Helping fate could be a real pain. "Find . . . Sammael." He used all of his energy to blast at Carlos.

"Sammael," Carlos repeated, voice soft and subdued.

"He'll take you . . . to the Fallen." Projecting out of his realm was nearly impossible. But, at least he was dealing with a shifter. Humans hardly ever heard the whispers, well, *roars* of angels.

With his strength dwindling, he left the shifter and hoped that Carlos would be successful in his hunt.

It grated that he had to leave his fate in the hands of a cold-blooded killer.

But sometimes, you couldn't really choose your allies . . . or your enemies. You just had to be ready to fight, to kill, or to die.

He was ready.

Was Keenan?

CHAPTER FIFTEEN

Sam's place was as quiet as a tomb. The lights were off, the silence thick and deep. As soon as he walked inside, Keenan knew they were alone.

He'd taken five steps up the stairs when Nicole caught his hand. "Keenan . . . wait."

Her voice was weak, breathless. They'd run back through the city, moving so fast humans wouldn't remember them.

"I need . . ." Her husky voice had his body tensing. He knew what she needed. He turned, took her into his arms, and pressed her up against the stair railing.

"Drink from me," he whispered as he urged her head closer to his neck.

Her lips pressed against his skin. Her mouth trembled and then he felt the slight sting of her teeth.

At her bite, the whisper of pain disappeared and pleasure pumped through his body. Had she really been close to biting Sam earlier?

A growl built in his throat as his hands tightened on her.

But then he froze. Ice poured through his veins, and he pushed her away.

"Keenan?" Her tongue swiped out and licked away the drops of blood on her lips. "Wh-what's wrong? Was I taking too much?"

His hands clenched. "I . . ." He took a breath and tried to fight down the rage that had risen within him. "I was afraid I'd hurt you." A careless touch. An angry thought. Was it that simple? What if he crossed the line? *Control.*

One weak moment . . . could he hurt her so easily?

"You didn't hurt me," she told him. "We've been over this, remember? You have to *want* to kill."

"Right then," he admitted with total honesty, "I did."

Her eyes widened. "Me? You wanted to—"

"Sam," he bit out the name. "You had your teeth on his throat." The words rumbled from him. "You were going to drink from him."

Just drink. Not fuck. Why should he be jealous over a blood exchange?

He shouldn't be, yet he was.

"I wasn't." Her voice was soft and still managed to stroke right over his flesh like a caress.

His brows rose. He forced his fingers to unclench. "I saw you. You were *at* his throat."

"But I wasn't going to drink." Nicole shook her head. "I really wasn't that hard up. I'm not going to make your friends into meals." She shrugged. "He was playing some kind of game, and I wanted to figure out why."

"Sam's always playing games."

"He wanted you angry. Jealous."

"Then he'd be real thrilled right now." He could almost see the guy's smirk.

"He told me the trick was control, Keenan. You have to keep your control."

One slip, yes, he knew what would happen. What he didn't understand was . . . "You know what I can do, so why do you still want to be with me?"

She smiled at him and the sight almost broke his heart. "You know what I've done, so why do you still want to be with me?"

"Because I've wanted you . . ." Before he'd even really understood what wanting was. He cleared his throat. "Because I want you, everything that you are."

"And that's the way I feel about you." Her fingers slid down his chest. "I just want you."

"What if . . ."

She stopped him by leaning forward and kissing his lips. A soft kiss. Gentle. Neither of them had seen a lot of gentleness lately. "I trust you," she breathed the words against his mouth.

Her trust was precious, he knew that. It was also dangerous.

"I heal faster . . ." She eased back and glanced at her hands. There was no sign of bruises anymore. "When I drink your blood."

Angel blood was potent. The most magical to some—and the most deadly to others. Vamps would see a burst in healing from angel blood, while demons who ingested his blood—they'd die.

The Fallen blood had once given rise to the demons, but over time, that blood had diluted. The drugs the demons so often ingested had changed their bodies— time and mutation had done the rest. Now, if the demons took a hit of undiluted angel blood—they didn't get a healing rush. They only got death.

"When I drink your blood . . ." Her eyes tracked to just over his shoulder. Her hand lifted, slid down his back, and her fingers seemed to stroke the air. No, she was *stroking his wings*. "I see things," she said.

A shudder worked down his body. He felt her touch on wings he no longer had. What the—

Her eyes came back to him. "You're beautiful, Keenan."

"Men aren't beautiful." If he didn't have her soon, he'd erupt. "Men aren't—"

"You're a lot more than a man." She turned away and headed up the stairs, her hips rolling and making him want to touch and take. "So much more." Nicole tossed a teasing glance back over his shoulder. "So come prove it to me."

Then she laughed, *actually laughed*, as she ran up the stairs.

Right then, the truth hit him. He knew exactly why he'd fallen, and he knew that if the choice came again, he'd face the fire once more.

For her.

He'd kill and he'd burn for his temptation.

Sam didn't really know why he'd searched for the woman, but the dancer—Seline—had caught his eye that fiery night at Temptation, and since then she'd kept slipping into his dreams.

Normally, he only dreamed of fire and screams. But lately, he'd begun to dream of a woman who stripped . . . and stared at him with ice-cold eyes.

Finding her wasn't very difficult. Most of the girls from Temptation had just bounced right over to Sunrise, another of his clubs, this one in a less desirable part of town. He went in and wondered if he'd find Seline on stage.

She wasn't on stage—she was waiting tables, and

dressed in a slim black, very, *very* short dress that made him want to lick her.

He picked a table in her area, then waited.

When she came toward him, he saw her hesitate. Her eyes widened a little. He knew fear when he saw it, but she kept heading toward him. *Interesting*. He lifted a twenty. "I'll take a beer."

She swiped the money and turned away.

He caught her wrist.

"You're not supposed to touch," she said, voice tense.

He kept touching. He stared at her skin—soft, silken skin—then let his gaze rise. Yes, it was still there. A sensual appeal that lapped at the senses and wouldn't be denied. Even now, other eyes were on her, other men were waiting and watching. Sam nodded and let his touch linger a little longer before he freed her.

She stepped back and turned for the bar.

"I'd lay odds you're a demon," he said quietly.

The drink tray fell from her right hand. When she whirled around to stare at him with wide eyes, he smiled. "What? No one figured it out before?"

She shook her head and glanced around the club. "You . . . you shouldn't be here."

"Where else should I be?" His gaze dipped to her very long legs. "Besides, I like the view."

Seline marched forward and curled her fingers around his chin. Delicate fingers forced his chin up as her eyes locked on his. "Someone's hunting you."

Sweet. She cared enough to warn him.

"I'm telling you . . ." She glanced over her shoulder. "Because I've heard you pay your debts."

Not really, but he wanted her to keep talking so he kept his mouth shut.

"Tina . . . she talked to some guy after the fire—"

Tina? He vaguely remembered a blonde with big breasts who'd been semi-skilled at pole dancing.

"She told him about you, about that woman who was with you in the back at Temptation."

Ah, Seline *was* helping him now. Perhaps he would owe her for the information. "What did this man look like?"

"Six foot two, two hundred pounds, black hair, black eyes, with a Mexican accent." She bent and scooped up her tray. "And if I'm not mistaken, he's a shifter. He smelled like an animal, no mistaking that shifter scent."

Seline was just full of surprises. "Your memory's good."

Her lips tightened. "It should be. He was in here not thirty minutes ago."

His good humor vanished.

"I *told* Tina not to leave with him, but she wouldn't listen to me." Her knuckles whitened around the tray. "I didn't like the way he looked. I—I'm worried that Tina might not be coming back."

Possible. It was also possible that Tina had spilled every bit of information that she had on him. Tina wouldn't know much though, she'd only seen him at the club, she wouldn't—

"Tina's been sleeping with Ron."

Shit. He'd warned the demon to watch his guard with the girls, but Ron had a serious weakness for big breasts. And the demon had no power to speak of. *Almost as helpless as a human.*

Seline nodded. "Your right-hand guy, isn't he? If that shifter wants to know where you hang your dirty laundry, I'm guessing Ron can tell him."

Sam lunged out of the chair and towered over her. "If you see that shifter again, stay the hell away from him."

She laughed at that. "Do I look stupid?"

"You look like walking sex."

She blushed. *Blushed.* A stripper wasn't supposed to blush. Especially a demon stripper.

He turned away. There'd be time later to solve her puzzle.

"You owe me, Sam!" She called after him.

He didn't stop. Whatever payment she wanted, he'd give her. After all, how much could it be?

But now, he needed to find Ron, and he had to make sure that demon didn't talk.

Keenan raced after Nicole, stripping the shirt from his body. He went into the darkened room and found her waiting. Nicole knelt on the bed and she was already naked. *Yes.* He tossed his shirt onto the floor and finished stripping before her.

"You are the sexiest woman I've ever seen," he told her as he stalked toward her.

Her gaze had tracked behind him, and he knew she was staring at the wings she shouldn't see. *Only the dying or those with angel blood could see—*

Keenan stopped and laughed, because he should have realized the truth sooner. Thanks to him, Nicole *had* angel blood in her. He'd given up his blood plenty of times for her.

"What's so funny?"

The bed dipped beneath his weight, and he shook his head. He caught her hand, kissed the top of her knuckles. A shiver slid over her.

"Keenan . . ."

He brought his body closer to hers. His fingers feathered over her breast. Such a soft, pretty nipple. He bent his head and licked her.

She arched up to him with a sigh.

Soft. Gentle. He could give her that. No pain, no fire, no fury. Just a man and a woman.

He needed to give her that.

He laved her nipple with his tongue, loving her taste and wanting more. Keenan slid his legs between hers—the better to open her to his touch. As he licked her, his knuckles edged down her stomach. His hand slid lower until his fingers were right over her sex.

When he touched her, he found her wet. Ready.

He licked a path to her other breast. Pulled her nipple into his mouth and sucked. Her hips arched, a fast rise against his hand, and he let two fingers dip inside her.

Her sex clamped around him, and his cock jerked. *Inside.*

But . . . not yet.

One more swipe of his tongue over her breast, and then he pulled back to watch her. Pleasure rippled across her face with each flex and plunge of his fingers. He liked the way her breath caught when the pleasure hit. Liked the way her eyes gleamed and she bit her lower lip.

Most guys probably wouldn't have found biting fangs sexy. Those guys were idiots.

He pulled his fingers out of her tempting flesh. His hands curved around her thighs, and he spread her even wider.

For a moment, he just stared at her sex. Pretty and pink, plump with desire. Then Keenan bent and tasted her. At the first lick, he wanted—

All of her. *All.*

He pulled her tight to his mouth and took.

She came against his tongue. Once. Twice.

But he didn't stop tasting or taking. Right then, he was desperate for her, and whatever waited for them, well, he wanted her to remember this moment.

Pleasure. No pain. No fear.

For one night, he'd only give her pleasure.

"Keenan," Her nails dug into his flesh. *"I want you inside."*

He rose up, licking his lips, and still tasting her. He knew his eyes would be as dark as hers.

Her breath choked out as she stared up at him. Then her hands slid down and whispered over his back. The silken touch shot right through him. *Stroking wings that aren't there.*

He thrust into her and drove as deep as he could go. Her legs locked around him, her heels pushing against his ass as she arched toward him. Taking, needing, just as wildly as he did.

Her moans filled his ears. His hands wrapped tightly around her.

Thrust.

Thrust.

He took her mouth and drove his tongue inside, so hungry for more of her taste. Her tongue brushed against his as her sex squeezed him, clamping down with her delicate inner muscles.

His spine prickled. His climax was close, but he didn't want the release to hit yet. *Not yet.*

Her fingers slid over the ridges of his scars, and her light caress ripped right through his control.

He plunged into her harder. Deeper. The gentleness was gone now, when he'd wanted to hold on to it so badly. But then, he needed—

Her.

He exploded inside her and heard the gasp that came from Nicole as she climaxed. The pleasure was rough, pounding, racing through his blood.

He held her as tightly as he could.

Won't let go.

No matter who came calling.

Some things in this world were more important than duty, and some things were even stronger than death.

Sam caught the scent of blood as soon as he climbed the porch steps at Ron's house. The front door stood open, swaying brokenly on its hinges.

His jaw clenched, and he knew what he'd find even before he crossed that threshold.

Poor Ron had never been a particularly strong demon. Barely a level three on the power scale, he wouldn't have been much of a challenge in a fight against another paranormal.

Ron lay on the floor. His throat had been ripped open, and blood pooled around his body.

"Fuck."

Long clawmarks riddled Ron's arms and chest. Those marks weren't deep enough to kill.

No, the shifter who'd come after Ron had tortured him first, trying to break Ron to get the guy to talk.

"You broke, didn't you?" He whispered, then shook his head as he bent to close Ron's eyes. When it came to pain, Ron hadn't been strong. A fault many demons carried. *Pain was their weakness.*

Who'd come to collect Ron at death? Az? One of the guy's dozen minions?

Sam yanked out his phone. Sometimes, technology was even faster than magic. He called his house. It only figured that Keenan would take his vampire back there. Sam knew when fucking time was at hand—and Keenan had been burning for his vamp.

The phone rang. Once, twice—

"Hello?" Nicole's hesitant voice.

He turned away from the body. "Company's coming," he warned. "Be ready—"

He heard the shatter of glass over the phone line.

"I think company's already here," she told him softly and the line went dead.

In an instant, Keenan jumped from the bed. He grabbed his jeans, yanked them up, and whirled to face her even as Sam's warning echoed in her head.

Company's coming.

Sam's warning was too late.

"Stay here," Keenan told her, "You need to—"

"No way." She jumped from the bed and yanked on her own clothes. "We're doing this together. You're not fighting alone!"

"If you're with me, you'll distract me."

Hard words that froze her.

He lifted his hands. "They touch me, they die. I can take them out. I just need to make sure that you're safe."

But she wanted to be at his side. "I'm not weak."

"I didn't say you were."

No, he'd never said that.

"I'm saying you're too important to risk." He headed for the door. "Stay here."

While he fought the battle?

He was already gone.

"Dammit." He was gone but . . . she wasn't alone. The scent of flowers told her that, and when she looked toward the balcony, the doors flew inward and there she could see . . . *oh, crap*. Not just shadows anymore, but the solid form of a man. Huge wings rose from his back and fury hardened his face.

Az. She didn't even need him to speak to know she was staring at Death.

"You'll let him die for you?" Az snarled and stalked toward her.

She backed up. Yes, she wanted to be all brave and

badass and step right toward him, but she knew what he could do with a touch.

So she backed the hell up. "Keenan's not dying." She heard the yells then. Screams from downstairs. Not Keenan's screams, though. Her chin lifted. "He's not—"

"He could have come back." Az was still advancing on her. Not good. "All he had to do was *finish his mission.*"

Her elbows banged into the wall. Nowhere else to retreat. "You mean all he had to do was be a good soldier boy and kill me."

"You shouldn't matter." He stopped, less than two feet away. His perfect brow crinkled, and he stared at her as if he were trying really hard to understand what the hell Keenan was doing with her. "You're just a vamp. A parasite to be exterminated."

Now he was trying to piss her off. She grabbed the nearby lamp and threw it right at his head. The porcelain shattered but he didn't blink.

No weapon made by man. Right. And the lamp was probably made in China, and not forged by magic. Dammit!

Looked like she'd have to get creative them. "Maybe I'm not the parasite." She shoved back her hair. "I'm not the one who takes souls, that's you."

His eyes widened. "I'm an *angel*, created to be superior, created to—"

"Yeah, yeah, I've heard this spiel."

He blinked.

She smiled. "You ever think maybe you've got it wrong? Maybe you aren't the superior one. You can't *feel*, can you, Az? Keenan can. He can feel and need and want and—" *Love.* But she bit that part back. She *hoped* Keenan could love.

Because she was sure falling for him, but she wouldn't give Az that weapon over her.

"Maybe humans are the superior ones," she told him instead. "You're supposed to guard us, right? Protect *us*."

His great wings stretched back behind him and their black tips brushed the ceiling. "You're not human anymore."

He'd just taunted her. The bastard.

Her gaze dropped to the floor and measured that distance between them again. Yep. Two perfect feet. "You can kill me."

He smiled.

Bastard. He *could* kill her, so why wasn't he? Why was he waiting for her to die?

Because angels had to follow orders. They didn't pick the moment of death. They had to wait and follow the rules and touch only when—

"No." She breathed out the word and took a step closer to Az as the understanding crystallized. "You have the power to kill with a touch, but you *can't* kill me. Not yet. Because you have to follow your orders, right, Az?" *Another good soldier boy.*

His eyes narrowed at the corners.

"You can't touch me, not until it's time. You *can't* kill me, not until it's time." Her claws were coming out, and her teeth were sharp and ready. "You might *want* to hurt me—"

He took a step back. "I-I don't . . ."

Bullshit. "Right. You expect me to believe you don't want some payback after I took one of your precious angels away?"

She caught the flicker of his eyelashes. Ah . . . "I'm the one who took him. *Me.* Keenan fell." She let her own smile curve and knew that it would reveal her fangs. "He fell for me, a vampire, a *parasite*, and he doesn't want to go back with you."

"You will destroy him." Stark.

This was the guy who wasn't supposed to feel? Maybe all the angels were boiling with emotions—and getting ready to explode. "Are you worried?" She asked him. "Because it seems like maybe you aren't the perfect angel anymore, either—"

"I never was."

That stopped her.

His wings were still spread wide. His hands were fisted at his sides. "Do you care for him, vampire?"

"Yes." Absolute truth.

His head tilted. "How much?"

She stared back at him, her brows pulling low. *What was he doing now?*

"Do you care enough to trade your life?" A brief pause. "Because that's what he did for you. He gave up everything he had. He *burned* as he fell. Keenan crawled through hell, just so he could come to you."

Hell? Wait—

"So I ask . . . *what would you do for him?*"

She realized the shouting from downstairs had stopped. *Too quiet.* Her heart seemed to freeze in her chest. She ran across the room and saw a big black bag near the nightstand. She yanked it open and found her clothes. *All* of her clothes had been brought over from Keenan's place—*Sam had known she'd be back.* She yanked out the clothes—and she found her gun nestled inside. *Thank you, Sam.*

"Would you fight for him?" Az pressed. "Kill?"

"Yes." Said without hesitation as her fingers curled around the base of a gun—the same gun she'd taken from that vamp feeding room in San Antonio. *Got the silver this time, asshole.*

"Would you die for him?"

Anger boiled in her blood as she whirled back to him. "I don't know what kind of sick game you think you're playing—"

His gaze didn't so much as drop to the gun. Right, 'cause why would he fear a gun? He wouldn't . . . but Carlos should fear the silver bullets that were still inside.

Az watched her with his bright gaze. "We both know Carlos isn't hunting you. It's Keenan's blood he wants because he needs an angel's blood to get power. So I ask again . . ." His voice seemed to whisper through her, "Would you die for him?"

That silence was too thick. Her hand tightened on the gun. There were only a few bullets left.

"Angels can die," Az told her, still in that whisper that sent chills over her. "*Everyone* can die, and believe me, vamp, you won't both survive the night."

Keenan?

She sprang for the door.

"Get ready to choose!" Az called after her. "I see death coming. *I see it.*"

The image of that last moment. Dammit, sometimes angels sucked.

"I see you and Keenan. I see the stake, and I see blood." He shook his head. "The blood is on Keenan."

No. He wasn't supposed to die. She nearly tripped over the stairs as she raced down them. "*Keenan!*"

"Death will come." Az's voice followed her. "Before the sun comes, *death will take a soul.*"

"Stay away from him!" Nicole shouted, but she didn't know if she was shouting the words to Az or to Carlos.

Then she hit the ground floor and she saw the broken glass that littered the floor. Two naked men—had to be shifters, they were always supposed to be naked when they transformed back to human form—lay on the floor.

But Keenan was gone, and there was no sign of Carlos.

"Better hurry . . ." She glanced up the stairs and saw Az staring down at her. "Time's running out."

Damn him. She ran out into the night, shouting Keenan's name.

CHAPTER SIXTEEN

Keenan caught her when she raced outside. He yanked her close even as he put his hand over her mouth to stop her screams.

He pulled her back into the shadows and covered her with his body. "Easy, sweet," he breathed the words against her ear and she sagged against him. "We're being hunted." And that knowledge had the fury ripping through his skin.

Two coyote shifters were already down—they'd been the welcome party that had launched at him with claws and teeth. They'd managed to make him bleed, spilling his blood all over the foyer, but he'd made sure they paid for those bites.

The fingers of Nicole's left hand curled around his arms. "It's you," she whispered, and he tilted his head so that he could see the fear in her eyes. "They're not stopping until they get your blood."

They'd already gotten all he felt like giving.

"Az told me—you could die tonight."

He nodded once. "Stay here while I hunt." He turned away.

She jerked him back. Hard. "What the hell? Did you just hear me?" She shoved something—a gun—behind her.

Carlos probably heard her. The woman wasn't trying to keep her voice down.

"We thought I was Az's target, but we were wrong, Keenan! It's you!"

He'd always been aware of that possibility. He knew Az liked to put down the Fallen who walked the earth. Sometimes, Keenan really wondered if Az was killing as ordained—or killing whoever he wanted.

But then he'd fall, too. And Az hadn't fallen. He'd been sitting up at that heavenly right hand for years.

Her claws bit into his hands. "You're not dying for me."

So fierce, his vampire. He brushed back her hair and let his palm linger on her face. "You worry for nothing. Az is trying to frighten you." He could feel the eyes on him, watching in the darkness. Another strike would come soon. He needed to get Nicole back inside. As long as she was inside, any attackers had to go through him in order to get her.

"Yes, well, he succeeded. I'm scared. I don't want to lose you!"

Footsteps shuffled to the right. Had to be a human on the street. A shifter wouldn't make an obvious sound like that. Shifters could retreat and attack in perfect silence.

The game of hide and seek was getting old.

"The coyote is out there," he told her, "and I'm not letting him get away." Because if he did, there would just be another attack. Carlos wasn't going to ever back off. Not until he got what he wanted.

My blood.

Too bad for Carlos . . . Keenan only planned to bleed for his vamp.

Her gaze trekked over his shoulder and scanned the darkened street. "You mean *we're* not letting him get away."

"Nicole . . ."

"*We're not.*" Said fiercely and the woman was so beautiful. Pale skin. Dark hair. Lips that he wanted beneath his mouth. Her gaze blazed into his. "I'm not letting you risk yourself out here. You're the target. I'm going to be watching your back."

Because of Az. Az had sent her racing into the darkness. *You'll pay, Az. Soon enough.*

"Then let's get hunting." Before the dawn came and weakened her.

He kissed her, one fast kiss, because he wanted to taste those lips. Then he turned into the night.

They hadn't gone far, though, before Nicole stopped him. He heard the swift inhale she gave before she whispered, "Blood."

He stared down at the dark cement and saw the tiny drops. "Maybe the bastard is hurt."

"No, that's human blood." She hurried forward. "There's more. It's—"

A trail.

So the coyote was playing dirty. Carlos was willing to sacrifice a human in order to bring in his prey. Not really surprising.

They followed that trail—light drops at first, then deeper spatters on the ground. Fresh blood. The humans they brushed by had no clue about the blood they stepped in as they stumbled down the street.

Dawn would come soon. Even in New Orleans, the party was slowing down now. Keenan needed to find his prey before Carlos came at him again.

Hunt or be hunted.

Only two choices here on earth.

The rounded a corner. Jackson Square waited before them, heavy with dark shadows. Just beyond the Square, the triple steeples of the St. Louis Cathedral pointed high into the moonlit sky.

When Nicole tried to advance, Keenan stopped her. "Sweet . . . you don't have to face what's waiting."

Not just Carlos, but her past.

She glanced his way and he was surprised by the hard edge that glinted in her gaze. "Yes, I do."

Then she was gone, snaking ahead of him and maneuvering easily through the darkness. She knew this place, knew every turn, and he followed behind her. Staying close, Keenan never let her stray more than a foot away from him.

"The trail goes inside," she whispered as she stared up at the stark turrets. His gaze followed hers, and he couldn't help but remember another night, one stained with more blood.

Slowly, Nicole crept forward, her eyes now on the crosses that adorned the top of the cathedral. "Why did he bring his bait here?" She whispered. "He can't know . . ."

No, the bastard *shouldn't* know what this place meant to them, not unless someone had tipped him off.

Her fingers trembled as she reached for the cathedral's left-side door. She pulled lightly and the air rasped from her lips. "It's not locked tonight."

He caught her hand. "Don't go in." He didn't know what waited but with all that blood . . . *death.*

But she shook her head. "I should have gone in long ago."

Then she went into the cathedral, and he followed instantly, not about to lose her to anything or anyone.

Their feet shuffled over the marble tile. The candle-lights and the chandeliers gleamed, though Keenan knew the cathedral should have been shut down at this hour. Images of angels and saints stared back at him. Seeming to weigh him. *Judging*.

"There." Her whisper. The blood led into the wooden confessional booth.

For Carlos to have left a body here, dumped in a church—*you'll regret this move, I promise*.

Some sins truly were never forgiven.

Nicole's head tilted to the left. "I hear . . ." She gasped and raced forward. She yanked open the confessional door and a scream echoed through the cathedral.

Not Nicole's scream.

The bait was alive. The woman was screaming and shaking. Thin, bloody slices covered her arms and legs. Keenan knew those slices had been made with a coyote's claws.

"It's okay," Nicole told the woman, holding up hands that no longer sported claws. "We're here to help you."

The woman, with tangled blond hair and a short black dress, blinked. Mascara and tears stained her cheeks. She looked familiar to Keenan. He knew he'd seen her before . . .

Running from the fire at Temptation.

He stepped back and his gaze swept over the wooden pews.

"Where's the man who did this to you?" Nicole asked. "Where is—"

"N-not . . . man." The woman fell to her knees and made the sign of the cross. "D-devil . . ."

No, just a coyote shifter. The devil had died long ago. Now someone else ruled for him.

"H-hurt me . . . wanted to know . . ."

"Let's get her out of here," Nicole said and Keenan noticed that she kept her head angled away from the woman. Right, *the blood*. That smell would be tempting Nicole.

He lifted the woman, holding her easily.

"H-help me . . ." She whispered. The woman's name—had it been Tina?

"We will," Nicole promised. "We'll get you to a doctor. You'll be okay."

They hurried for the exit. Nicole shoved open the door and the hot night air spilled inside. Dawn hadn't come, not yet, but it was edging closer. Nicole hurried down the stone steps. "Come on," she called out. "We can get—"

A growl broke the night.

Nicole whirled around and faced the dark alley. Pirate's Alley. The alley she'd nearly died in six months ago.

No, she *had* died in that alley. No getting around that truth.

And now Keenan knew that Carlos waited in that darkness for her.

Carefully, he sat the woman on her feet. "Can you walk?" He whispered.

She just cried. Her bloody hands wrapped around his neck as she held on tight.

He tried to pry her hands loose but she started screaming, "Don't leave me! *Don't leave me!*"

Nicole flinched as she glanced back at him. He saw her swallow and she said, "Keep her safe."

No, no, she wasn't—

"I'm not afraid of the monster in the alley anymore," she told him before she gave a hard nod. Her canines were lengthening, her claws sharpening. "This time, he'll be afraid of *me*."

Then she was gone. Nicole raced into the alley and ran right toward that darkness—and Carlos.

And while she ran, the bloody woman kept clinging

so tightly to him. She was shaking, and—and laughing?

"Kill her . . ." She whispered and she lifted her head to reveal the smile on her bloodstained lips. "He'll k-kill the bitch."

Fury had him shoving her away. Her head whipped back with the sharp push. "What are you talking about?" He barked.

But she just kept laughing, and he realized he'd forgotten a lesson he'd learned so long ago.

Humans lied. They often lied very, *very* well.

She smiled at him—smiled right through the blood. A willing sacrifice. "She'll be dead," she told him, the blood dripping down her body, "long before you can even—"

He didn't hear the rest. He was already racing to the alley and roaring Nicole's name.

When he saw her, the present and the past blurred. She was on the ground, fighting, struggling. But not with a vampire—with a full-on shifted coyote.

The coyote's teeth were in her shoulder, and she was pushing her arms between their bodies, trying to pry him off her.

No, not pry him off her . . . she was wedging something between them. Something small and black and—

The explosion shook the alley. The retort of gunfire echoed in the night.

The coyote fell off her. The fur began to melt from his body.

She lifted her gun, aimed, and fired once more.

The animal's body jerked. Not really an animal anymore. A man now. Naked. Hurting. The man twisted and cried out in pain as he bled out on the stone beneath him.

Nicole rose. Her eyes darted to Keenan. "This time," she told him quietly, "I was ready."

"*Sil . . . ver!*" Carlos's furious yell. "F-fucking bitch . . . *silver!*"

"Good thing we stopped by that feeding room in Texas."

The feeding room. He hadn't even realized she'd kept the gun.

"I've got one bullet left." Nicole stood over Carlos. The gun pointed right down at his chest, and her hand was perfectly steady. "That one's for your heart."

His body writhed. Keenan knew Carlos couldn't shift back with the silver in him. Carlos clawed at his flesh as he tried to pull the bullets out.

"Why did you want him so much?" Nicole asked. "Why didn't you just stay away? Leave us alone?"

Carlos threw one bullet into the gutter. "*Fuck you!*"

The second bullet was deep in his chest, but Carlos was digging for it, ripping and tearing into flesh and muscle.

"Nicole . . ." Keenan rushed forward. "*End it!*" The woman should know better than to play with the hunter.

"Why here?" She whispered. "Damn you, why pick *here?* Why this alley?"

The coyote shifter's breath rasped out. The minute Carlos got that second bullet out, Keenan knew he'd shift.

"Because he wanted . . ." Carlos licked the blood from his lips. "To fuck . . . with your mind."

Then he smiled, a smile as wild as the beast he carried, and Keenan knew the shifter had found the second bullet.

Behind the shifter, Keenan saw the shadows thicken. He heard the soft rush of wings.

Time for death.

Nicole fired and the bullet drove into Carlos's heart.

The shifter fell back, eyes wide. Not dead, not yet. Still struggling to breathe, the shifter fought hard to hold on. But Death was coming. Walking right there with his arms outstretched.

Az stalked from those shadows. His face was tight and remorseless. The shifter was gasping, choking as he labored to live. Shifters didn't always die as easily as they should. The beasts inside fought hard for survival.

A footstep whispered behind him. Keenan didn't glance back. He didn't want to take his eyes off Carlos. Not until Az touched him. But . . .

"Blood," Nicole whispered and she stepped back. "The woman—Keenan is she—"

"Don't worry about her." *Willing bait*.

Az was almost right over Carlos then. Only a few more moments.

"Choose," Az said.

Keenan blinked. *What?* There was no choice. Never had been. What was he—

But Nicole was moving, spinning around and screaming as she shoved Keenan to the side.

The woman—the bait—she'd followed them. When Keenan flew back, the bait's right hand lifted and she plunged a thick, wooden stake right into Nicole's chest.

Keenan grabbed the woman. Touched her—and she was dead in the same second. He ripped the stake out of Nicole's chest. *Not her heart. Not her heart, not—*

"It's too late," Az said. "It's time for the vampire to pass."

Then everything got very quiet as time seemed to slow. Keenan could hear the harsh gasp of Nicole's breaths. He could feel the warm weight of her body against his.

He looked up and Az was right there, standing over

him and reaching down. Az wasn't there to take the shifter because that asshole was still alive. Carlos was still alive when he should have been *dead*.

And now Carlos was rising to his feet. He'd dug all the bullets out of his chest. *A walking dead man*. Death hadn't taken his prey, because Az had broken the rules.

Bastard!

"No," Az said, shaking his head, and Keenan realized he'd yelled his accusations at the angel. "You're the one who broke the rules." Az shrugged and his wings flared behind him. "I'm just cleaning up the mess you made."

Carlos shifted then, transforming with a crunch and crack of bones into the thick, furry beast that was the coyote.

"Don't make this harder than it has to be." Az didn't glance at the coyote. His eyes stayed on Keenan. "I know you lust for her, but Keenan, she's isn't worth what you—"

"You're *not* touching her." He pulled Nicole closer and edged away from Az. Keenan pushed Nicole's lips against his throat. "Drink, sweet. *Drink*."

Az sighed and shook his head. "I've done this for you, Keenan. I risked wrath because I know you're better than this mortal world."

"Better, huh?" She wasn't biting him. He could feel the edge of her teeth, but she wasn't biting. Nicole barely seemed to be breathing. "Fuck you, Az," he yelled. "She's the only thing I want!"

"A vampire." Az's lips tightened. "A killer."

"You think we're so different from her?" Why wouldn't she drink? "How many souls have we taken, Az? *How many?*" He held her so tight, but her body was limp in his arms.

"We carry souls. Humans and *Other* kill themselves. We are just—"

Carlos howled behind him. The shifter was fully an animal now, and that shift would have helped him to heal. *He should have died from that last gunshot. Az was changing the game.*

"You're stepping over the line," Keenan grabbed Nicole's hand. Her claws were still out, barely. He used them to slice his neck and then he forced her mouth back to his throat. *Drink.* Even if the blonde had missed Nicole's heart, his vamp could die from blood loss. There was so much blood.

Her lips began to move on his throat. Lightly, but, she *was* drinking. *Yes.* "Stay with me, sweet," he whispered. "Just stay with me."

Az's eyes narrowed. "Why does she matter? You were an angel—and you can be again. This world, the hell here, you don't need it."

The coyote began to shift once more as he transformed back into the form of a man. Every shift would bring him strength. That was the way of the beast.

Keenan said, "I might not need the world." The pain. The hate. The wars. "But I need *her.*"

Az's wings stretched. "*Why?*"

The angel seemed lost. Probably because he was. "Because I love her." Simple.

"Angels don't love!"

"I do." Nicole's breath blew lightly against his throat. Good, she'd taken enough blood to keep her alive until he could get them out of there. Keenan pushed her behind his body, positioning her so that he was in front of her and the brick wall was at her back.

"You can't stay down here." A muscle jerked in Az's jaw. "This isn't the place for you."

"Wherever she is . . . *that's* where I'll be."

Carlos stood now, strong, grinning, his claws out and his sharpened teeth glinting.

"You going to sic your dog on me?" Keenan demanded, and Nicole's fingers pressed into his back. "You're the one who sent him here, after all." Yes, he'd figured that out. *The alley. The cathedral.* "You're the only one who knew what this place meant to Nicole."

Az's smile held an evil edge. Damn. This guy was supposed to be the good one?

"I thought angels helped people," Nicole said, her voice weak but clear. "I thought you were supposed to protect humans, to keep them safe!"

"Told you before, you're not human." Disgust had Az's lips twisting. "You should have died that night. Couldn't you see? We were trying to be merciful!"

Carlos stalked closer.

"How?" Nicole demanded. "By letting that bastard rape me? By letting him rip out my throat?"

"The cancer inside you would have broken your body. You would have suffered for months. Just like your mother, you would have withered away." Az lifted his hand and snapped his fingers. "Instead, your pain lasted only a few moments."

Cancer?

"Didn't know that, did you, Keenan? Why did you think your charge was racing for those church steps that night? Humans always turn to God when they need something." Az stepped back and cleared the path for Carlos. "Then they turn away when he needs them." Az pointed at Keenan. "*You* shouldn't have turned away."

Keenan held Az's stare and felt the fury rise even higher.

"This is your last chance." Az expelled a hard breath. "You can still come back."

You just have to kill her.

Keenan smiled. "Fuck you, Az."

Az blinked, then his jaw tightened. "Then you've

chosen. I wonder what waits in the next world for an angel that fell?"

Carlos ran toward them, his claws out, long, sharp, and deadly.

Keenan wasn't afraid. The rage was too strong. He could touch and kill and he'd take Carlos out.

But would Carlos manage to kill him in that instant, too? It just depended on who could strike first, who would be fastest . . .

But the rush of wings filled his ears before he could attack. Az grabbed Keenan and hauled him away from Nicole. The bastard's grip was unbreakable and they rammed into the side of the alley.

And Carlos—grinning bastard—swiped out with his claws and struck Nicole.

"No!" Keenan leapt for him.

Az tightened his grip. "You can't kill me with just a touch." Az held him pinned to the building. The faint rays of sunlight spilled into the alley. "This time, you *will* watch her die."

No, he wouldn't. Keenan rammed his head into Az's. But Az just laughed.

Nicole screamed.

Keenan's gaze flew to her. More blood flowed. Carlos had sliced her arms and chest with his claws.

"A vamp, especially one so new, is no match for a shifter." Az sounded so detached.

"*Nicole!*"

She swiped out with her own claws and managed to catch Carlos in the side. He grunted at the pain and promised, "I'll kill you, then I'll take your lover's blood."

"The sunlight will speed up her death." Az smiled and told Keenan, "Don't worry, she won't suffer long."

Fucking crazy bastard.

"No," Keenan agreed, "she won't." And the rage poured from him—

In a ball of red-hot flame that blasted into Az.

This time, Az was the one who screamed—a loud, pain-filled cry as he flew back. Az hit the ground and rolled over and over, trying to put out the fire.

"That fire didn't come from man, asshole." *From me.* "I conjured it and I damn well can control it." *Not you.* So it would burn the flesh right off Az. Az would heal, eventually, but first, he'd hurt like hell.

"*I'll take his blood . . . and he'll be my weapon . . .*" The shifter's taunt.

He spun and saw Carlos still circling Nicole.

"I'm no one's weapon!" Keenan roared. "Not anymore." Then he grabbed Carlos.

The shifter died before he could scream.

Carlos's body fell to the ground and thudded into the earth. Nicole's shoulders slumped.

"It's okay." Fury cracked Keenan's voice. "It's over now."

Her gaze darted over his shoulder. Pain and fear flickered in her gaze. "No," she said very definitely. "It's not."

She grabbed his arm and tried to yank him to the side.

Too late.

Fire slammed into his back.

CHAPTER SEVENTEEN

Keenan had covered her with his body. When the fire hit, he'd launched at Nicole and protected her. *Always protecting me.*

Now he was on the ground, rolling, trying to put out the fire that had burned his flesh.

She glanced up and had to shove the hair out of her eyes. Az was on his feet. The angel's body was covered in blisters and burns just like Keenan's, and Az was advancing on them.

"I didn't want it to end this way, Keenan. I wanted you to come back."

Keenan pushed to his knees.

But Az flew toward him and slammed his feet into Keenan's injured back, driving Keenan into the ground. Then the angel rose up, probably to better prepare for another hit.

Nicole reached for Keenan and wrapped her arms carefully around his body. "Keenan . . ."

He was so weak. She could *feel* the weakness pushing at her. He'd given her his blood and put himself at a disadvantage so that she'd live.

Her right hand touched her chest. The stake had come close to her heart, but, lucky for her, the psycho bitch had a really crappy aim. Blood had soaked her clothes. Her blood, his.

Sirens wailed in the distance. Finally, someone had noticed all the hell breaking loose in that alley and thought to call for help. *Finally*.

"Help won't come in time," Az said as he touched down a few feet away. "I've got a job to do—*and I will do it*. I won't hesitate. I won't make the mistake you did. *Emotion* won't stop me."

Then he came at Keenan again. Az grabbed him and yanked him right out of Nicole's arms. Az tossed Keenan onto the other side of the alley. Keenan flew into the bricks, and a thick crack appeared to run the length of the wall.

"*Stop!*" She ran after Az with her claws out. "Damn you, *stop!*"

Az spun toward her. And smiled. "Ready to choose?" he whispered.

She stumbled to a halt.

"I told you before . . . it's all so easy. Your life . . . or his." His wings eased down. "We can make this right. Your soul should have been taken. Order has to come back."

She glanced at Keenan. He was struggling to rise. If he could just get to his feet . . .

"You don't care enough about him to die, do you?" Az laughed at that. "Keenan *loves* you, but this time, you'll be the one who stands there and watches death come."

"No." She wouldn't have much time. She'd have to be fast. Fast . . .

"You won't give your life for him!"

Keenan was on his feet. His eyes were wide and desperate as he lunged at Az's back.

"I'll do better than that," she said softly, and it was her turn to smile and show her fangs. "I'll kill for him."

Az blinked. "Wh—"

She leapt forward and grabbed him. Nicole's teeth sank into his throat and her claws ripped into his chest even as Az's hands closed tightly around her.

One touch . . . just one . . .

Cold spread from his hands and sank into her flesh. *Death.*

But Az was trembling against her and his blood was in her mouth. The angel wasn't getting away unscathed this time. Actually, he wasn't getting away at all.

Time to kill . . . and time to die. For both of them.

Right there, in that damn forsaken alley. *Right there.*

Az had been right. Six months ago, she'd gone to the cathedral to pray. To ask God for strength, but his house had been closed to her.

Then the devil had come into the alley.

But she hadn't turned away from her faith. Az had been wrong about that. She'd prayed and she'd hoped and she'd gotten her angel.

I'll kill for him. I'll die for him.

Because Keenan had given her a reason to live. Hope. Love.

"*No!*" Az shoved her back, a shove that sent her flying ten feet and thudding into a window. Glass crunched around her.

And Az hit the ground. Or rather, he hit when Keenan crashed into him and drove the guy down. Then Keenan started ramming his fist into Az's face, again and again. The brutal thuds filled the air and almost drowned out the approaching sirens.

Nicole pushed to her feet. She took a step and staggered.

Strong, hard hands caught her. "You okay?"

Sam.

She blinked and realized that blood was dripping into her eyes. She could hardly see him—

Sam lifted his hand and pulled a chunk out of glass out of her brow. "Easy . . ."

Now wasn't the time for *easy*. Two angels were trying to kill each other, and one of those angels—*I love*.

Wind whispered against her body as she fought against Sam's hold. "We have to help Keenan!"

"I don't think Keenan's the one who needs help," Sam muttered. "Where's the coyote? We need to stop him. If he gets his hand on any angel blood . . ."

She broke Sam's hold. "He's dead." She hurried for Keenan as she tossed that bit out.

Az didn't seem to be fighting anymore. The angel just lay there, taking the hits, as he stared up at Keenan with swollen, confused eyes.

Then his gaze drifted to her. "You . . ." He licked busted lips. "Should be . . . dead."

Keenan yanked him up. "No, *you're* the one who's dying."

"T-touched her . . ." Az shook his head and managed to stand up on his own. "She should *die*."

Yes, he had touched her and she was sure he'd touched with the intent to kill.

But she was still breathing. How about that?

"Maybe it's not her time to die," Sam drawled as he stalked closer.

Az weaved on his feet. The blisters and burns on his body weren't healing. Keenan already seemed fine once again. Powerful and strong, with not a mark on him, but Az . . .

"She was on the list." Az shook his head and tried to straighten. Two fallen angels surrounded him on either side and Nicole saw the fear in his gaze. "I *saw* her death. Here. Tonight."

"Really?" Sam didn't sound convinced. "If you were so sure she was gonna die, then why team up with the coyote?"

Az didn't answer. He did spit out a mouthful of blood.

"Maybe you weren't so sure she'd die," Sam said. "Maybe you were just trying to change fate your own damn self."

"I was trying to give Keenan a chance at *redemption!*"

Nicole's claws dug into her palms. "You didn't see my death," *so good at twisting truth,* "and you didn't see Keenan's."

His eyes hardened. "*I saw death!*" His brows furrowed. "Should have died . . . *should have died!* The touch only doesn't work on those with angel bl—" He broke off and his gaze lazered on Keenan. "You—you gave her your blood, *damn you!* You made her stronger so she could hold off the touch!"

Nothing was stronger than angel blood.

Az took a step forward. "I'll touch her again . . . she won't be able to hold off the Touch. *I'll touch her again!*"

"You're not touching her." Keenan's hands were fisted and bloody. "And the death you saw . . . maybe that was your *own* death, asshole."

That had Az blinking. "I was trying to help you. We've worked together for two thousand years, I didn't want to see you lose everything for a damned soul!"

Damned? Goose bumps rose on her flesh. She didn't want to be damned. She wanted a second chance. When she looked up, Nicole could see the crosses over the cathedral. Black against the pink dawn. *Before the sun comes, death will take a soul.*

Keenan's body vibrated with fury. "I don't want your help, Az. I don't want redemption."

"*What do you want?*" Az screamed.

Seemed to her that the angel was losing control of his emotions.

"Now you're sounding human." The drawl was Sam's, but his words echoed her thoughts.

Keenan caught Nicole's hand and smoothed his fingers over her knuckles. "I have what I want."

Those sirens were nearly on them. The cops would be bursting into the alley any moment. They wouldn't see Az, she knew that. The cops would just see her, Sam, and Keenan—and two dead bodies.

"You have nothing." Disgust tightened Az's mouth. "You think she'll stand by you? The bloodlust will get to her again, and she'll take any man who comes her way. She'll kill, she'll—"

"Who are you to judge me?" Nicole's voice came out ice cold. "You've killed. You set up these two—" A jerk of her head toward Carlos and the woman "to die tonight. You *knew* they wouldn't make it out of this alley. But you put their deaths in motion. If you'd left them alone . . ."

"Instead of baiting a damn trap!" Sam charged, looking ready to do some killing of his own. Probably because he was.

"They'd be alive," Nicole finished.

Az laughed then. He threw back his head and laughed long and hard.

The laughter mixed with the sirens. She could see the flash of the police lights now.

"I'm a ranking angel. One of the first created. *Favored*—"

A burst of wind whipped through the alley. The wind grabbed Nicole's hair and tossed it into her face.

And Az staggered back a step beneath the force of the gust.

"You real sure about that favored status?" Keenan asked.

Nicole saw the sudden pallor of Az's skin. He tried to retreat, but Sam caught him and held tight.

"You're not going anywhere, *brother.* Nowhere but hell." Sam told him.

Az turned and his wings knocked into Sam and sent the Fallen hurtling back.

Then Az faced Nicole and Keenan once more. "You'll both die," he promised. "I *saw* it!" Then there were flames in his hand. Conjured flames that he threw right at them.

Keenan jumped in front of her and shielded Nicole with his body.

But the flames didn't touch him.

The flames didn't touch anything or anyone.

That wind whipped again and the fire vanished.

This time, the laughter that rang out was Sam's.

Nicole pushed Keenan to the side and saw that Sam was rising.

Az stared down at his hands. "How could—"

"I think that's a definite," Sam broke over his words, smirking. "Your ass isn't favored anymore."

Az's body jerked, contorted, and flew five feet up in the air, as if he'd been yanked on a puppet string.

"Did you ever think . . ." Sam's voice was pitched high to carry to the rising angel. "That Keenan didn't fall because he was being punished?"

Keenan's arm was around her, holding her close. She could feel the warmth of his body and the strength of his muscles. *Safe.*

Az was screaming, struggling, but rising higher and higher.

"Maybe . . ." Sam yelled to be heard over the howling wind and the sirens. "Just maybe he fell because *he* was favored."

Keenan stared up at Az. When he spoke, his voice was grim. "Beware, my friend, this will hurt."

It looked like Az already was hurting. Was it wrong that that made her happy? No, she figured it wasn't wrong at all.

"I've heard," Keenan called, still staring up at Az's rapidly disappearing body, "it's the fire that makes you scream the loudest."

Az screamed again, a long, desperate cry that echoed through the streets. He shot upward and his wings flapped uselessly. Then he vanished.

"The fire won't be all he has to worry about." Sam turned to them with a shark's smile. "Once his ass hits earth again, he's mine."

"No," Keenan said, "for all that he's done, I'll—"

"*Police!*" A hard voice barked. "Turn around and *put your hands up!*"

Dammit. Could they not get a break?

They turned, slowly, and Nicole was all too aware of the carnage around them.

Her gaze met the cop's. The first responder on the scene, and, oh, no . . . his face that was familiar to her.

Greg Hatten. The cop who'd come to rescue her six months ago. The cop who now bore deep scars on his throat.

His eyes widened and she knew he recognized her, too. Some nights, you just had bad luck.

He fired the gun without another word. The bullet plowed into her chest. Right into her heart.

"I know what you are!" He screamed. "You won't hurt me again, vampire!"

Her chest was smoking. Why was her chest smoking?

"Holy water," Keenan yelled. "Sam, take care of the cops!"

Then Keenan lifted her into his arms, held her

tightly, and ran as more bullets blasted around them. One bullet hit her leg and burned like a bitch. Other bullets flew right for Keenan but never broke his skin.

Over the gunfire, she heard the sounds of screams. "Don't . . . kill . . ." It was so hard to speak, but she had to try since they were cops. Scared cops who thought they were fighting monsters.

Because they were.

Her chest *hurt*. A stake and now a holy water bullet—*too much*. Nicole's eyes sagged closed. She wasn't real sure she'd make it through much more.

The sun hit her when they broke clear of the buildings. Bright, strong rays of sunlight poured on her. The weakness instantly weighed down her limbs, but she held on to Keenan.

She wasn't letting him go.

She ignored the fire that burned through her heart. "I love you." She wanted him to know that, always.

His head jerked, and he gazed down at her with wild eyes.

She tried to smile.

His hold tightened. "You're not dying."

She didn't want to die. He might have fallen for her, but she was living for him.

"We have to get the bullet out!" He rounded another corner and sat her down on the ground. Keenan ripped open her shirt and stared at her chest. She didn't want to look at the wound so she just watched him.

His eyes widened, and then all emotion vanished from his face. *Still trying to protect me.*

"I know," she whispered. The stake might have missed, but that cop had great aim.

Keenan shook his head.

"Just get it out," she told him. "Get it out . . . before it kills me."

But she knew, even as she said the words, just how dangerous such an act would be. The knowledge was there in Keenan's eyes, too. In the daylight, she wouldn't heal. And if he dug into her heart and the bleeding couldn't be stopped—she could die while he tried to save her.

Dying by Keenan's hand would be just what Az had wanted.

Keenan shook his head.

She grabbed his hand. "I trust you." Nicole wet her lips. "And I love you," she said again.

His fingers were trembling.

"If you love me, save me." She knew she was asking a lot, but there was no choice. *I'm dying.* "Save me."

He touched her heart.

But then, he'd done that from the beginning. Touched her heart, touched her soul, and marked her as his.

The pain blasted through her. The agony stole her breath and the last sound she made was the whisper of his name.

Then she saw paradise.

The sun set and Nicole's eyes didn't open. Keenan sat by the bed and kept his stare trained on her. He'd been there, watching, waiting, all day.

Open your eyes. Look at me.

She still breathed. Her chest rose and fell. Her heart beat.

He glanced down at his hands. The blood was gone now. Finally washed away. He'd held her heart in his hands. *Her heart.*

His fingers clenched.

"She'll wake." Sam's voice sounded confident.

Keenan didn't look at him. His gaze was back on Nicole. "I gave her my blood. She should have been up by now."

"She will be." Sam's hand slapped on his shoulder. "Give her time."

He didn't want *time*. He wanted her.

The floor squeaked as Sam turned away.

Keenan reached for Nicole's fingers. He smoothed his hand over her flesh. "Sam . . . why did you fall?"

Things were clear to him now, and he wished he'd realized sooner . . .

Keenan was the favored one. Sam's words echoed in his head.

He hadn't even realized how lucky he'd been. Nicole hadn't been his temptation. She'd been his reward. He'd just needed to be strong enough to fight for her.

"Maybe I became a power-hungry jackass like Az," Sam said.

Maybe. But "maybe" wasn't an answer. "The stories . . . they said you killed nearly a hundred men. Men who shouldn't have died." So long ago . . .

"Those bastards deserved death more than anyone I've ever seen." From the corner of his eye, Keenan saw the ripple of Sam's shrug. "Falling was a small price to pay in order to get them off this world." He paused. "Wasn't it a small price to pay for her?"

Yes. For her, he'd burn again.

"I thought so." He sighed. "Now I think you're finally understanding this game." The floor squeaked as Sam left.

Silence reigned and the minutes ticked by. The darkness grew heavier. And then . . .

Nicole's lashes began to flutter. He forgot Sam and leaned forward, holding her hand tighter. "Nicole?"

Her lips curled into a smile even before her eyes fully opened. "I was dreaming about you," she whispered and blinked slowly.

His heart raced in his chest and he kissed her, a quick, hard kiss. "You scared me."

She shook her head and her hair brushed over the pillow. "I wasn't leaving you." So simple and sure.

His gaze searched hers. "If you had, I would've just followed you." The angels wouldn't have been able to keep him away from her.

"I know." Her grin widened a bit.

He brushed back her hair and knew that he had to tell her everything now. "I . . . didn't realize what was happening. Why I watched you so much . . ."

Her eyes didn't judge. Didn't question.

"I should have stopped the vampire sooner." That would haunt him. "I should have—"

"We can't go back, and I don't want to."

She pushed up so that her face was only inches from his. "I meant what I said before. I love you, Keenan."

She was . . . everything to him.

"Az was right," she said, and the words had his head jerking in immediate denial. "I've killed. I'll probably kill again. And I'll always need blood."

She'd always have him to give that blood.

"I'm not perfect—"

To him, she was. Fangs, claws and sinful lips— *perfect*.

"But I want to be with you. I just want . . . *you*."

He swallowed. "I've seen everything this world has to offer." Good and bad. Nightmares, battlefields, and miracles. "And you're the only thing in my existence that has ever made me *feel*." That should be a warning to her, but she was looking at him with soft eyes.

She didn't understand the danger.

He forced his hands to lift from her. "You're all that

matters to me here, Nicole. Your life, your happiness—I'll do anything to protect you." He'd killed for her before and would do it again because he knew those times would come. The world wasn't an easy place. Too many hated vampires. Too many hunted.

No one will take her.

"Don't mistake me for a normal man," he warned her. "I'm not human, the feelings I have—" Lust, need, jealousy. "Sometimes they can make me very dangerous."

"You're not dangerous to me."

One touch to kill, one touch to give pleasure.

"You're *not* dangerous to me," she said again. Her eyes seemed to see straight into his soul.

"No, sweet." He'd sooner burn again than hurt her. "But I'm no angel." Not anymore. He knew his eyes would be darkening to black.

"Neither am I," she whispered as she twined her hands around his neck. *"Neither am I."*

She kissed him, sliding her tongue into his mouth and giving him that perfect taste of sweet sin.

Die for her—*yes*.

Kill for her—*yes*.

Love her?

Yes.

Heaven and hell could wait. He had paradise right there in his arms.

She was a temptation he'd never be able to resist. And, oh, hell, yes, she'd been worth the fall—and the burn.

For her, he'd fall again.

Any damn time.

EPILOGUE

Az had told Nicole that she would be dead within ten days, and angels didn't lie.

But a month had now passed and she was feeling as strong as ever.

She stared up at the St. Louis Cathedral. Her gaze drifted slowly over the thick crosses and then down to the round head of the white clock on the front of the cathedral.

Midnight.

Her gaze didn't stray to the alley that had shown her hell and heaven. No point in going back there.

Keenan had never asked her about what happened that night when the holy-water-laced bullet had thudded into her heart. Maybe he hadn't wanted to know.

I died.

No, angels didn't lie. And when Az spoke of her coming death, *he* hadn't been lying.

She didn't worry about her soul being damned anymore. She'd seen what waited after this life. She'd heard the whispers of angels and felt the flutter of wings.

No, she didn't fear death. She'd *chosen* to live.

And decided to come back to earth for the man she loved.

"Nicole?"

She turned at his voice and found Keenan striding from the shadows toward her. Handsome and strong.

She still saw his wings, dark shadows that stretched behind him. She loved the sight of those wings and she loved the way he trembled when she stroked them.

Loved him.

"Are you ready to leave?"

Because they were leaving New Orleans. Heading north to snow and strangers who would never recognize her. "Yes." She wasn't afraid anymore of what the future would hold for her.

Her future was right in front of her, and he was the best thing she'd ever seen.

She took Keenan's hand and they walked away from the cathedral and the ghosts that haunted that old alley. She didn't look back. She didn't want to see the memories anymore.

She just wanted her fallen angel—good, bad, and everything in between.

Not perfect. Not pure.

Hers.

Forever. And for a vampire and a fallen angel, forever would be one very long, hot time.